"A dizzily compelling story of love, lust, addiction, faith, maternal longing, and ... frozen yogurt." —*Vogue*

"*Milk Fed* is a romp ... a pageant of bodily juices and exploratory fingers and moan after moan of delight." —*Los Angeles Times*

"A thrilling examination of hunger, desire, faith, family, and love." —*Time*

"A delectable exploration of physical and emotional hunger." —*The Washington Post*

"Anything by Melissa Broder is an immediate must-read. . . . A precise blend of desire, discomfort, spirituality, and existential ache." —*BuzzFeed*

"A bold and luscious story of desire in all its forms." —*Esquire*

"Captivating ... delicious and depraved and unlike anything you've read before ... You will eat this up." —*Glamour*

"Broder has a rare ability to ground her fantasy in reality without undermining her imaginative vision, making it feel personal and raw and relatable." —*The Boston Globe*

"One of the strangest and sexiest novels of the year." —*Entertainment Weekly*

"A revelation . . . one of the strangest and sexiest novels of the year: a harrowing, exhilarating, and frankly obscene exploration of all the ways we endeavor to make ourselves disappear—and the untold liberty that comes when our appetites are freed at last."

—Leah Greenblatt, *Entertainment Weekly*

"Bravely questions the particularly female lionization of thin and loathing of fat, landing on fresh explanations . . . deliciously droll . . . a celebration of bodily liberation."

—Lucinda Rosenfeld, *The New York Times*

"Profoundly sexy . . . *Milk Fed* gathers strands of faith, hunger, queerness, lust, and loneliness and braids them into a fully risen challah of human experience."

—Emma Specter, *Vogue*

"A sensuous and delightfully delirious tale . . . Filled with an unadulterated filthiness that would make Philip Roth blush, Broder's latest is a devour-it-in-one-sitting wonder."

—*O, The Oprah Magazine*

"An erotic, singular experience that could only come from Broder's fascinating mind . . . this book is sensual, brimming with tension and food and fantasies."

—Isaac Fitzgerald, *Today*

"Anything by Melissa Broder is an immediate must-read. . . . A precise blend of desire, discomfort, spirituality, and existential ache makes Broder's depiction of the human experience so canny."

—Ariana Rebollini, *BuzzFeed*

"A delicious new novel that ravishes with sex and food . . . Broder has a rare ability to ground her fantasy in reality without undermining her imaginative vision, making it feel personal and raw and relatable. . . . With humanity, sardonic wit, and erotic scenes so potent that the heat of my blushing face made my NYC apartment radiator's seem tepid, *Milk-Fed* vividly evokes the lives of each woman, so that we're fully invested in them."

—Kera Bolonik, *The Boston Globe*

ALSO BY MELISSA BRODER

Death Valley

Superdoom: Selected Poems

The Pisces

So Sad Today

Last Sext

MILK FED

a novel

MELISSA BRODER

SCRIBNER

New York London Toronto Sydney New Delhi

Scribner
An Imprint of Simon & Schuster, Inc.
1230 Avenue of the Americas
New York, NY 10020

First Scribner paperback edition August 2021

For information about special discounts for bulk purchases, please contact Simon & Schuster Special Sales at 1-866-506-1949 or business@simonandschuster.com.

The Simon & Schuster Speakers Bureau can bring authors to your live event. For more information or to book an event, contact the Simon & Schuster Speakers Bureau at 1-866-248-3049 or visit our website at www.simonspeakers.com.

Interior design by Wendy Blum

Manufactured in the United States of America

7   9   10   8

Library of Congress Cataloging-in-Publication Data has been applied for.

ISBN 978-1-9821-4249-0
ISBN 978-1-9821-4250-6 (pbk)
ISBN 978-1-9821-4251-3 (ebook)

To Nicholas

My mother gave birth to twins: myself and fear.

—Thomas Hobbes

It didn't matter where I lived—Mid-City, Mid-Wilshire, or Miracle Mile. It didn't matter where I worked; one Hollywood bullshit factory was equal to any other. All that mattered was what I ate, when I ate, and how I ate it.

Every day at 7:30, my alarm went off. I'd remove the night-soaked piece of nicotine gum from my mouth, put it on the nightstand, and replace it with a fresh piece. I'd begun smoking at sixteen and was never without a cigarette. But when I started working at the talent management office, I was no longer able to smoke all day. I switched over to nicotine gum, which provided me with a way to "chew my cigarettes" and always be indulging. Now I was never without a piece of the gum. It helped me skillfully restrict my food intake, providing both a distraction for my mouth and a speedy suppressant for my appetite. I bought the gum on eBay, stale and discounted, so that I could afford it. At market prices I would have had a $300-a-week habit.

After popping a fresh piece, I'd get in the shower and drink a little water from the spigot, letting it mix with the coating from the gum. I preferred the coated varieties, Fruit Chill or Mint Blast, and did not count the coating in my daily caloric intake. Some days I worried how many calories the coating was adding. After the shower, I popped another piece of gum. Two more followed as I drove to work, heat blasting. This procession of gum was Breakfast One.

Between Breakfast One and Breakfast Two there was a stretch. Sometimes my blood sugar dropped so low that I'd feel dizzy and panicked. It was still worth it to postpone Breakfast Two, my first real food of the day, until 10:30 or 11. The later I started eating, the more food I could hoard for the back half of the day. Better to suffer now and have something to anticipate than to leave a big chunk of my day's food in the rearview mirror. That was a worse kind of suffering.

If I made it to 11 with no food, I felt very good, almost holy. If I ate at 10:30 I felt bad, slovenly, though any negative feelings quickly gave way to the rapture of consuming Breakfast Two. The meal consisted of an 8-ounce container of 0% fat Greek yogurt with two packets of Splenda mixed in, as well as a diet chocolate muffin top that could only be purchased at Gelson's supermarket. I was so emotionally dependent on these muffin tops that I feared what would happen in the event of a shortage. I bought six boxes at a time and stored them in my freezer.

The muffin top was 100 calories, and the yogurt was 90 calories: a perfect one-two punch of creaminess and sweetness, a symphony of flavor that couldn't hurt me. My fondest time of the day was that instant I first put my spoon into the yogurt, just after having sprinkled half a Splenda packet on top. In that moment, there was so much left to eat, the muffin top not even touched, only a promise of chocolate. Afterward, I always wished I'd eaten more slowly, so I could still have something left to look forward to. The end of Breakfast Two was a sad time.

I ate Breakfast Two seated at my desk, directly across from another assistant named Andrew, who enjoyed NPR, natural peanut butter, and obscure Scandinavian films for the sake of their obscurity. Andrew's head was one size too small for his gangly body. He had pinched nostrils, poised for disapproval, and he styled his hair in an ornate, indie-rocker shag that sat on his tiny head like a fright wig of cool. I knew he judged my use of chemical sweeteners, so I built a blockade with file folders, Ikea cacti, and a battalion of coffee mugs at the front of my desk to block his prying eyes. I at least deserved some privacy to fully enjoy my ritual.

Lunch was even trickier. At least two days a week, I was forced to join my boss—Brett Ofer—for lunch with clients, agents, and other industry people. I didn't like eating with others. Lunch was the crown jewel of the day, and I preferred to savor it solo, not waste it on foods I hadn't chosen. Ofer always made us go to the same restaurant, Last Crush, which shared a parking garage with our office. He insisted we get a bunch of small plates and split everything, "family style," as though sharing a meatball made our clients feel like brethren. Who wanted Ofer as a relative? He acted like family was a good thing.

At Last Crush, I was forced to contend with macaroni and cheese, sliders, veal meatballs. Even the vegetables were tainted by interloping fats: Brussels sprouts choked with butter, mushrooms fried in bread crumbs, cauliflower lost to a shiny glaze. The arugula salad that I requested as my contribution to the smorgasbord was but a slippery cadaver: death by oil, goodbye.

On these outings, I would eat tiny portions of three of the dishes, assigning 100 calories to each portion and then adding an extra 100 to the total for anything I'd missed. While the algebraic formula was imperfect, it allowed me some illusion of control. But Ofer was always trying to haze me into eating more.

"Who wants the last slider? Rachel, I know youuu're thinking about it," he taunted, before breaking into chant. "Do it! Do it! Do it!"

Ofer was an eternal frat brother. He believed in loyalty, community—not because we had any real connection as individuals, but because we were part of the same something. As he extolled the virtues of our "collaborative office culture," his bald head gleaming, a fleck of veal meatball on his lower lip, I imagined him delivering the same spiel to the Alpha Epsilon Pi pledges two decades prior.

"Do you know how lucky you are? You could be working at Management180, where nobody shares a goddamn lead on anything! You could be in Delta Upsilon, drinking your brother's piss!"

Ofer had started in the mailroom at Gersh and worked his way up to agent. Nine years later, he'd left the cutthroat agency world to open a talent management company—The Crew—which made him think he had a soul. Worse yet, his wife had just given birth to twin daughters and he now identified as a "feminist." Ofer was acquiring a perfunctory knowledge of social justice, as dictated by thinkpieces on diversity, inclusion, and equal pay in the *Hollywood Reporter*. He made constant references to his "privilege," also our privilege to be working there. It bothered him that I didn't feel lucky to be part of the family. Talent management was not my dream, and this hurt him.

When I wasn't forced to go to Last Crush with Ofer and the clients, I was on my own for lunch. These were the good days. First, I would go to Subway, where they listed the calories for everything online. I would get a chopped salad with double turkey, lettuce, tomato, banana peppers, pickles, and olives. It was a magic salad, packing explosive flavor into a modest caloric total of 160. Most of the time, my sandwich artist was a cute USC kid who piled his dreadlocks on top of his head to give him four inches of extra height. He always asked if I wanted "sauce," the word for dressing at Subway, and I always told him no. Thankfully, he never questioned my choice. But sometimes he failed to incorporate the abundance of lettuce that gave the Subway salad its crucial bulk.

Occasionally, I had another sandwich artist, a ginger-haired teen with Invisalign. This guy made a mean salad, the lettuce really flowed, but he was far too interested in connecting with me as a person. The moment I walked in the door, he would call out, "Hey! Double turkey!" and I'd be like, "Hi, thanks, no photos." I didn't have to tell him that I wanted no sauce, because he always remembered, muttering, "No sauce, no sauce." But every few salads, he felt the need to interrogate me, asking, "Yo, why you don't use the sauce? It's free!" to which I would say "I just don't like it." "Too spicy? Too wet?" he'd ask. "Just salt and pepper, please," I'd say.

I always ate the salad at one of the little outdoor patio tables outside Subway, though that wasn't ideal. On the one hand, there was no way I was going to eat inside the restaurant with the sandwich artists watching me. But when I ate outdoors, I became prey for any of the passersby, including people from my office.

It wasn't that eating a Subway salad was inherently shameful. But I liked my food rituals to be protected—fully differentiated from my work life as much as possible. This was mine and mine alone. It was not to be shared. So I ate outside facing a stucco wall. I ate hungrily and greedily, sometimes shoving forkfuls of the turkey-pickle-pepper mixture in my mouth, other times seeking out a single ingredient, like just one olive on my fork.

The triumph of my lunch was that it contained two courses: the grand salad and then frozen yogurt. I loved food that came in multiple parts, prolonging the experience. If I could be infinitely eating, I would be. I had to restrict my intake, or I'd never not be putting something in my mouth.

Subway was flanked by two frozen yogurt shops, Yogurt World and Yo!Good. At Yogurt World you got to serve yourself. No one manhandled your yogurt or toppings, and checkout was even automated. The grace was zero social interaction. At Yo!Good, you had to order through a server, but their yogurt made it worth it. Yo!Good had banana, caramel, and cake-batter flavors that were fat free, sugar-free, low-carb, and just 45 calories for a half cup.

This meant that I could get a 16-ounce serving for 180 calories. At Yogurt World, the lowest-calorie yogurts were 120 calories for 4 ounces. I had to get the kids' size to rival Yo!Good's numbers. So I sacrificed privacy for mathematic soundness and quantity.

I was grateful that the counter boy at Yo!Good had little interest in talking to me. He was an Orthodox Jewish boy who looked to be about nineteen or twenty. He was very quiet, polite, and wore a blue yarmulke and curly peyos. His gentleness made me feel sad—also, the way he pronounced the word *yogurt* as *yuh-gort*. I felt like I could cry between the two syllables. There was an innocence there, an earnest desire to please the customer, a recognition of yogurt as a substance of great import, a calculated precision with the yogurt machine that felt like care. You didn't find that kind of focus in food service every day. He also possessed a contained isolation, never handing me the yogurt cup directly, always placing it on the countertop in front of me, pointing to the counter to receive my money, no hand-to-hand, our worlds not to touch. It was as though he were a ghost from a lost time. Or maybe it was just a time lost to me.

CHAPTER 2

The Reform synagogue I'd attended growing up in Short Hills, New Jersey, was way more Chanel bag Jew than Torah Jew. I felt most Jewish when my grandparents, also Reform but deeply obsessed with Jewish food, would drive me to New York and take me on a tour of all the old culinary haunts of our tribe. My grandparents were considered medically obese. They'd both developed diabetes as a result of their weight, but food remained something to be celebrated. There were delicious warm buttered onion rolls and creamed herring at the kosher dairy restaurants, cabbage borscht and hot pastrami sandwiches at Second Avenue Deli. There were black-and-white cookies from William Greenberg Desserts, pints and quarts of pickles—sour, half sour, and sweet—from Guss' on Essex Street.

When I got back from New York, my mother would ask for a full report of all I had eaten. "Do you want to be a chubby or do you want boys to like you?" she'd say.

My grandparents were only a brief respite from the universe. My mother was what the universe was really about. My mother the sun, my mother the rules, my mother, god herself! My mother the high priestess of food, the religion of our household: *abstain, abstain, abstain!* My mother with her archaic ideas about dieting: melon and cottage cheese, tuna and carrot sticks, melba toast. My mother the judge storming into the dressing room at the children's clothing shop, me age six, her whispering, "Look at Amy Dickstein in that dress. Now look at you." It was a whisper that implanted itself in me, a whisper that stuck.

I was softly plump, like a dumpling, and short. She feared the shortness would lead to more weight gain, that it would make the weight show. She saw future pain, frightened that I would grow up to be like her parents, whose obesity had caused her shame, or her fat cousin Wendy, who was unhappy. I wondered, if I could go back and rescue myself from that dressing room, would I do it? I probably wouldn't. I thought that soft little girl was disgusting too.

The more my mother restricted my food intake, the more I binged in secret. She didn't understand why I was expanding, that I was stealing candy from convenience stores, eating other kids' lunches in the coatroom. She eyed me from across a birthday party as I chewed a bite of cake. She threatened to ask my teachers what I was eating if I gained more weight. Once a month I was weighed on a scale at the YMCA. She didn't yell in public, but in the car I would cry in the back seat.

At sixteen I began restricting my food intake for myself. I developed an arsenal of tricks: Diet Coke, cigarettes, fake-sweetened everything, meal delay, steamed vegetables, never eating with others. My grandparents and I took our trip to New York, but the restaurants that were once my temples had become a threat. I fended off cheese blintzes, knishes, and schnecken, replaced cherry hamantaschen with Dr. Brown's diet soda. I slurped around matzo balls, set boundaries with bagels, found safety in pickles—so low-calorie, *baruch hashem*.

For years I couldn't be thin enough. Then, in an instant, I was too thin. If I had 20 pounds to lose, I lost 45. I wanted to stay there forever. I pared my food back further: spinach, broccoli, steamed chicken. I called it my Spartan regimen. I felt high on my sacrifice.

But I was freezing all the time. I lived in the bathtub. A downy fur grew on my body. My period stopped. At night I dreamt of wild buffets. My hip bones chafed against the bed. At school there were whispers. My mother said nothing.

One night, I was shivering so badly I got scared I would die.

"I have to tell you something," I said to my mother. "I think I have an eating disorder, anorexia maybe."

"Anorexics are much skinnier than you," she said. "They look like concentration camp victims. They have to be hospitalized. You aren't anorexic."

"I haven't gotten my period in months."

This troubled her. My fertility was important; she wanted grandchildren one day. She sent me to a nutritionist, who helped me increase my daily calorie intake. We did it slowly, methodically, with charts and lists that reduced every food to its serving size and caloric value.

I went from freezing to just cold. The shaking stopped. The fur disappeared. I could sleep on my stomach. The whispers got quiet. I bled again. But I remained engrossed in calories. The constant mathematics in my head never went away.

CHAPTER 3

As I waited in line at Yo!Good, I plotted the concoctions I would create if I ever found myself magically immune to calories. I envisioned red velvet yogurt dripping in caramel, freckled with slivers of Snickers. I buried a dulce de leche yogurt in marshmallow sauce, then poured a stream of crumbled Oreos over its sweet head. On a Dutch chocolate planet lived every species of gummy: bear, worm, fish, penguin, dino, and peach ring. It snowed Reese's Pieces and chocolate sprinkles on a cake-batter-flavored mountain.

They had everything: strawberries in syrup, cookie dough balls, and tiny white chocolate nonpareils in a rainbow of pastel shades. They had hot fudge, warm caramel, and a butterscotch sauce that hardened at the moment of impact. They had a diet version of the hot fudge that made me consider, *What if? What if I just had a drizzle?* But the nebulous calorie count of a drizzle posed too many variables. I feared that if I tried the sauce once, I'd never eat my yogurt without it again. I didn't trust myself to taste the fudge and let go.

Thankfully, the Orthodox boy didn't say, "No topping?" the way the Subway sandwich artist always said, "No sauce?" I watched him closely as he pumped the yogurt, inspecting to make sure that he didn't go over the top (that airspace was calorically uncountable). When he reached the top, I called out, "Stop!"

He stopped right away, brought the cup to the register, and pleasantly issued the total for the *yuh-gort*. Other than in his politeness, he showed no recognition that I was a regular customer. I was thankful for that.

I consumed the first three-quarters of the cup at the back corner table inside Yo!Good facing two walls. I was always cold, but I preferred to eat inside the chilly yogurt parlor than outside at the sunny tables, because they were popular. I had a specific style and rhythm with which I liked to eat the yogurt, and I didn't want anyone watching me. First, I licked around the sides of the cup to get the melty parts. Then, I put spoonful after spoonful of the cooler stuff in my mouth and squeegeed it back and forth between my teeth to liquify it.

For the final quarter of the yogurt, I abandoned my method and headed outside with what remained in the cup. Those last five minutes in the sun felt like Eden, the end of Eden really, because the freezing office awaited. They kept it so deeply air-conditioned that I wore a puffer jacket at my desk. But in those last few moments of warmth, I communed with the dregs of the yogurt and imagined the sun was penetrating me—creating a force field that could live internally and heat me throughout the rest of the day. Then I reentered the office and puffered-up again.

The afternoon was mostly spent obsessing about my forthcoming snack: a chocolate chunk protein bar that contained 180 calories. On good days, I could delay the bar—a beacon of sweetness and hope to look forward to—until I left the office at 6 for the gym. On bad days, I opened the wrapper at my desk "just to sniff it," and gobbled it up.

I was so enamored of that protein bar: its candy bar taste, the creaminess and powers of satiety it packed into its body. I'd recently been devastated when, in studying the wrapper, I discovered there had been a sneaky increase of 20 calories. When did this happen? How long had I been in the dark? Was there a change in recipe, or had they willfully been misleading everyone all along? It seemed a public apology was in order. Now I was in the process of healing: learning to trust the protein bar again.

I delayed the protein bar consumption by having "afternoon teatime" in the office kitchen. I liked drinking tea with Ana, the office manager, a busty woman in her midfifties who dressed in exquisite, low-cut silk blouses tucked into high-waisted pants that showed off her slender middle. Most women Ana's age who worked in the entertainment industry were Botoxed within an inch of their lives. But Ana's enhancements were elegant—subtle fillers, gentle relaxers—allowing for fine lines around her pretty mouth and big brown eyes, but no deep creases or folds: a feigned realness, rather than an outright fake.

"Shhhh," said Ana, quieting me so we could hear Ofer on his phone down the hall. "Listen, it's the sound of movies getting stupider."

"I know. Is there anything worse than entertainment?"

Ana's ex-husband produced a hit trilogy of vampire movies in the early 2000s: *Night's Sundry, Enigma's Descent,* and *Wicked Shroud.* During the postproduction of *Enigma's Descent,* he'd left her and their nine-year-old son for a special-effects makeup artist. Now, Ana saw it as an insult that she had to work in the industry for a living. She only remained in Los Angeles because her son and his girlfriend lived in Highland Park.

"I'm older than you, so I get to hate everything more," she said. "Wait, tell me you aren't drinking the house Lipton. Please, take my Harney & Sons, I beg of you."

I was pleased that Ana wanted to give me the good stuff. I actually loved Lipton, plus one teaspoon of creamer and four Splenda, like a "milkshake." But I craved any nurturing I could get from her. It wasn't so much that she was kind to me. She just hated everyone else more. We had become an "us" because our coworkers were such a "them." Still, I really liked being an "us."

I wondered if she talked shit behind my back the way she did about everyone else.

"At least you don't eat the slop they leave around here," said Ana. "The other assistants are playing it a little too fast and loose with the pastries. That Kayla, especially, is looking one cheese Danish over the line."

I hoped I was far, far under the line. People said that Ana and I resembled each other. She looked more like me than my own mother did. We both had an abundance of coarse, wavy brown hair, olive skin that tanned easily in the sun, and dark brown eyes. My mother had fine black hair, gray eyes, and skin so fair it was translucent. But in their equation of thinness with goodness, my mother and Ana were so like-minded. My mother persuaded me to stay thin by insulting me. Ana did it by insulting everyone but me. This absence of rejection felt like an embrace.

CHAPTER 4

My therapist in Los Angeles, Dr. Rana Mahjoub, wore sensible clogs and said insight-adjacent things like "put on your oxygen mask before helping others," but I didn't entirely respect her because she accepted my insurance. How good could she be if she was willing to deal with Blue Shield? I couldn't help but see our sessions as disposable soap samples handed out for free at a mall.

Dr. Mahjoub's office was filled with elephants: elephant lithographs, elephant statuary, elephant carvings. I wondered whether she genuinely loved elephants and had collected them over the years, or if Pier 1 was having a sale and she thought, *Yes, thematically cohesive decor fosters ego integration in patients*, and purchased them all at once.

I'd entered therapy hoping to alleviate the suffering related to both my food issues and my mother, but without having to make any actual life changes in either area. I'd hoped that Dr. Mahjoub and I could pursue a subconscious, hypnotherapeutic modality, like learning to go comatose while still appearing alive. But Dr. Mahjoub wanted me to take real action.

"I suggest that you take a communication detox from your mother," she said.

"Sure," I said. "No problem."

"I suggest ninety days of no contact."

"Ninety days! No contact?"

"That's right."

"Like, not even an emoji?"

"Try," she said.

I laughed, as they say, out loud.

"She'd never let me go more than four days without talking."

"She won't *let* you?"

"I guess she can't force me to talk. But the guilt would be excruciating."

"Setting boundaries doesn't always feel good," said Dr. Mahjoub. "Just because it feels bad doesn't mean it's wrong."

Maybe it wasn't wrong to set boundaries. But I knew that my feelings would be intolerable. I kept thinking, *My mother is going to die someday.* I would die too. Dr. Mahjoub couldn't stop death. What did she really know?

At our last session, she'd encouraged me to learn to "parent myself." Amidst the Mahjoubian elephants, this idea seemed positive, doable, maybe even fun. I was going to speak gently to young Rachel, tell her that everything was going to be okay in hushed, empathetic tones. I'd be a mother to me.

Then I left the office and thought, *Wait, what am I supposed to do?* Something about self-soothing, offering up compassion for the young Rachel who lived inside of me. But I hated that young Rachel.

Young Rachel was always getting excited and then being popped like a balloon animal. She was always being deflated. She wanted too much. This week, young Rachel wanted a little acknowledgment from her mother.

I had just been chosen by a low-trafficked entertainment blog as one of 25 young female comics to watch. When I'd texted the link to my mother, she wrote back: *How did they find you?*

A few minutes later she followed that up with: *Can't opem link*

And then: *I hope there's nothing embarrassing in it*

And then: *You didn't embarrass me did you??!*

Dr. Mahjoub said that if her daughter came to her with that kind of news, she would be incredibly proud.

"My daughter is only eleven," she said. "But I only hope that she can one day have your success."

"Let's not get carried away," I said. "It's a blog."

It seemed strange that mothers like Dr. Mahjoub existed in the world—mothers who supported their daughters. I felt jealous of her daughter, that she got to have a mother like that. I told Dr. Mahjoub I hadn't expected fanfare from my mother. But I'd thought she would at least be a little bit proud.

"You were going to the hardware store for milk again," said Dr. Mahjoub.

"Well, maybe just a tiny bit of milk," I said.

"That's the problem," she said. "You have to expect nothing."

Expect nothing. The simplicity of that directive, its bare-bones, self-contained power was intoxicating. Expect nothing. It was so clean, so potent.

It was a phrase you'd associate with a person who didn't need anything from anyone; a closed system, an automaton. I wanted to be that person. I wanted to be that automaton.

"Okay," I said. "I'll try it."

"Try it," said Dr. Mahjoub.

"Okay!" I said again. "Why not?"

I left the office feeling strong, hopeful, a bit high. I kind of sashayed across the parking lot. Expect nothing. Why expect something if you could expect nothing?

In my car, I texted my mother.

Hi. I will not be reachable for the next 90 days. Thank you.

She wrote back immediately: *What are you talking about?!?*

Sorry, I replied. *Unavailable.*

Then she called.

"I'm detoxing," I said.

"What do you mean, detoxing?"

"From our relationship," I said. "It's emotionally unsafe."

"What do you mean, emotionally unsafe?"

This was the thing about boundaries: they made sense in therapy, but when you tried to implement them in the real world, people had no idea what you were talking about. Or, deep down they knew exactly what you were talking about and immediately set to work reinforcing their case of denial.

"So I've been a terrible mother," said my mother. "I guess I've done nothing right."

I could feel her opening an emotional spreadsheet that began with the womb. This was why I never confronted her. Now we'd have to go traipsing through it together, cell by cell, until I retracted everything.

But what if I just refused to traipse?

"I can't," I said. "I'm sorry, but I can't."

I closed the spreadsheet.

CHAPTER 5

This Show Sucks was a Silverlake comedy night started by my ex-boyfriend from college, Nathan. In Madison, Nathan always drove us to and from open mic night at a bar called Blind Willie's Hideaway. I began dating him by default when one night, in his car, he put his hand on my thigh and I was too hungry and tired to deal with moving it. I ended things a few months later, when I got the energy to move it.

Nathan had achieved quick success in LA and was now in his first season hosting a Comedy Central show called *Assplainin'*, an Internet meme-based charades game. He never came to This Show Sucks anymore, but he had them book me every week— even though it was obvious I didn't fit in with the regular comics on the bill.

The other comics emanated Moon Juice, organic lip tint, and cocaine, whereas I used only cancer-causing cosmetics and sweated Coke Zero. They wore ugly clothes on purpose: mom jeans, dad sneaks, serial-killer glasses, neon visors. I maintained a uniform of all-black everything, the bulk of it from Saks Off Fifth. I was an alt JAP; they were just alt.

The crowd was mostly tourists. They loved it when I said shit like, "I'm thinking of freezing my eggs at a fertility clinic in Beverly Hills, so my eggs can live in the 90210."

But if thirty people laughed and three people didn't, those

three were clearly the most important. I wanted to write the kind of mixed bangers that tickled the out-of-towners while simultaneously signaling a scathing core of outré cred to the comics. My newest bit was about natural disasters.

"Anyone here from the East Coast?" I asked.

I was met with cheers from the crowd, a scowl from the light dude.

"Why do you guys know more about our weather than we do? My mother texts me every day from New Jersey about my impending death. 'You have now entered the dry season! The Weather Channel said someone in Pasadena just lit a candle! Be careful!'"

The mother part was sort of true. It had only been a day since the detox began, and I was now receiving cautionary weather missives in rapid-fire succession:

Just read about the Santa Anas on Yahoo! Remain alert!!
Earthquuke in Mojave Desert!!! 1.6 Did u feel it??
Tsunami warning in effect!! Do NOT sleep on the beach!!!

I tried to give the crowd a version of my life seasoned with enough "but really it's fine" bravado to make the underlying desperation that compelled me to stand there in the first place seeking validation from strangers a palatable experience— delightful, even! When they laughed at my sort-of truth, I felt the thrill of being sort of seen.

My college degree was in theater. I'd started as a freshman at the University of Wisconsin, spouting feverish diatribes about the dramatic arts as an agent of social change, inspired by a hot streak of high school roles as Abigail Williams in *The Crucible*, Nora Helmer in *A Doll's House*, and Sheila in *Hair*. This *was* the dawning of the Age of Aquarius, and I was going to usher in the new era.

But by the time I completed my first year, I'd learned two things. One was that I wasn't quite as talented as my high school drama teacher, Ms. Dannenfelser, seemed to believe. Another was that I fucking hated theater people. I hated the way they enunciated every consonant, even offstage. I hated their studied, deliberate movements, the idea of the self as craft, the body as instrument. By my third year I was only hanging out with the props people. I began doing open mic stand-up comedy at Blind Willie's Hideaway to take the edge off my dead dreams. I was good at comedy, or at least the patrons of Blind Willie's thought so. After the artifice of theater, I wanted something real. Drunk laughter felt real. I decided that after school I would move to Los Angeles and pursue it.

My LA life began with a job waitressing at a vegan diner on La Brea, followed by the realization that I was a terrible waitress. I was too easily distracted, obsessing about what the customers were eating: seitan-chorizo nachos, avocado tostadas, spinach-artichoke dip. I didn't have the energy to be on my feet all day. Sometimes, when no one was looking, I would stand there and touch all the food: stroking a bun, caressing a stuffed potato, massaging a warm flour tortilla. When somebody's uneaten soysage patty made its way into my mouth, I went home and applied to all of the sitting-down jobs I could find online.

I interviewed with Ofer, feigning excitement about "supporting" other artists—the same actor types I'd fled in college. Really, I just wanted a chair for my ass, a place of refuge from the avalanche of vegan donuts that threatened to suffocate me.

CHAPTER 6

I was required to burn 3,500 calories a week, a number I'd arrived at via an interactive equation of old Weight Watchers data, my daily caloric intake, and the way my clothes fit over time. I clung to my 3,500 like a winning lotto ticket. No one could lay a hand on it. The number guaranteed my security, physically and emotionally.

I was no athlete. I didn't run, swim, ski, or play soccer. I didn't fuck around with anything that could be defined as "sport" or "game." I was devoted to only one thing: the green glow of ascending numbers—147 cals, 215 cals, 319 cals—as I pedaled nowhere frantically on the stationary bike or elliptical machine.

I went to the gym every night, even Thursdays, when I'd change into spandex after work and then change again into an all-black outfit for cold-shouldering by the neon visors at This Show Sucks. I spent a good three hours at the gym most days: an existence defined by calories per minute, time elapsed, and stride length. My gym schedule, conveniently, precluded me from having to engage in any real human intimacy. Even if I'd wanted that, there simply wasn't time.

It was only after I'd served my gym sentence for the day that I could soften a little. Hunkered down at night, alone at home, having successfully completed the day's calibrating and calculating, I could reward myself with a culinary parade, a procession of delicacies rolling in one after the other.

First came a 240-calorie light frozen spaghetti dinner mixed with one tablespoon of Sriracha. Next was a medium sweet potato, microwaved for seven minutes, with three packets of Splenda poured into its guts. If I ever seemed to be gaining weight, the primary suspect was the size of the sweet potato—and so I would be forced to downgrade to a smaller potato for a few weeks: a sad, but necessary, alteration.

Following the sweet potato came Dessert One: a 100-calorie diet muffin top crowned with four tablespoons of Cool Whip Lite. All of this was eaten standing up in my empty galley kitchen, on paper plates, with plastic silverware. I owned no dishes or cutlery, no pots or pans. I did have a set of four extra-large Christmas glasses—printed with a lovely holly and berry motif—which had been left behind by the prior tenant.

Right before bed, I capped off the orgy with a pint of 150-calorie diet chocolate ice cream, microwaved for 45 seconds then mixed with half a cup of Special K Red Berries cereal. This delicacy I consumed under the covers in bed, converting my sheets into a temporary tablecloth.

Ending each day on such an abundant high note felt like freedom. Was it real freedom? Unlikely. But my rituals kept me skinny, and if happiness could be relegated to one thing alone, skinniness, then one might say I was, in a way, happy.

CHAPTER 7

"**C**an you believe how well I'm doing?" I asked Dr. Mahjoub.

It was day 3 of the detox, and I was still holding strong, but I'd come to her office for an extra reinforcement session when the weather alerts from my mother suddenly took a darker turn. Now I was receiving allegations of ungrateful daughterhood in the form of rhetorical questions:

Who took you to Baby Thespian classes at the Paper Mill Playhouse?

Who was there for you when you didn't get Éponine??!

Who cheered for you when you got into Wisconsin??

Am I such a horrible person!?!!

She texted repeatedly, then stopped and waited a few hours, then texted again. The silent times were the hardest. That was when I had to mourn. I would close one eye and look at my phone, imagine it cracking in half, the way people sitting shiva ripped a piece of clothing. I didn't want to mourn. I didn't want to accept my loss—not only the loss of communication, but the loss of an idea that my mother was going to be the one to change. It made me feel like a loser. It meant I had wanted something and hadn't gotten it, that I'd been, in some way, rejected. It meant my needs were too big for this world.

"This is a good first step," said Dr. Mahjoub. "But if you're really serious about getting free of your mother's voice, we've got to work on your eating."

I could tell by the breathable cotton tunics she wore, the cropped, wide-legged pants in organic linen, that Dr. Mahjoub was a woman who ate when she was hungry and stopped when she was full. Occasionally I spotted a package of Fig Newmans on her desk. She was probably someone who genuinely enjoyed a nice pear.

"Why can't I leave things the way they are?" I asked.

"Are you satisfied with just surviving?" asked Dr. Mahjoub. "Or do you want to get well?"

I glanced at a papier-mâché elephant kneeling on her end table with his trunk in the air, then at a multicolored elephant triptych hanging on the wall. She'd definitely bought all the elephants at once.

"I'm well enough," I said.

On my way out of the office I checked my phone again. No new texts. What would happen if my mother just showed up at my apartment? Rationally, I knew this was unlikely. She was terrified of flying and had not been on a plane in over ten years. But all night, I kept expecting her to materialize. In some way, I even wished she would just appear.

I was aware that the mother I truly desired would not be the one who appeared. I'd learned that from Dr. Mahjoub, who I never wanted to see again. I felt resentful toward Mahjoub, exhausted by my mother. I wished that I could procure, from nowhere, an incarnation of a mother I wanted. This interplay between hope and reality was also part of the mourning.

CHAPTER 8

Ana was the only maternal figure I had left. I wanted to please her more than ever. I wanted her to soak me in praise. I also recognized that I was physically attracted to her. This was something I'd tried to conceal, especially from myself, but it was bursting out of me. Every time I masturbated, Ana popped into my head; and when she surfaced—her giant breasts and slender waist, the little bulge just above her pussy, her heady white floral perfume—I always blocked her image out. I felt ashamed, as though it were my own mother I was fantasizing about. But on night four of the detox, as I masturbated drowsily in bed, I allowed myself to imagine being with Ana fully for the first time.

I was her daughter and had menstrual cramps. Mommy Ana had cajoled me into bed with a cup of Harney & Sons tea. I lay still under the cool sheets as she spoke to me in a hushed voice, almost a whisper.

"Can I rub your belly?" she asked.

She was wearing a pink bathrobe, which was slightly open, and I could see the length of her abundant breasts in the dim light.

"Yes," I said. "That would be nice."

She really wanted to comfort me. She was just aching to soothe me. She was dying for it. I felt beautiful and treasured as she cooed and rubbed my lower abdomen over my cotton pajamas (I was wearing cotton pajamas as I touched myself in reverie).

"I'm going to take this off," she said of her robe. "So I can be more comfortable in rubbing you."

"Okay," I said.

When she opened her robe, a waft of her white floral perfume came toward me like a sweet and filthy wind. There was also the smell of her pussy in the air, salty and a little fishy. Her breasts were gorgeous pendulums with big nipples the color of dusky valentines, ample and perfect. But that bump below her waist, just above her pussy, where the flesh had gathered in her aging, drove me the craziest. I wanted to rub against it, then work my way down to her pubic hair: unshaved and unwaxed, a thick mound of dark and coarse femininity.

I could hear her breathing as she rubbed my abdomen softly.

"How does that feel?" she asked.

"Good," I whispered.

"Good," she said.

I was beginning to get the feeling she liked me as more than a daughter. I mean, she was naked. But she hadn't yet touched any parts of me that a mother wouldn't touch.

"I want you to feel good," she said, as she continued to tenderly stroke my tummy.

She moved her body over me so that her face was by my face, her hair brushing against my cheek. She nuzzled my forehead, the tip of my nose, my neck. Then she kissed me very lightly on the lips. There was a pause. Then she kissed me again, this time with her mouth open. Her tongue was in my mouth, tasting for mine like a ripe strawberry.

So it was confirmed. Mommy wanted me! She was seducing me, and she didn't even seem the least bit ashamed. If she wasn't ashamed, then I wouldn't be ashamed. I was merely the seducee. I was the innocent one here.

"You are the innocent one here," she said.

I loved being the innocent one. I heard a soft moan come out of my mouth, filling hers. Gently, she lifted up my shirt and moved her lips to my nipples. I felt like I was made of liquid, viscous, throbbing with ache. I continued to rub myself frantically, imagining what would come next. I replayed that first tongue kiss again and again. Then she let her tits dangle over my face. I suckled on each one, thinking: *Feed me, Mommy! So that I may live!*

My real mother had not breastfed me. She said I hurt her nipples too much. I knew that if Ana were my mother, she would have breastfed me as a little baby. Now she was doing it again. I sucked as much as I could of her nipple into my mouth. I wanted to choke on her, to gag on her, to be filled up entirely with her breast, all the way down my throat. I made little squelching noises as I sucked.

Her legs straddled my thigh. Then she began to ride me. Her thigh moved on my pussy in a circular motion. Her pubic hair was thick and wiry. I could feel her wetness, how much she wanted me. I could smell her fish and flowers. She was doing everything. I only had to lie there and be myself.

Every time I got close to coming, I would stop masturbating and let the wave of my pleasure simmer back down.

I want you to eat me, I thought as I edged closer.

The consuming mother, I thought as I pulled away.

I want you to eat me, closer, closer.

The consuming mother, further, further.

Then I got so close that I could not pull myself back from the edge. I spilled over, dissolving into pure light.

When the wave of pleasure receded, Mommy Ana had disappeared. In her place was office manager Ana. She was seated in a Staples ergonomic chair, headset on, eating a shrimp Caesar from Simply Salad, answering the phone.

"The Crew, please hold."

CHAPTER 9

Ofer was unhappy with the company that sold the fake Instagram followers we purchased for our clients.

"They aren't paying enough attention to diversity along the lines of race, ethnicity, and gender," he said as we sat down together at Last Crush.

"But the followers are fake," I said.

"They should look real. When we get back to the office, I want you to start researching other companies. Find out prices, longevity, the diversity of the fake followers, and—what's that crinkling sound?"

The crinkling sound was me. I was attempting to extricate a piece of nicotine gum from its foil wrapper in my purse. Usually, I'd remove at least five pieces of the gum and place them bareback in the purse, along with a ball of toilet paper for the chewed ones, prior to any client lunch. This enabled me to access the gum soundlessly. But I'd forgotten to pre-release the gum, and was now forced to extricate in-booth while we waited on the arrival of Ofer's prize pig—an actor named Jason Blagojevich, who called himself "Jace Evans"—and his two agents.

Jace had a lead role as "Liam" on a hot new CW show, *Breathers*, about three sexy young people who survive a zombie apocalypse. The show had become a phenomenon in the teen market and was growing popular with the types of adults who acted ironically anti-intellectual but were maybe just dumb. *Breathers* had just been renewed for a second season, and Jace was sitting pretty. He'd only been out of Akron for less than two years.

Ofer began repping Jace before he had an agent. He managed to secure him the part without agency representation, which was rare. Jace's agents, two heat-seeking sheep named Josh and Josh, had "joined the team" just in time to do the contract. They never would have touched Jace without a pilot, but now they acted like they'd birthed him.

"My duuudes!" grunted Ofer, rising to greet Jace and the Joshes. He secretly hated the Joshes, claiming they lacked a moral compass, but I knew the real reason for his animosity was because they thought he couldn't hack it in the agency world. I was happy the Joshes were in attendance. The more people at the table, the less anyone paid attention to what I ate.

I was there to take notes on my phone. Mostly, I googled calorie counts and tried not to stare at Jace. I couldn't decide if I was attracted to him. His hair was exhausting, a shaved under-cut with a skyward floof on top. The floof was straining to stay erect, while the overall look struggled to find itself: punk or pompadour, skinhead or sculpture, it didn't know what it was. Jace clearly invested a lot of time and money in his hair, though I didn't imagine any salons survived the zombie apocalypse.

Jace was the type of dude who always seemed like he was wear-ing a fedora—even when he wasn't. He wore two rosaries around his neck, which I assumed were from Fred Segal. His motorcycle jacket appeared new, yet pre-distressed, and the stacks of leather and metal bracelets on his wrists suggested he was headed off to battle in an ancient war right after lunch. On his left hand, he had a freckle the size of a pencil eraser. I decided it was ugly.

"I'm concerned about Liam's love triangle going into next season," said Jace, caressing his own jaw with his freckle hand. "I hope the writers don't make it the central conflict of the show."

I typed the words *central conflict* in my notes. I was surprised he knew what that was.

"Agreed, it's a show about survival, not love," said Josh.

I typed: *survival not love.*

"Ofer, let's find a constructive way to express Jace's concern to the network," said the other Josh.

"On it," said Ofer. "Though I think the tone change is flattering. When Jace was cast, no one had any idea what a star he would become. Except me, of course."

I would not have called Jace a star. A glow-in-the-dark sticker, maybe.

"We just have to make sure the world of the show stays authentic," said Jace.

I typed: *authentic.* It was a show about zombies. How authentic could the world be?

I could never tell if other people genuinely believed their own bullshit or not. I felt genuinely perplexed about it—especially at work lunches, but frequently in my nonlunch life too. At times like this, I longed to break the fourth wall, to whisper, *Hey, just between us: Is this a performance or is it really what you believe?*

I decided that Jace was objectively attractive. I didn't necessarily want our genitals to touch, but there was a certain place in my mind, or maybe in my solar plexus, where I liked him. I felt programmed, like a drug-sniffing dog, to seek his approval.

What I wanted most was for this certified hot person to see a hotness in me, thereby verifying, once and for all, that I was hot. It wasn't that civilians didn't find me attractive. But for a licensed hot person to verify me? That was the real shit.

"Maybe we need to remind the network that Jace has fans elsewhere," said Josh.

I typed: *fans.*

"He's got fans at Netflix, fans at Universal," said the other Josh. "Big fans at Universal, and on the movie side too."

I typed: *fans fans. big fans.*

Jace turned to me.

"Thanks for taking notes," he said.

He acted like I was doing this voluntarily. Still, he seemed nice. But he could afford to be nice. All of the attention was on him. If he were in my position, if he weren't the one being feted, would he be so nice?

"No prob," I said, looking at the word BEEF printed on the back wall over his head.

Last Crush had a farm-to-hell look that always made me think of death by hanging: wooden beams, lightbulbs dangling from the ceiling like ligatures. There were enough upcycled bulbs to illuminate a stadium. Nobody needed that much light.

"Bread?" asked Jace, extending a basket of carbs threateningly close to my head.

I imagined a pack of zombies infiltrating the restaurant, smearing blood and pus on the stone floors, the fake-rustic walls, soaking the bread. Whose brains would they eat first? Probably Jace's because he had the most fans.

"Thank you," I said. "But no."

CHAPTER 10

Dr. Mahjoub wouldn't let me break up with her by phone.

"If you're going to terminate, it's important that we honor the work we've done together with a final processing session," she said.

I didn't want to honor anything. But now I was seated across from her, and between us were four containers of something called Theraputticals Anti-Microbial Modeling Clay.

"Rachel, if this is going to be our last session together, I'd like us to try something a little different," she said. "I was hoping that you might be amenable to doing a bit of art therapy work."

I wasn't amenable. But the clay seemed ready to go.

"Over the course of our sessions, I've written down some words you've used to describe your body," she said, clearing her throat. "Amorphous. Out of control. Disgusting. Exploding. These kinds of words reveal to me a deep dysmorphia—"

"No," I said. "I don't feel like I'm exploding."

"That was the word you used."

"I was talking about the future. I just don't want to get to that point. Of exploding."

"So, it would be more accurate to say that these descriptors are what you . . . fear becoming."

"That's right."

"But not how you see yourself now."

"Not today."

"Okay," she said. "I'd still like to try this approach, if we may. I was going to ask that you use the clay to sculpt an image of yourself. I was hoping that we might identify, in a visual, tactile way, the discrepancy between how you perceive yourself and how you actually appear to others—"

"You mean, like a self-portrait?"

"Yes," she said. "But now I'm thinking it might be more productive, and lead to greater insight, if you would be willing to sculpt for me—well, for yourself, really—a rendering of those future fears you describe. Who is that 'out of control' woman you are so afraid of becoming? What does she look like?"

"You want me to make a body?"

"Well, yes," she said.

Did I look like Michelangelo? I was annoyed. But there were still 36 minutes left until termination.

I opened the container of pink Theraputticals, took out the whole blob, smushed it with my hand. I broke off a chunk and shaped a round head. Then I put the head down on Dr. Mahjoub's glass coffee table. I took the rest of the clay and started mushing it into a torso. I began shaping an immense belly, huge tits. But there wasn't nearly enough clay, so I opened the blue container. Then the green. I made massive thighs, weighty calves, a voluminous ass. I layered more and more clay, swirling it into an immense psychedelic woman.

I lost myself in the sculpting. I actually enjoyed the sensation: the cool of the clay, the way it warmed in my hands, the not-thinking, the feeling my way around, the enlarging of my woman. I also realized, as I sculpted, that I wasn't so much making what I was scared of becoming, a future, but a shape I already knew very well. It was a shape that had always lived inside of me. It was destined to come out. What was even scarier was how much my hands liked this.

I used the last of the yellow clay to give her hair. Then I held the figure up to Dr. Mahjoub.

"There," I said. "Happy?"

"Well done, Rachel. I really appreciate your willingness to try that. You seemed to rather enjoy the exercise, no?"

"It was fine," I said.

"Good. So let me ask you. This body—this creature you've sculpted—this is what you mean when you say 'amorphous, exploding, out of control'?"

"I don't know," I said. "I just made it because you told me to."

"Uh-huh," she said, adjusting a sensible clog. "And let me ask you, do you imagine this is what you will look like if—"

"No," I said. "It's just a thing."

I didn't want to tell her that I did feel, in some way, like the figure was part of me—that I'd made her from the inside out.

"Well, I think she's rather lovely," said Dr. Mahjoub. "Don't you think she's lovely?"

"She's fine," I said.

"Yes, I think she's quite lovely. And I think she's worthy of love—more than worthy of love, actually? Don't you think so?"

"What?"

"Don't you think that she's worthy of love?"

"Yeah," I said, my cheeks burning. "I guess so."

I was crying. I felt angry, tricked. This was supposed to be closure, not some psychological art show.

I stormed out of the office without even paying my copay. When I got to my car, I realized I still had the stupid clay figure in my hand. I opened my trunk, then buried the thing in a trash bag of old clothes.

"Fuck insight," I said, and slammed the trunk shut.

CHAPTER 11

On day 7 of the detox, I went over to Yo!Good for my usual 16-ounce no-topping delight, only to discover that the Orthodox boy wasn't working. In his place was a woman who looked to be my age—maybe a little younger, twenty two or twenty-three. She was very pale, with light blue eyes and a braid of wheat-blond hair. Her eyebrows were gold, eyelashes nearly white. Her fair complexion made her other features seem surprising— as though I forgot that lips could be pink, and then, in looking at her mouth, remembered again.

On one of her round cheeks was a small brown beauty mark, like a caramel chip from the toppings bar. There was a rosiness to her cheeks, a natural flush that swept over the beauty mark, interacting with it, bathing it in a wash of color. On her neck was a triangle of three darker moles: a dark chocolate drop on her Adam's apple, framed by two milk chocolate drops to the left. She looked both Jewish and not Jewish at the same time—but there was something distinctly Jewish about her, a shtetl essence that perhaps only a fellow Jew could detect.

Above all, she was fat: undeniably fat, irrefutably fat. She wasn't thick, curvy, or chubby. She surpassed plump, eclipsed heavy. She was fat, and she exceeded my worst fears for my own body.

But it was as though she didn't know or care that she was fat.

If she were concerned with hiding her body, she could have worn something baggy and black. Instead, she'd stuffed herself into a straight-cut, pale blue cotton dress, modest in its long sleeves and ankle-length skirt, but otherwise revealing every stomach roll, side bulge, and back fold of her body. The soft fabric stretched and sheered as it detoured her hips and ass. Her breasts were enormous—an F cup? a G cup?—but the dress did nothing to flatter them. The dress was there and the breasts were there, and neither was cooperating with the other.

When she caught me staring at her, she said, "What can I get for you?" She said it nicely and briskly, as though she didn't care that I'd been staring.

"I'll have the sugar-free, fat-free cappuccino swirled with the sugar-free, fat-free cheesecake," I said. "Medium."

She reached for a large cup.

"No," I said. "Medium. The sixteen-ounce one."

She put the large cup back and picked up a medium cup.

"Oh," I said. "Also, I—only want it filled to the top of the cup. Like, not over the lip."

She nodded that she understood. Then she pulled the lever and I heard the whirr of the machine. I watched closely as she rotated the cup under the swirling yogurt. She was good, precise, leaving no pockets of air, just how I liked it. But as the yogurt approached the top of the cup, she showed no signs of slowing down.

"That's enough," I said softly.

She didn't stop. The yogurt took a full lap above the rim.

"That's enough!" I called out, loudly this time.

She released the lever on the machine, halting the flow of yogurt. Then she turned to me.

"It's priced by cup size, not by weight. We won't charge you for the extra."

"Oh," I said casually. "Okay."

She pulled the lever again and the flow of yogurt resumed. The swirls piled higher and higher, forming a creamy, glistening castle that towered high above the cup.

"What toppings do you want?" she asked, clearly not yet finished with destroying my life.

"Um, none. That's okay as it is," I said.

"Nothing?" she asked.

"Yeah, I like it plain."

She looked at me incredulously, but I couldn't worry about what she thought, because I had other problems. There were 32 ounces of yogurt in my 16-ounce cup. I needed a strategy.

I could eat the Northern Hemisphere of the yogurt down to the rim, then throw the southern half away. But that seemed sad to me. Who wanted to stop? It would be much more pleasant to lop off the top half and then have the rest of the cup to enjoy. But where could I get rid of it? I couldn't just throw the offending portion away in front of her. I was going to have to go outside to do surgery on the yogurt.

I found a trash can by the curb and was then met with another problem: it had no hole. It was one of those California-architectural sanitation masterpieces with a puny slot. There was no way to dump out the offending portion of yogurt all at once. I could scoop off small spoonfuls gradually, but then I needed leverage—something upon which to tap the spoon and release the blobs of yogurt into the slot. I wasn't about to touch the spoon to the can.

I scooped a small spoonful of yogurt out of the cup. Then I rapped the spoon against my phone, just over the slot. This rapping motion provided enough friction to dislodge the yogurt. I scooped again. Then rapped. Scooped. Rapped. I became so focused in my work that I didn't see NPR Andrew walking right by me.

"Hi, Rachel," he said.

I looked up, mid-rap. He was wearing earbuds and sunglasses. He had a smirk on his tiny face. He continued walking.

So the little shit had witnessed my process. I felt violated, disgraced. I prayed that he couldn't fully comprehend what he had seen. At the very least, he knew it was something freaky.

Well, my yogurt was ready. I could eat in self-disgust and peace. I stood in the sunlight, licking the melty parts first, then transitioning into the ritual of spooning and squishing it against my teeth. Coffee and cheesecake was a good combo. Sublime, really.

CHAPTER 12

The trash can incident marked the beginning of a new phase: the era of yogurt interruptus. In the days that followed, the Orthodox boy never returned to work. In his place was always the zaftig girl, and there was no controlling her.

Each time she reached the lip of the cup, I'd call out, "Okay!" or "All good!" or "Whoa Nelly!"

But my Mayday cries only inspired her to hit the accelerator. Then she'd bring me my heaping yogurt and remind me, "We charge by cup size, not by weight."

I tried going to Yogurt World instead. The cup was the size of a fucking thimble.

An amuse-bouche, I said to myself. *Petit, chic, just a taste, lovely in a Parisian way.* But I was no Parisian.

I returned to Yo!Good with a new plan. After my yogurt was served, I would go around to the alley behind the store and eliminate the surplus in their spacious dumpster. Then I could enjoy my dessert blissfully, surrounded by flies and the stench of hot trash.

It was a vile, genius solution, and it worked as anticipated— until I got busted decapitating a peanut-butter-and-cake-batter swirl.

"The yogurt isn't good today?" asked the zaftig girl.

She was carrying two big bags of garbage.

"No," I said quickly. "Guess I should have stuck with coffee-cheesecake."

She nodded, then pulled out a cigarette and put it in her mouth. It was strange to see someone smoking in LA. The cigarette was a clove, which was always one of my favorites. In my anorexia heyday, I'd smoked clove cigarettes with diet hot chocolate and counted it as a meal. But this woman probably wasn't smoking as a meal. She was smoking because—she liked it.

I stared at the smoke moving in and out of her mouth. It looked as though she were exhaling a tree shape, one thick stream like a trunk and then little streams blowing off of it like branches.

"Do you want one?" she offered.

I did want one and said yes. She lit the cigarette for me, and I thought about the fact that she was always giving me things to put in my mouth. Was this girl my worst nightmare?

My eyes went to the three moles on her neck. I felt a strange desire to suck on them.

As a kid I'd had three moles just like that. They'd lived on the inside of my right arm, below the inner elbow crease. Her moles were bigger than mine had been, but both hers and mine—if connected with a pen—formed a shape like the Big Dipper.

I'd hated those moles: their prominence, their strangeness, the way I felt they called attention to my arm chub. I always wished they were on the outside of my arm instead. The inside was such a soft, vulnerable place, more shameful than the outside.

It hurt when the dermatologist shot me with novocaine, then lopped them off with something that looked like a hole puncher. But I felt elated to have them gone, free. Now, on the inside of my arm, there were three little white scars—each a tiny cloud. I hadn't noticed them in years.

"You're working here full-time now?" I asked her, trying to suss out the situation.

"I'm filling in for my brother Adiv," she said. "He's traveling in Israel."

That was all she said about that: *He's traveling in Israel.* She issued no disclaimers. There was no: *He has mixed feelings about the political situation* or *He's not on Birthright or anything* or *I'm personally for Boycott, Divestment, Sanctions.*

"My family owns this place," she said. "All of the Yo!Good shops. I fill in whenever they need me. I'm Miriam, by the way."

That was my Hebrew middle name. I was Rachel Meredith, and in Hebrew, Rachel Miriam. I didn't tell her.

"I'm Rachel," I said. "I'm surprised you smoke."

"Because I'm religious?"

"Yeah," I said. "And because it's LA. It's nice to see someone who isn't afraid of cancer. I mean, life is long enough."

"You're funny," she said without laughing. "Orthodox people smoke. And drink. I love to drink. Mai tais."

"Mai tais?"

"They're tropical."

"I know what they are. It's just an interesting choice."

"Are you Jewish?" she asked.

"Yes," I said. "But bad. I'm a very, very bad Jew."

"Me too." She laughed. "But you keep kosher?"

"No," I said, taking a puff of clove: warm, sweet, and cinnamon-y.

"Oh," she said. "I do."

When she said she was a bad Jew, she definitely did not mean it in the way I meant it.

"There's a kosher Chinese restaurant on Fairfax that makes the best mai tais. The Golden Dragon. Ever been there?"

I shook my head no. I tried to imagine what it would be like to be her: drinking and eating her way through a smorgasbord. I wondered if she got egg rolls, scallion pancakes, all that good fried shit. I bet she did.

"Do you drink?" she asked.

"Definitely," I said, even though I didn't really, because I didn't want the extra calories.

"I love it," she said. "Especially getting drunk with my family. There are eight of us, six kids. It's a lot of fun."

I'd never thought of Orthodox Judaism as fun—more as sexism and rules.

"Sounds fun," I said.

"It's total *mishigas*." She laughed.

Then she exhaled another smoke tree.

"So," she said. "You're close with your family?"

CHAPTER 13

O n day 13 of the detox, my father called.

"To what do I owe the pleasure?" I asked.

I was standing in my bathroom with wet hair, having just finished Breakfast One in the shower.

"Rachel, I don't know what this is about a 'detox,' but you better call your mother immediately."

If she was bringing my father into this, she had to be desperate.

"Tell her I'm fine," I said.

"I'm glad you're fine. That's not the point. The point is that now she's calling *me* every day and I have to hear about it."

Displeasing my father was painful. He rarely expressed disapproval about anything. When my parents were together, he never confronted my mother about the way she policed my food. Instead, he would sneak me out for all-you-can-eat junk food benders to compensate. When they divorced, he remarried a ceramicist named Christina (not a Jew) and moved to the Berkshires. I only saw him a few times a year, but I had no real daddy issues to speak of. Even in his absence, I at least knew where I stood.

When he'd come to town on my birthday or for Chanukah, we would gorge all day. We'd do lunch and dinner out: the diner and the Chinese restaurant, or a farm place in a real barn where they served plate after plate of creamed spinach, creamed corn, waffles. Then we'd go to the candy store and the 7-Eleven to load me up with bags of junk food. My mother gave me 24 hours to keep my stash before it all got thrown out. I wished I could hide my riches, but she took an inventory of all of it when I walked in the door.

The only time I remember feeling sad about my father's absence was on my tenth birthday. After he dropped me off back at home, I changed into my pajamas and went down to the kitchen for a round of junk food. I had 23 hours left to eat, and I was determined to get in as much as I could.

Rifling through the 7-Eleven bag, I found a box I hadn't seen him buy. It was one of those packages that contains all different little bags of chips: Cheetos, Doritos, pretzels. On the box, in big red and yellow letters was printed: VARIETY PACK.

What was this? It seemed he'd chosen a special, secret box just for me. While I'd been busy with the Slurpee machine, he must have been inspecting the shelves, his glasses falling down his nose, ruminating on the question: *What's something Rachel would really like?*

Suddenly, his Dad eyes had spotted it: Variety Pack. With his Dad hand, he reached out and touched it. Variety Pack! Maybe he'd even whispered out loud, "The Variety Pack—yes, she might really enjoy that."

"Variety Pack, Variety Pack," I said, as I stood in the kitchen, eating and crying.

The words were beautiful to me. Also devastating.

"Rachel, am I on speaker? Can you hear me?" asked my father.

"Sorry," I said.

Water was dripping from my hair onto the screen, and I knew it would fuck up my swiping for days.

"Please talk to her," he said. "As a favor to me. For my sake."

"I can't," I said. "No more hardware store."

"What?" he asked.

"Nothing."

I looked at my wet face in the mirror. Was my face getting more annoying? My neck looked like it had somehow gotten thicker.

"This isn't easy for me either," I said.

"So then—"

"But listen. Just because something feels bad doesn't mean it's wrong."

"Huh," said my father. "Who said that? Benjamin Franklin?"

CHAPTER 14

A great miracle occurred. Adiv returned.

"Shalom!" I called out when I saw him behind the counter.

"Shalom," he said, looking confused.

Never, I was sure, had any customer been so happy to see Adiv back at it. This was my burning bush, my Noah and the Ark and the dove. I was to be captain of my dessert realm again: no more peer-pressured extras or yogurt in conversation.

I wondered how his experience in Israel had been, what his views were. But a food-service interaction seemed an inopportune time to say, *Hey, any thoughts on a two-state solution?*

"I'll have the cheesecake," I said, omitting any discourse on land disputes.

Then Miriam emerged from the back.

"Hey, Rachel!" she said, signaling that she'd handle me.

"Oh, hi," I said.

"Be useful and go unbox the pretzel cones," she said to Adiv.

Adiv complied. I watched her grab a 16-ounce cup and pull the lever on the machine.

The yogurt began its ascent, swirling upward until it overtook the brim, entering the unsafe space above it. But then it transcended that realm, soaring to a new, unthinkable altitude before reaching a summit that was miles above where she began. Even for Miriam's style, the serving was absurd.

"I want to give you a free topping," she said. "Because you didn't like your last yogurt."

"That's okay," I said. "I don't want one."

"Come on," she said. "There has to be something you like. What about sprinkles? I'm just going to put sprinkles on it, just a little."

"Rainbow," I said instinctively, then thought, *Fuck*.

I watched her spooning on the sprinkles and noticed, for the first time, that she had lovely fingernails: smooth and egg-shaped, trimmed neatly. She wasn't a biter like me, a compulsive habit that began in childhood as something of a snack. Now I painted my nails red as a deterrent, but I only ended up biting off the polish too—spitting flakes of crimson.

When she handed me the yogurt, every inch of that mammoth peak was covered in rainbow sprinkles. It was gorgeous, seamless, as though the yogurt were a rainbow itself: no separation between dessert and topping. Its beauty made me think for a moment that it should have always been this way.

I stared at the sculptural masterpiece in my hand. I wanted to kiss it, to make out with it, to touch it with my tongue and lips and explore what those tiny textures felt like. Simply holding the cup, I was rocketed back to sprinkles past. I remembered that they were actually made of tiny bits of dried frosting, and the way you could dissolve them in your mouth, suck until they softened back to frosting once again, completing one of life's great cycles of transformation.

"See?" said Miriam. "Everybody loves a topping."

I smiled at her and felt weak. Then, as though compelled by an otherworldly force, I brought that majestic mountain to my mouth, licked it, and took a bite.

"Mmmmmmm," I said with my mouth full. "Thanks."

I closed my eyes. The sprinkles were so delicious, melting there on my tongue, that my throat began to call out for them.

What would be the harm? What would be the harm? said my throat. *What would be so bad about just swallowing?*

Of course, I knew what the harm would be. Sprinkles were loaded with sugar, and there was no way of knowing how many of them were packed into any given mouthful. From one bite to the next, it would be impossible to calculate a caloric load.

Panicking, I spun on my heel and headed for the door. I hoped that I could keep the concoction in my mouth long enough without swallowing to get to the trash can on the curb. But when I reached the can, my lips would not open to relinquish the mouthful. I stood there and swallowed it down my gullet.

Then, to my horror, I found myself sticking my tongue into a crevice between yogurt and cup, where a small pile of naked sprinkles had fallen. I licked them out. I didn't stop, but pressed on to where the sprinkles and some drips of melted yogurt had formed a viscous union. I chewed these bites up quickly and swallowed again and again, as though this were the fastest way to get rid of them.

While I ate, I watched myself—like I was hovering up above, split into two beings. One of me was the one doing the eating. The other observed myself in shock as I continued to devour it all. *Stop! Stop!* called out the observer me, but it was no use.

I was consumed by the yogurt, all five senses bathing in its drips and swirls, as though I had entered some yogurt door, no thought, no vision or sound but the yogurt and its sprinkles, any fear or hesitation fully eclipsed by sensation, the crunch, the slurp, the melt, the heavenly feeling of cleaning each side evenly with my tongue—hardness and softness, sweetness and more sweetness— a prism of beauty on Earth and above it, and me, the me on the ground, nothing but a giant mouth and tongue, eating and eating for nothing, not one thing, except sheer pleasure alone.

I don't know how long I stood there in front of the trash can: devouring, licking, swallowing. I only knew that when my mind and body were finally united again, the first thing I noticed was the sour smell of trash in the warm sun. I felt afraid, then a hot shame. It had really happened. I'd eaten the whole thing. All that remained was a dribble at the bottom with two sprinkles floating in it: one pink and one blue. I dug them out with my spoon and put that last little bite in my mouth.

Something had taken me over, possessed me, some phantom transmitted from Miriam to me, or a demon lurking latent all these years, now suddenly awakened. I had not lost control like that with food since I was sixteen. I'd thought the demon was dead.

No, that wasn't true. I'd sensed the demon in me all along, waiting for the right moment to open my mouth, suck the world down my throat. All of my restriction, my efforts at control, as I tiptoed daily around the edge of hunger, were enacted in the name of keeping that demon shut up: sleep late to delay calories, write everything down, eat ice, avoid friends. But in all that busy-work, I'd forgotten what made the demon space so dangerous in the first place. When you were in it, it felt fucking great.

On the way back to the office, I stopped off at my car in the parking garage. I opened the trunk and rifled angrily through the trash bag of clothes where I'd dumped the sculpture I made in therapy. Fucking Mahjoub. I'd show her honoring the work! I pulled out two black dresses, a dirty black T-shirt, and a pair of old Nikes. No sculpture. I took out a black blouse with a hole in the sleeve, a bralette, one black patent leather high heel, a black skirt. Now the bag was empty. Still no sculpture. Maybe it had fallen out of the bag and gotten loose in the trunk?

My trunk was filled with so much shit. The thing could be anywhere under all of that crap! I began pulling items out and placing them on the floor of the parking garage: sunglasses, a box of broken planters, my college diploma, a case of Coke Zero, wiper fluid, a spare tire, my missing copy of *The Fran Lebowitz Reader*, three empty cans of Coke Zero. No sculpture. It was gone.

CHAPTER 15

We were invited to a party for the cast and crew of *Breathers*, to celebrate their second season renewal. I dreaded these kinds of events. The rooms were always filled with the professionally skinny, the skinny-for-pay, the ultra-ultra-skinny. I knew it would be impossible to shrink myself down to that next tier of skinny without suffering more than I was already suffering. On the suffering scale, I was currently at about a seven-point-five. I felt unwilling to go up to a nine or ten. But when I observed the ultra-ultra-skinny, I forgot about that suffering and saw only the ways they appeared to be protected—cocooned by an absence of flesh—from judgment, hurt, or shame. When I looked at the ultra-ultra-skinny, I thought: *safe*.

Ofer acted like he was doing me a favor by bringing me along, as though I actually gave a shit about this circus. Once we arrived, he was in full networking mode and had no use for me. I tracked his bald head as he made his way around the room, sniffing out the dissatisfied talent: the actors and actresses whose managers weren't doing enough for them—their eternal cry.

I was starving. I feared that at any moment my hand and mouth could form a secret shared alliance, wherein my hand would unconsciously reach out and make a grab for the butlered hors d'oeuvres: the pigs in a blanket, chicken-and-waffle bites, and small rustic pizzas that mined the whole room. I had my protein bar stashed away in my purse, ready to safeguard me from hunger. But I couldn't just whip it out in the crowded room when there was so much other food available.

I would have to consume the bar in the bathroom. I had no qualms with eating in bathrooms, really. If given the choice, I'd much prefer to eat a protein bar alone on the toilet than do cocktail hour under the watchful eyes of others. At least a bathroom was a room of one's own.

Unfortunately, this bathroom had two stalls. Another woman already occupied one of them. I entered my stall, sat down, and waited. I wanted to hold off until she left in case my chewing made any noise. The protein bar was soft, consisting of whey proteins, not loud like a granola bar, or anything in the crunchy family. Still, I craved total privacy.

When the woman finished peeing, another woman came in and took over her stall immediately. When that woman finished, a third woman entered. This third woman made no noise. She simply sat there silently for a very long time. I knew she was waiting for me to leave so she could do her business. We were locked in a stalemate, and neither of us was moving.

I was starving. It was now or never—I would have to let her win. As quietly as possible, I took the protein bar out of my purse. The wrapper made a loud crinkling sound when I opened it. I hoped that my neighbor would think it was a tampon wrapper. Gingerly, I took a bite and tried to chew quietly. The saliva in my mouth made juicy, squelching noises. It was time to just say fuck it and surrender. I took my next bite with more gusto, chewing heartily.

Suddenly, I heard a series of farts erupt from the stall next door, then the sound of shit plopping, unmistakably diarrhea, then more farts. I wondered if the woman felt ashamed, knowing that I was there to hear it. What an exciting feeling! I was happy not to be the one who was ashamed for once. Then the smell hit me. I didn't know what to do. Should I finish the bar, steeped in diarrhea smell? Should I go back to the party light-headed with low blood sugar? As more shit fell, I was unable to continue eating. I swallowed my bite, put the bar in my bag, and flushed even though I hadn't peed.

I washed and dried my hands, then took the remainder of the bar out of my bag, unpeeled it, and shoved the rest in my mouth. I swung open the bathroom door, mouth full of bar like a chipmunk.

"Hi, Rachel."

It was Jace Evans. There was no way I could open my mouth. I already felt a little puddle of drool forming in the right corner of my lips. I gave him a little wave and tried to keep walking, but he stopped me.

"Is anyone in the women's room? Some guy locked himself in the men's for the past ten minutes," he said. "I have to talk to media, but I really gotta go."

"Mmm-hmm," I said, lips still clenched and bulging like I had a mouth guard in. I held up two fingers to indicate that there were two people in there.

"Oh, okay," he said. "You all right?"

"Mmm-hmm," I said again, trying to suck the giant ball of bar farther back in my mouth. There was no way I could swallow it without choking. It had the consistency of a Tootsie Roll. Instinctively, once it reached my molars, I started chewing.

"Do you always eat in the bathroom?" he asked.

CHAPTER 16

"Where's Adiv?" I asked, as Miriam greeted me at the counter with a big smile.

"Packing his stuff," she said.

"Oh?"

"He's going back to Israel. Basic training. He's going to be serving in the IDF."

"Oh."

The IDF?! The situation was more alarming than I'd imagined. Maybe it shouldn't be surprising. Adiv did seem like the "follows orders" type. He took commands well with a yogurt machine at least, which was more than could be said of Miriam.

"Listen," I said, before she went over to the machine. "I only want the yogurt to the top of the cup, no higher."

I said it firmly and solemnly.

"Okay," she said, shrugging.

She filled the cup, exceeding the rim by a few centimeters—probably out of spite.

"What toppings do you want?" she asked.

So we were still playing this game.

"I don't want any toppings," I said.

"Didn't you enjoy the sprinkles last time?"

Oh, I'd enjoyed them, all right.

"They were fine," I said. "But I prefer it plain."

"Maybe try a different topping this time," she said.

"No, that's okay."

"How about this? Why don't you let me make you something special? If you hate it, I will just give you your plain cup to the rim, exactly the way you want it."

This was coercion, intimidation by butterscotch. I wanted to tell her to go away, that she was ruining something secure and delicious in my world. But another part of me —that same wild part that had lapped up the sprinkles, the demon of my old insatiable hunger—felt liberated by her enthusiasm.

I opened my mouth and said, "Okay."

And when I said, "Okay," Miriam said "Okay" too.

She gave me a huge smile, her face flashing like a candle. I felt my anxiety dissipate. Gone was the fear that she was out to ruin me, the suspicion that she wanted to disappear me from myself, to make me hate myself, to send me spinning out into infinity, a nothing, a blob, so big I could be seen only in fragments, so unwieldy I could never be held, just an overwhelming void, just devastated, just dead. I looked at her smile, and I thought: *love*.

She moved silently to the toppings bar in her long blue dress, the same dress she wore the first time I'd seen her. I traced the many curves of her body around and around all the way to the floor. I wondered what she was going to do. I was scared. How many times had I made sundaes in my mind, never thinking the fantasies would actually be realized? I'd never even *wanted* the fantasies to be realized. I'd thought it was safe to fantasize, because my inner wall was so strong. My wall was thick, under my control. But now she was lifting the metal lid off the hot fudge with her pale hand, this sorceress at the cauldron, and not a low-calorie cauldron either, but regular hot fudge. She was taking up the ladle.

I watched her spoon three large puddles of fudge on top, the yogurt plateauing beneath the warm sauce, the sauce dripping down the sides, wildly volcanic. After each ladle, I thought she was going to stop, but she did not stop, she added a fourth, then a fifth ladle of fudge, the yogurt going totally Vesuvius. She paused for a moment, then dusted the entire thing with a layer of chopped peanuts. I was stunned. Never in my topping daydreams would I have thought to incorporate a peanut. She finished with whipped cream—just a dollop—and then a drizzle of strawberry syrup on top of that.

Miriam had made me an ice cream sundae. It was the perfect sundae you might see at a 1940s soda fountain or in a vintage housekeeping magazine. It was a throwback, food of another era, time-traveling to the Yo!Good counter. There was an innocence about it, a childlike quality. It was a treat that a child would receive from a caring older person who wanted to reward them just for existing.

When she handed me the cup, our hands touched. Her fingers were incredibly soft.

"Thank you," I said.

I didn't know what to do. I had forgotten how to say no, but I had also forgotten how to eat. I felt my hand tingling; the yogurt was heavy. I was unable to move the cup closer to me or farther away. Her hand touching mine had somehow paralyzed me. Maybe she'd cast a spell that was conveyed through touch.

Spoon, I thought. *Get. Spoon.*

I saw myself pick up a pink spoon from the dispenser on the counter. Stiffly, I lifted it up, then plunged it into the sundae. I penetrated the whipped cream and fudge down to the yogurt below. I wanted to taste all of it at once: yogurt, fudge, strawberry sauce, whipped cream, and peanuts. I brought the bite to my mouth. My mouth knew what to do. It opened. I shoveled the bite inside.

The taste was orchestral, so many different flavors in one. First the nuts blended with the strawberries, à la a peanut butter and jelly sandwich. Then the fudge cavorted with the nuts to create a candy bar essence. The whipped cream and strawberries were their own heaven: a strawberry shortcake of pleasure. I tasted them all in unison, but also separately. They coexisted in harmony, while each ingredient maintained its own identity.

"Good?" she asked.

"Uh-huh," I said.

I took another bite, savored it, then swallowed.

"I love it," I said. "You're really good at making sundaes."

"Thank you," she said. "When you work here, you start to know which flavors taste really good together. Next time you come I'll make you my personal signature. I call it the Peppermint Plotz."

"Yeah, that sounds really great," I said.

Then she pointed to her mouth and said, "You have a little chocolate on your lip," and giggled.

I admired how pale pink her lips were, like the pastel nonpareil white chocolates sold as toppings. When I wiped the chocolate off my lip and said "Thanks," I realized that my messiness caused me no embarrassment. I hadn't been propelled back through the portal from pleasure to shame. I felt like an innocent, a little girl who had done nothing wrong. I was cute in my joy and mess.

When I said goodbye and walked out, I already knew what was going to happen next. There was no way that I could calculate however many calories were in that sundae. I could get close, but the strawberry syrup and chocolate fudge and peanuts made it difficult, if not impossible, to discern quantities. I had crossed a line, if only for today, and there was no point in turning back now.

I would give myself just this one day to eat everything I wanted: all the things I had deprived myself for years. The day had already been claimed by the sundae, and the only logical next step was to bury it under more food. It would be like cutting off my head because of a headache. But I was so tired of my head.

CHAPTER 17

The first spot I hit was Immaculate Confection, a bakery I passed on my way to and from the office. I went inside and bought a slab of chocolate mousse cake covered with dark chocolate fondant, a slice of carrot cake with cream cheese frosting, an M&M cookie, a yellow cupcake with chocolate frosting, a chocolate chip cookie the size of my face, and a lone cannoli. It all cost $34.20, but I felt so proud to be a skinny person ordering all this cake—some fucking wonder of nature who ate and ate and showed none of it on her body—that I paid happily.

I brought the bakery boxes to my car, deep in the bowels of the parking garage. Then I got in the driver's seat and turned the heat on blast. I opened each of the boxes, waving my fingers like a pianist. I stuck two fingers in the carrot cake icing, then licked. I began mixing and matching, dunking and shoveling: the M&M cookie in the chocolate frosting, the chocolate chip cookie in the cannoli cream.

"Hrrrrrrrrrrrm!" I made a sound as I jammed the baked goods in my mouth, feeling loose and primal.

I lifted the cupcake, stuck my face in it like it was a pillow. Then a wave of nausea hit. I wished that for just this one day, I could have infinite room in my stomach. I wanted to take the memory of the day and put it in a snow globe full of frosting.

Then, when I returned to my calorie-counting life, I could always recall this binge and revel in the magnificence of it.

I decided I needed something savory to break up all the sweets. I put the half-eaten cookies and cakes in the boxes, then shoved them all under the passenger's seat.

"See you soon," I said to the baked goods, licking my fingers a final time.

I stopped inside Dr. Burrito. I had seen people eating burritos in there, so casually, and I wondered how they did it—just calmly ate something so fattening. The burritos always looked delicious, like warm babies swaddled up tight in blankets. I'd wanted to take a burrito and hold it to my cheek, or put it over my shoulder and soothe it.

I ordered the verde chicken burrito: strips of pulled chicken simmered soft and juicy in green sauce, guacamole, sour cream, cheese, Spanish rice, and black beans. I wasn't physically ready to consume my baby yet, so I decided to just carry it.

"There there, sweet bundle of beans and cheese. You are wanted."

Two blocks from the office, a cheese pizza called out to me from a window.

Rachel, said the pizza. *We should be together.*

I went inside and ate a huge slice in a front booth. I wanted the other customers to see what I was doing. I was a pizza-eating woman who somehow stayed slender. I was an amazing creature, a miracle. The sauce was sweet, and the crust was crispy. But it was becoming difficult to swallow. I felt like a landfill. Everything I'd consumed—the yogurt and baked goods and pizza—were piled on top of one another, teetering toward my throat.

I thought about ancient Rome, how they supposedly made themselves throw up so they could make room for more feasting. I had tried to purge many times, particularly when I was young and bingeing, but I'd never been successful. I'd jam my fingers down my throat and bring on tears, spit, mucus, a red face, the sensation that my head was going to fall off into the toilet. I'd come out with a few coughs into the toilet water, maybe a wet burp, but my guts refused to budge. Once a morsel of food made its way down my esophagus, my body took it prisoner and refused to surrender.

I'd been more successful with laxatives. I'd eat them just before bed at night, the chocolate-flavored ones, a hint of cocoa melting on my tongue as I eased into sleep. Then, in the morning, my ass would sound an alarm. I'd race to the bathroom still half-asleep, awaken fully on the toilet shitting forth streams of fire. For the rest of the day I'd be out of commission, hopping from toilet to toilet like a manic toad. Laxatives were a major time commitment, a second job, and the effort was never worth the payoff. I'd lose half a pound of water weight, only to gain it back the following day. In the end, I quit the purging game—revisiting it only very occasionally with diuretic pills or a lone secret suppository.

I was feeling sick. I threw away my paper plate and gathered up my burrito. But instead of returning to work, I found myself standing inside a candy store called Yummies.

I'd been there once and allowed myself exactly 180 calories' worth of candy. Now I dove in without counting: jelly beans, Hershey's kisses, candy corn, *laissez* sweets! I was exuberant in the Cadbury eggs, wild with the Haribo cherries.

I lingered over a bin containing little white and purple discs, chalky and nickel-size. The discs had appeared in a movie I'd once seen about a boy who was dying of a terminal illness. I'd forgotten what illness he had, but I remembered clearly the way his mother snuck the discs into the hospital to try and get him to eat.

"I brought your favorite cahndies," she said, pronouncing it like that, *cahndies*. Was there a more melancholy way to pronounce anything?

As a child, I'd seen a wide range of nonterminal illnesses amongst my young friends, as well as the delicious food cures their mothers provided. I'd prayed that I would contract tonsillitis (ice cream), a stomach virus (ginger ale), chicken pox (oatmeal bath), the flu (chicken noodle soup), swollen glands (lollipops), tooth pain (Popsicles), the common cold (more chicken noodle soup), strep throat (raw honey). But I was cursed with perfect health.

I made retching noises in the bathroom, choked on faux phlegm, blew empty air into a tissue, clutched my throat.

"Ack-ack! Ack-ack!" I hammed it up. "Honey. Must have raw honey."

"You're fine," said my mother. "Honey is fattening."

It was like I'd spent my entire life trying to get honey and then trying to avoid it. I wondered what I would have done with all that life if it hadn't been defined like that. The freedom seemed enormous, monstrous.

I brought my bag of candy and the burrito into the office and put them in my desk drawer. Then I stopped at Ana's desk to see if anyone had noticed I was gone.

"I don't think so," she said. "Ofer is on a panel this afternoon, something about 'queering the script.'"

"Ofer is queer?"

"No, he's speaking from the perspective of the ally."

"Oh."

"Not that anyone wants him as an ally."

I laughed, feeling the weight of my stomach heavy with food. It was strange to be so changed yet know that I looked no different to her. I made sure she was on a phone call before I went and microwaved my burrito in the kitchen. I didn't want her to see me using the microwave like one of the office commoners, stinking it up in there.

After the burrito was microwaved, I placed it on my desk

with a few of the salsas. The cacti that sheltered me from NPR Andrew's view were still standing guard, but it didn't matter. I felt so languid and self-contained with my burrito, already full from the rest of my feast, that I could simply take small pieces and dip them in the salsa like a normal person. I wanted him to absorb my portrayal of ease. Yes, I was performing a one-woman show about a person who could simply take or leave a burrito, no biggie, just coolly have a burrito at rest on her desk, no obsession, no fear, a sane food woman, a woman to whom food was only one facet of a very expansive life, the burrito simply a prop, a trifle to be toyed with, a second thought, a third thought, even.

The day went so much faster with the burrito and candy to pick from. I imagined how much more pleasurable my life would be at work if I had this every day. Life was a lot less bleak when you were staring straight down the barrel of a burrito. Was this how some people lived all the time?

At home, I continued to eat throughout the night: Easy Cheese in a can, SpaghettiOs, half a large bag of Cool Ranch Doritos—all purchased from 7-Eleven—plus the remainder of the candy and baked goods, and a large container of takeout pad thai. I ate and ate until the clock struck midnight, then threw away all of the remaining food. I took the trash bag out to the garbage cans on the street and let everything go into the trash.

Then I got into bed, feeling like a blimp, a whale, but perfectly done: sated, tranquilized, as though I'd been fucked very well. The only thing left to do was pop a piece of nicotine gum. I smiled, parked the gum between my molars and my cheek, and drifted gently off to sleep.

CHAPTER 18

I woke up to my alarm in a great terror. I couldn't remember exactly what had happened the day before, but I knew it had been bad. As I pieced together what I'd eaten, I could taste some of it in my mouth, in the sour, acidic parts of undigested food that came up: a hint of salsa, a lone SpaghettiO. My stomach hurt from the bottom to the top, like I had to take a massive shit that snaked itself in coils and knots and would never end. But the worst pain was in the middle, where I felt a strange emptiness despite the incalculable food that I had eaten. I had stretched my stomach, made too much space. I felt like I still needed more food, to return to what had hurt me, to soothe all that I had done.

Put something in me, said my stomach. *Give me something calming.*

But I could not and would not oblige. I no longer kept a scale in my apartment. In my laxative years, I'd weighed myself ten times a day: every time I shit or pissed. If I'd learned anything from that self-torture, it was that if I owned a scale I'd never get off it. But now I felt I had gained at least ten pounds. I made a resolution that for the next three days, I was only going to eat protein bars so I could keep perfect track of my calories. I felt disgusting. I imagined the food I had consumed simmering in my stomach, just beginning to make its way slowly out to different parts of my body: my hips, my stomach, my arms. Was I going to look like Miriam? Was I becoming a frozen yogurt girl: soft, sloppy, melting?

I thought about Dr. Mahjoub and the missing clay figure. I didn't believe in *The Secret* or vision boarding or creative visualization or any of that other LA drivel. And yet, I wondered if it was possible that I had somehow *The Secret*–ed this woman.

That night, I googled *voodoo doll*. I ended up on someone's Etsy page, featuring an array of ugly gingerbread-man-looking stuffed dolls—said to be handmade in Brooklyn. I googled *Jewish voodoo doll* and found an article about anti-Semitism in Turkey. I googled *Jewish Frankenstein* and read a biography of Mel Brooks. Then I googled *Jewish monster*.

> A golem (/ˈɡoʊləm/ GOH-ləm; Hebrew: גולם) is an animated anthropomorphic being found in Jewish folklore that is created magically from inanimate matter—usually clay or mud. The golem possesses infinite meanings, and can function as a metaphor for that which is sought in the life of its creator.

Well, I certainly hadn't sought out yogurt sundaes, that was for sure. I continued reading:

> The most famous golem was said to have been created by Judah Loew ben Bezalel, the late-sixteenth-century rabbi of Prague, who made a golem to defend the Jews from anti-Semitic attacks. Some think the golem is real. Others believe it is symbolic and refers to a spiritual awakening.

In one picture, the golem looked like King Kong. In another, it looked like something of a hulk: the Jolly Green Giant or Andre the Giant. In no picture did the golem look anything like Miriam or me or a young me or the psychedelic woman I'd made or Dr. Mahjoub or even frozen yogurt.

I googled *Rabbi Judah Loew ben Bezalel* and found a painting of him. He was old and had a beard down to his feet. He was smiling. He looked nice.

CHAPTER 19

They say the perfect is the enemy of the good, that if you strive for perfection you will overlook the good. But I did not agree. I didn't like the good. The good was just mediocre. I wanted to go beyond mediocre. I wanted to be exceptional. I did not want to be medium-size. I wanted to be perfect. And by *perfect*, I meant *less*.

But enforcing my protein bar regime was not as easy as it used to be. I felt like I was moving through the stages of grief. In the morning there was pain, because of the emptiness. It was as though I had expanded the inside of my stomach to a giant stadium and I was dying to fill up the seats. Next came resolve, me feeling like a champion, slogging my way to my lunchtime protein bar, powered by self-hatred. In the afternoon came hunger again, then exhaustion. The hours between each protein bar felt endless. At the gym, I thought I might collapse. At night I lay awake, envisioning vegetables, tomato juice, pickles, salt—anything that wasn't the sweet, cloying whey of the bars.

After two days, I returned to Subway and let the salad caress me with its vegetables. I walked back to the office slowly in the sunlight and decided that a few things were true. I decided that love is when you have food in your mouth that you know is not going to make you fat. Lust is when you have food in your mouth that is going to make you fat. Fear is the day after you had food in your mouth that is going to make you fat. Fear is when you eat your allotted calories for a given time and you find yourself still hungry. Fear is when you no longer trust yourself to stick to your prescribed regimen.

As I approached the front door of the office, I froze. My mother's car was parked at a meter out front. I knew it instantly: a white Volvo with New Jersey plates. She had driven all the way across the country to come find me.

"Oh no," I moaned.

But it wasn't my mother's car. It belonged to some dude who looked like Jay Leno. He was sitting in the front seat, vaping. The thought occurred to me that my mother had somehow transformed herself into a vaping Jay Leno, or that this dude had stolen her car. I checked the passenger door. My mother's Volvo had a dent on the passenger door, but this one was dent-free. I felt an urge to knock on the dude's window anyway, to talk to him, as if having the same car connected them somehow. As if it connected us.

I thought about how I used to watch my mother sleep sometimes, how innocent she looked with her hands tucked under the pillow. In those moments, I saw her as a little girl, and I felt that nothing was her fault—just a chain of fears and feelings passed down from generation to generation. In those moments I thought, *You can show her how to love you better by being loving to her.* But it was easier to be loving when the person was asleep.

I took a step toward the office, then I looked at Jay Leno one more time. He was on his phone, yelling at someone. He exhaled in frustration, shrouding himself in a massive cloud of vape smoke: a Los Angeles apparition. I reached for the handle of the office door. Then I turned around and headed for Yo!Good instead.

CHAPTER 20

When I opened the door to the shop, the bells jangled and I thought I was going to faint. I was accustomed to light-headedness. This was the price of calorie restriction. Sometimes I even enjoyed the experience, because it was proof that what I was doing was working. There could be a physical high too, from the actual sensations, when I let go and agreed to just be there. Other times the stars took a while to clear and I worried that I had been blinded. But this time, my vision cleared quickly, or so I thought, except what I saw when the stars dissipated was something of an inner vision projected outward.

What I saw was an enormous braided challah. The loaf of bread was taller and much wider than me, maybe seven feet tall and four feet wide—a giant. A challah golem. It was a plain challah, no raisins, and its outsides shimmered and shone with honey. The challah did not have a face, but in all other ways I felt it to be smiling at me, each shining cord of the braid like a smile itself. The challah shook and shimmied back and forth as if beckoning me to come dance with it.

I saw myself move toward the challah as if to take up its offer to dance. I wanted to hug the whole bread, to rest my face against the glazed crust, to dive into that eggy, doughy center headfirst. But the challah, magic as it was, had something even better in store for me. The closer I got to its honey-scented body, the more weightless I became. It was as though the challah was some kind of moon that was disrupting my sense of gravity. I saw myself rise up into the air, levitating, rotating sideways, then upside down with my feet over my head, flying above the beautiful top of the bread. I was merely a satellite in the challah's orbit. I felt at once celestial, mystical, part of a magical painting, like a Chagall, where people soared over one another in glorious dance. Except I wasn't dancing with a person, but a bread.

I heard Miriam call out, "Hello!"

The bells on the door were still chiming. I realized that my feet were on the ground. In place of the challah stood Miriam. Her face glistened with sweat, prismatic, as though she herself had a honey coating. I felt happy to see her.

"You couldn't resist my sundaes, could you?" she asked.

"No," I said, grinning. "I could not resist your sundaes."

"I'm going to make you an even better one," she said. "Think you're ready for the Plotz?"

"Let's do it," I said.

I watched her survey her kingdom of yogurt. She licked her lower lip several times, and with each lick, I felt something course through me that was greater than the peace of her presence, greater than the joy of my challah vision. It was desire. I felt a desire to put my mouth on her mouth, to suck on her lower lip, to bring her close to me, her body against my body, to smell her neck and know what she smelled like, to feel her big belly against mine, to sway against her a bit, rubbing up on her.

Oh fuck, I thought. *I like this girl.*

CHAPTER 21

I had only slept with two women in my life. The first was Zoe, a theater acquaintance in college, during my second year. By graduation she'd fucked everyone in the theater department, and my turn came the night of a cast party for Chekhov's *The Cherry Orchard*. I was excited. I had fantasized about women and wondered if I was bisexual, or even a lesbian. I'd always preferred masturbation to having sex with men.

Zoe wore a newsboy hat over her blond bob. I remember taking the hat off her head and putting it on mine, feeling like I had swagger. I liked the way her neck smelled when I kissed it, musky and aromatic. But when we went to her house, I quickly grew bored with the experience. Her skin felt strangely gummy. She was skinnier than I was, and her hip bone kept stabbing me. Her pussy didn't taste like I'd hoped it would. I had imagined her to be mossy, cheesy, maybe oceanic. But she was tangy, almost bitter, like a kumquat. I tried to avoid putting my tongue deep inside her and just stayed on the clit. I did well. I gave her two orgasms, which I knew were real, because I could feel her pussy muscles clenching as she came.

By the time she got to me, I was ready to go home and eat the nine pretzels I counted out for myself each night. She honestly tried to get me off and I honestly kept thinking about those pretzels. Finally, I faked it—pretended to come in her face the way she had in mine, clenching my vaginal muscles intentionally so that she would think it was really happening. I wanted my snack.

In my third year at school I pursued a woman named Cait for half a semester in a state of complete infatuation. Cait was a vocal activist on campus, and I followed her to climate change protests and conscious capitalism symposiums. I took on a timekeeper role at the LGBTQ alliance meetings, promoted an electro Arabic Dabke concert sponsored by Students for a Free Palestine, and helped facilitate a video installation project in the cafeteria called "Spring Forward: the eMPower Sessions" aimed at "exploring the relationship between emotional trauma, synesthesia, and the tyranny of the iPhone."

I pursued the idea of Cait so doggedly that the real Cait could never compare. When I took off her bra for the first time, I discovered we had the same exact tits. It was crazy! Our tits were literally replicas of one another: about the size of large tangerines, with small red areolae and big gumdrop nipples. When I pinched and sucked on her titties, I felt like I was pinching and sucking my own. I didn't like myself enough to suck my own tits.

Cait sensed my reticence and became clingy. The less I texted her, the more heart emojis and *u ok??* messages she sent. It was like being asphyxiated by a part of my own self—the need for approval and validation I so despised. More of me? That was the last thing I wanted!

I began dating men again, usually fantasizing about women while I was with them. It was easier. If the actual experience of being with a woman wasn't as good as it was in my fantasies, why bother coming out as bisexual or pansexual or whatever the hell I was? Nathan would eat my pussy for a full half hour in the back of his Kia Sorento and I could fantasize about Cait, only with different tits and ignoring me, until I came. It seemed that as long as I wasn't actually having sex with a person, I could get off to them. But once they embraced me it was over.

CHAPTER 22

The Peppermint Plotz was a Candy Land fantasy, using chocolate yogurt as a base with a swirl of peppermint around the border. Miriam piled on the hot fudge again, jacked it up with Junior Mints, sprinkled chocolate chips on top of that, then finished with marshmallow sauce on top. It was what a magic winter fairy would make if she had the pleasure of serving herself at Yo!Good.

I felt giddy as I ate, like a kid. I felt more like a kid than I did when I was a kid. All of my childhood interactions with other children were about going to their houses and trying to get a taste of their junk food. Often there was shame in it, because the other little girls were skinnier than me or cared less about food. Amy Dickstein would bribe me with different foods so that we could play "prom" together. Amy said that every prom had "refreshments." She promised we could have something delicious to eat, but only after we did the other parts of prom night. She promised potato chips. She promised apple fritters.

She let me be the girl. She was the boy. I had no problem with that. We would slow dance in her bedroom, and she would tell me I looked very pretty. She would ask if I was having a good night. Then we would have an after-prom moment, before refreshments, and she would lay me down on her bed and softly brush the hair off my cheek. This felt good, it really did. Then she would put toilet paper between our mouths, lie down on top of me, and kiss me. One time, she kissed me without the toilet paper, and it was nice and soft. Sometimes she moved against me or rubbed our pelvises together. She said that since I was the girl, I was not required to move.

I enjoyed the caresses and attention. But what really turned me on was the anticipation of getting to eat forbidden foods after. As Amy kissed me and rubbed up against me, I thought: *apple fritter apple fritter apple fritter.*

"Good?" asked Miriam.

"I've plotzed," I said, spooning up a bite of melted yogurt and a bit of hot fudge.

"Good."

"What do you do when you aren't yogurting?" I asked.

"I go to the movies," she said. "Old movies."

"With friends?"

"Usually by myself."

I imagined her in an antique movie theater, sitting up in the balcony, smoking. Of course, you couldn't smoke in any theaters in Los Angeles, but that was how I pictured her: blowing rings into the light from the projector as it cut through the darkness of the theater. Between puffs I imagined her eating a bag of Red Hots, spicy like the clove cigarette.

"I'm going tonight," she said. "*Charade.* A late showing, ten p.m. Do you like Audrey Hepburn?"

When I was seventeen, at the apex of my starving, I had a big, vintage poster of *Breakfast at Tiffany's* in my bedroom. My goal had been to become as narrow as Audrey, but no matter how little I ate, I could still feel meat on my abdomen, cushion on my thighs. Audrey was practically sculpted from bone. She was starved during childhood, World War II in Holland, which was why she was so skinny. I knew it was fucked up, but I found myself envious that she'd had skinniness fully thrust upon her.

An enemy had inflicted her starvation, which made it heroic. She hadn't had to starve herself to become a star.

"I'm sort of over Audrey," I said to Miriam. "But I do love Cary Grant."

"Want to go with me?" she asked.

"Okay," I said, though I meant to say no.

"Great," she said. "We'll go to dinner first. A kosher Chinese restaurant near the theater, the one with the tropical drinks."

"I can't."

Chinese food was impossible to keep track of mathematically: so many disparate items, shared plates, fried foods, starchy sauces.

"No?" asked Miriam.

"I have a work dinner," I said.

"Oh," she said. "Well, that would be the whole fun of it. Dinner and a movie. What about tomorrow?"

I thought about the possibility of all these calories bleeding into the rest of the week: a sundae now, Chinese food tomorrow. The whole month could be infiltrated if I wasn't careful! No, it was better to keep this madness confined to today, Day of the Peppermint Plotz, as it would now be known in the Hebrew calendar. Tomorrow I could get back to my regime again and stay there forever.

"You know what?" I said. "I think I can get out of the dinner tonight."

"Great!" she said, smiling. "Let's meet at the Golden Dragon in Hollywood. Eight p.m."

CHAPTER 23

wanted to bring Miriam a gift, but I had no idea what to get her. Flowers seemed too obvious, too date-y. I didn't even know how she felt about me. Was she crushing? On the fence? Totally platonic? She probably just wanted to be friends. Maybe this was how normal women made friends with other women. They invited them to do shit like eat in public.

I stopped at a beauty store after work and bought her a red lipstick, Ruský Rouge. I told myself I was getting her the gift as a thank-you for how generous she had been with the sundaes. Really, I knew that I was testing her, seeing how far she was willing to dip into my side of modernity, at least aesthetically. I assumed that she never wore makeup because of religious reasons. But if she'd be willing to put Ruský Rouge on her lips, what else would she be willing to try? It seemed significant that the gift was a girly one: a sexy, creamy tool passed from woman to woman.

The first time I'd ever masturbated, I'd straddled my pillow and fantasized that I was being passed between women this way. I imagined a roomful of women, each a different classmate's mother, moving me from lap to lap, thigh to thigh, taking turns rocking and soothing me. Their gestures seemed nurturing, rather than lusty, and so, when I came, and came again, I was able to avoid thinking about what my pleasure could mean.

Over time, this fantasy became more overtly sexual—escalating from lap sitting into kissing, dry-humping. Every time I came, I would think, *Oh god, please don't let me like women.* I forced myself to change the narrative, imagining the women with their husbands instead of me. I imagined the married couples rubbing against each other in abandoned offices, or the men eating their wives' pussies in their backyards at night under the stars, poolside. In these fantasies, I got to be both woman and man: shifting my consciousness from the wife to the husband to the wife to the husband. This felt less shameful than two women.

In college, I'd been all bravado with Zoe and Cait, the adrenaline of novelty and the velocity of intrigue propelling me through my encounters with each of them. I was moving so fast that I didn't really have time to be afraid. But now, going to meet Miriam, I felt the same *Oh god* I'd felt when I was young.

The truth was, I knew very little about Miriam. I knew that she was Jewish, a bit younger than me. I knew that she was very, very nice to me. I knew that around her, I felt like I could eat a sundae, or two sundaes, and maybe even Chinese food. I knew how she made me feel, which was full of confetti instead of blood. And so I reasoned, as I paid for the lipstick, that while my illusive pursuit of Cait had been based on an idea, at least with Miriam I was following a feeling.

CHAPTER 24

I stood outside the Golden Dragon, chain-chewing nicotine gum and waiting for Miriam. The evening air was cool, the sidewalks, cars, and buses cloaked in pink light. It was LA's magic hour. The Golden Dragon looked to have once been magic too, but now it was in a state of disrepair: the corpse of somebody's 1950s Hollywood regency-tiki dream.

The façade was a ranch-style stucco painted with banana leaves. It had survived the Cold War, only to fall prey to black mold. Two cracked lacquer Foo dogs, one missing an ear, stood guard at the red pagoda entrance. A turquoise neon sign over the pagoda blinked: G LDE DRA N.

But the place was surprisingly popular. Women in wigs kept entering and leaving with takeout. A party of ten drunk Chassidic men clambered in. There were also nonreligious patrons: an aging Hollywood rocker couple with full sleeves of ink, a group of what looked like set designers in paint-covered jeans. Each time the doors opened, I heard the sounds of animated voices buzzing over notes of Hawaiian guitar music.

I waited for ten minutes, then went in. It was dark and fragrant with fried food, a fun house of gilt bamboo mirrors and pink leather banquettes. I didn't see Miriam, so I sat down at the rattan bar, beneath strands of lights in pinks, blues, yellows, and greens. A gold dragon hung from the ceiling over my head.

Every minute or so, the dragon exhaled a stream of light and steam.

What was I doing here? It was like the place existed in a cipher—zero Yelp reviews, a web page with only a name and a menu, and then the place itself—a glowing black hole. I'd always wanted to escape to a black hole. I felt awed by the glow. And who was this random person I was meeting at a Chinese food restaurant bar? Technically, it was less random than a Tinder date or something. But it seemed weirder to go out with my yogurt scooper than with someone whose picture I'd only seen online.

Just calm down, I said to myself.

I am calm, I replied.

The bartender brought a bowl of fried, crunchy noodles, primed for duck sauce and spicy mustard. I hadn't tasted those noodles in over a decade, and quickly commenced a parade of them, dipping and crunching and dipping again. I didn't remember them being so delicious. Then Miriam walked in. I licked my fingers quickly and waved.

She was twenty minutes late. But she seemed completely unconcerned with time as she walked languidly toward me, opulently corpulent in a floral yellow robe-dress with kimono sleeves, a smile on her pale face.

She really exists, I thought, as though up until this point I'd thought the yogurt shop were an alternate reality, which vanished along with everything in it when I left.

"This is kind of funny," I said when she sat down beside me.

"What?" she asked.

"This," I said, motioning to her, then to me.

"Have you looked at the menu yet?" she asked, ignoring my assessment of the situation.

"No," I lied.

I was afraid to let her know that I had been anticipating our time together. But she seemed to find nothing awkward about the situation, because she said, in a cheerful voice, "Well, in that case, let me order for both of us."

She snapped her fingers at the bartender in a commanding way. This seemed like an odd thing for someone who worked in the service industry to do. People must have been doing that to her all day.

"Two Scorpion Bowls," she said.

The drinks were brought to us in giant green ceramic bowls shaped like half watermelons, filled to the brim with maraschino cherries, pineapples, chunks of orange. The calorie count in one bowl alone was probably more than I allowed myself in two days.

"Try it," said Miriam, smiling.

I put the pink straw to my lips and sipped. It was exquisite, like drinking a neon airbrushed rendering of a fruit punch island. It was its own tropical cosmos complete with coconuts, sea, and sunset. The drink warmed my chest and stomach immediately. Suddenly, I was way more at ease.

"Well, Aloha," I said.

She laughed. "Stick with me."

"Gonna fuck me up."

"That's a blessing."

"I do feel chosen," I said, taking more sips.

"What kind of Jew are you again?"

"I was Reform," I said. "But now I'm sort of nothing."

"Do you like being nothing?" she asked.

"It's not a question of *like*. I didn't feel—connected to Judaism spiritually."

"That's funny," she said. "I never thought about feeling it. Maybe because I've always felt it. You do believe in god, though, right?"

"I don't know," I said.

This was getting kind of heavy for a first date or whatever we were doing. I swigged the drink.

"You don't?" she asked.

"I mean, how can I know? God isn't, like, texting me *Hi* or anything."

"What do you think all this is?" she laughed, pointing to the lights and the dragons and the mirrors and the lanterns and the other diners and her and me.

I was silent.

"It's god," she said, as though it were obvious.

"Is this god?" I asked, pointing to the Scorpion Bowl.

"Oh, definitely." She giggled. "That's maybe the most holy of all. Half of my family are lushes."

"Really?"

"No. But everybody loves to drink. People come over on Shabbat and hang out, and we all have too much. Happens every Friday. You should come. You'd really like it."

Why was she so certain about everything?

"Do you live with your family?" I asked.

"Of course," she said, as if this was the most normal thing in the world. "Don't you miss yours so far away?"

"Definitely not," I said casually, as though that were true.

"Oh," she said softly.

I examined the shapes and shades of her face, studying her. Each feature was its own inhabitable world. Her hair was the color of cream soda, or papyrus scrolls streaked with night light. Her eyebrows were the color of lions, lazy ones, dozing in sunlight or eating butter at night with their paws by lantern. Her eyes: icebergs for shipwrecking. Lashes: smoke and platinum. Her skin was the Virgin Mary, also very baby. Her nose: adorable, breathing. Upper lip: pink peony. Lower lip: rose. The teeth were trickier, but her inner mouth was easy—Valentine hearts and hell.

I reached into my purse and got the lipstick I had bought for her. I wanted to bring that inner mouth out, make everything red.

"I got you something," I said, handing it to her.

The lipstick was in a little bag with some tissue paper.

"Oh, how nice," she said, the way a stuffy old tourist lady might say when coming upon a scenic hayfield.

This was getting weirder by the minute. I took another sip of my drink and watched her lick her lower lip as she opened the package. Her papyrus hair shone in the bar lights.

"Oh," she said when she pulled out the lipstick.

"I noticed you don't wear makeup, but—"

"I don't know how to do it right. My mom gets on me sometimes about wanting me to wear it. She said if I want to find a husband I'll have to learn. She has no idea how to put it on either, so she can't judge."

Oh, great, a husband, I thought.

"You think I need it?" she asked.

"No, no," I said.

"Put it on me, then."

"Okay."

I unwrapped the plastic and took the tube out of the cardboard box. I clicked it open.

"Pucker up," I said.

She parted her lips. I'd never been so close to her face before. Her scent was very clean, soapy. The way she had her mouth open, just slightly, drove me crazy. I wanted to stick my finger in there. I wanted to touch her saliva, use it to trace the pronounced bow of her top lip, paint her with her own spit. Her lips were already so wet. They were too wet, in fact, for me to correctly put on the lipstick.

"Wait," I said. "Let me do something."

Gently I took my cloth napkin and blotted the moisture off her lips. Then I dabbed on the lipstick, lightly at first, then heavier, tapping out a gentle melody, then another. I put on way more than she needed, because I didn't want to stop.

"Okay, okay," she said.

I sat back on the bar stool and looked at her. It was witch-craft. She was transformed. With a few strokes of my hand, she'd gone from chaste lamb to pout mouth, suckling pup to pulp tart. Where before, her beauty was in her purity, the lipstick rendered her tramp-lipped, vamp-kissed, kind of a harlot. But what was hottest was the way her innocence still radiated, like a young girl who'd gotten into a woman's makeup bag and wasn't sure if she was going to get in trouble—but liked it.

"Wow," I said, revealing her to herself in the mirrored side of the lipstick case.

"Mmmmm," she said shyly, contemplating the small reflec-tion. "It does look nice."

"Vixen," I said.

She smiled widely, smearing lipstick on her teeth.

May I lick them clean? I thought.

"So," I said casually. "What's good here?"

CHAPTER 25

"We'll start with wonton soup," Miriam said to the waiter, after we'd moved over to one of the pink banquettes. "Then we'll have pepper steak, sesame chicken, chef's special pan-fried noodle, and duck fried rice."

The waiter blew air through his lips, as though doubtful we would eat all that food—or concerned that we might.

"Oh," said Miriam. "We'll also take a pu pu platter. Bring that after the wonton soup but before the rest of the food is served. Tell the chef to leave a little time."

"I'm sorry, the pu pu platter is only for four or eight persons," said the waiter.

"Four is fine," said Miriam, winking at me.

Her teeth were clean of lipstick now, but she'd gotten it all over her straw. It belonged there somehow, with the watermelon bowl and cocktail umbrellas, like a retro pinup girl was out for a night on the town, devastating everyone.

"Anything else, Rach?" she asked.

"Uh-uh." I shook my head.

"And two more of these," Miriam said to the waiter, pointing to the Scorpion Bowls. "Very cold."

"Oh, I'm okay," I said.

"Fine, then one. She'll share mine," she said.

Then she looked at me.

"Can't handle it?" she said, smirking.

She was more pleased with my reaction to the wonton soup. When I took my first bite, the soft noodle gave way to a garlicky inside, releasing a stream of salty broth in my mouth, and I moaned out loud.

"Good, right?" she asked.

"Oh my god," I said with my mouth full of food.

"I told you this place was great," she said. "Just because it's kosher doesn't mean it's bad."

"No, I wouldn't have thought that," I said.

Little did she know that any kind of Chinese food, good or bad, would have been amazing to me, as I had not tasted it in so many years.

"They do those wontons totally with chicken," she said proudly. "No pork."

"Wow."

I watched the way she wielded her spoon, orchestrating every bite. First, she added spicy mustard to the bowl of broth. Then she moved methodically, wonton by wonton, breaking them in half, dunking the halves in duck sauce, before popping them in her mouth. I followed her lead, copied her method. The wontons burst in my mouth, a sweet-and-spicy party.

Then the pu pu platter arrived.

"Make way, make way," called Miriam, as a wooden tiki bowl was set out before us, blazing in the middle with fire.

We began double-dunking everything on it: egg rolls, spring rolls, scallion pancakes, dumplings.

"We're going to need more duck sauce," she called to the waiter. "A lot more."

And then again when our main dishes were served.

"More duck sauce," she said, thrusting the bowl at him, as though it were his fault for not knowing we'd decided to bathe in it.

I wanted to be submerged in all the sauces. The pepper steak was so good I would have eaten the gravy on its own. I sighed audibly as I plunked a bite of the tender meat in my mouth, escorted by a slice of onion. Was there wine in this mother-fucker?

"Well?" asked Miriam.

"Moist," I said.

"And?"

"Juicy."

But my favorite was the sesame chicken. I liked the way the sweetness contrasted with the spice, also that there were no vegetables in it. I didn't need to see another vegetable ever again. It was so decadent to put sesame seeds and flour on chicken and fry it up in a fattening sauce. This was what made it so delicious—the knowledge that underneath all those carbs and fat was chicken, which could have been healthy, but for the sake of taste was not. It was like a Fuck You to chicken. It was a Fuck You to everything!

"Fuck *me*!" I said in celebration as I took a joyful bite.

Miriam laughed, taking a sip from the Scorpion Bowl. Then she cut carefully into a piece of chicken with the side of her chopstick, elegantly and with slow precision, as though nothing had to be inhaled urgently. There was plenty, and there would be plenty. She surveyed her plate, strategizing, map-making. This was how it was going to happen, then this, then this. She took one noodle and draped it around the chicken, then put a piece of egg from the fried rice on top. She dunked it all in some of the spare chicken sauce and sesame seeds on the side of her plate. Then she raised it to her lips, closed her eyes, opened them again, and bit in. I watched her chewing thoughtfully.

"You seem interested in my chopsticks," she said.

"I like the way you feed yourself."

"Yes, I *am* good," she said.

"You are."

"Want me to make you a bite?"

"Okay."

She used her chopsticks to assemble the same bite for me: chicken, noodle, egg, sauce. Then I used my chopsticks to take it off her plate. I popped the big bite in my mouth.

"Now chew," she said.

"Mmmm."

"What do you taste?"

"It's a miracle," I said. "A real simultaneous chicken-and-egg situation. It's like, what came first? Neither!"

"Yes." She laughed. "And?"

"I mean, the way the noodle is hugging both of them at the same time."

"I know," she said. "Now swallow."

I swallowed.

Proudly, she made another bite for herself. As she brought it to her lips, she stared at me with those ice-blue eyes. *Fuck*, I thought. *I might love this girl.*

Beside her, the pu pu platter was still burning. It was a big wooden bowl with a gun-metal grate in the center that released a steady blue flame. The blue was rimmed in red.

I stared at the fire. I squinted at it until it became two flames, twins. Then I blinked, and it became one again. I could see something in there burning, a little charred thing, probably a piece of an egg roll skin. But the longer I stared, the more the thing looked alive—like a tiny figure being incinerated. It had a torso and a neck. It had a skull. I hoped the figure wasn't a bad omen.

Just an egg roll crumb, I said to myself. *You're drunk.*

But I couldn't shake the feeling that the figure was a person, a symbol of something foreboding. Was the figure me? Was I being burned up in the fire? I felt dissociated, separate from myself. All my thoughts and beliefs, my little machinations and schemes, what were they? To calm myself, I tried to add up numbers in my head: 365 and 780 and 1,250 and 195. I could not remember how to do math. I couldn't add up anything. My certainty of what was what—it was turning to ash.

I felt a strange and terrifying loneliness in the midst of that crowded restaurant. I wanted to stand, to run to the bathroom, to try and puke everything up. But my legs were trembling. So I stayed sitting down.

I put my elbows on the table and took deep breaths. I held my hands up to my eyes. I could still see the flames in the spaces between my fingers. I counted eight.

"Are you all right?" asked Miriam.

"I'm a menorah," I said.

She laughed. I laughed too. Then I was more okay. I hadn't turned to cinders. I felt safer.

At the banquette next to us, I saw the set designers eating from big plates of noodles, talking animatedly. I felt a swell of tenderness for them. I liked their talking. I liked their noodles. At the table of Chassidic men, one man stood up to give a toast. Everybody clinked their glasses with their spoons. I also liked the men. I could hear music playing on a speaker overhead. The music sounded beautiful to me. I wondered if it was Beethoven or Mozart or something. I laughed when I realized it was an instrumental pan flute version of Santana's "Smooth."

The toasting man called out, "L'Chaim!" The table of men chanted, "L'Chaim!" The gold dragon blew another round of smoke. The pan flute swelled.

"Hey," said Miriam. "Did you have enough?"

I considered her question for a moment.

Then I said, "Yes. I did."

CHAPTER 26

As we walked down the street from the Golden Dragon to the movie theater, Miriam cracked open her fortune cookie. It was dark out now, but the sidewalk was lit up with streetlamps.

"'You know how to handle all situations,'" she said, reading hers aloud.

"Is that true?" I asked.

"Don't doubt it," she said, crunching down on the cookie, creating a downpour of crumbs on her breasts. "The cookie doesn't lie."

"Anyone who's seen you in action when Yo!Good gets crowded would never contest that."

"Oh, I've had far more intense jobs than Yo!Good," she said.

"Yeah?"

"Camp counselor. Five summers."

"Overnight?"

"Day camp. Camp Shimshon in Beverly Grove. Youngest bunk. Arts and crafts, basketball. I'm great on defense."

There were creases in her dress from where her stomach folded over when we were sitting down at the restaurant. As we walked, some of the fortune cookie crumbs floated down from her breasts and landed in the creases. I tried to picture her playing basketball.

"Parachute games, swimming," she continued. "Twice I had to save those little runts from drowning."

"Wow!"

"Yeah. Open your cookie," she said.

I obliged, cracking open the cookie and reading my fortune out loud.

"'Road work ahead. Expect delays,'" I read. "Great, of course I get the one about traffic."

"Oy."

"It's really the perfect LA fortune, when you think about it. Avoid the 405 and have a nice life! That's my fortune."

She laughed.

"Steer clear of the 10 East between five and eight p.m."

I put the two pieces of the cookie together and began making them talk, as though they were a bird's beak, opening and closing.

"You think you can just glide down Santa Monica on a Thursday morning?" asked the bird. "Ain't happening. And don't even think about taking Wilshire. Enjoy your future."

She laughed harder.

"Stop," she said, sniffling and wiping her face. "Do I have lipstick all over me?"

"No," I said, eating my cookie. "You licked it all off at dinner."

"Oh," she said. "I want to redo it."

We stopped under the awning of a furniture store, closed but lit from the inside with one glowing light. She pulled the lipstick out of her purse, a small turquoise leather Coach bag, something an old lady might own.

"Can you put it on me again?" she asked. "I'm terrible."

"Sure," I said.

I moved closer to her in the yellow light. I was so near to her that I could smell the soy sauce and garlic and sweet liquor on her breath. She stifled a burp, and we both giggled. I wanted to say, *It's okay, don't be embarrassed, let it out, I like you, the air inside you, all of you.* Instead, I said nothing in that yellow light.

There was an awning above us, a palm tree hanging over the awning, as though it were some kind of double chuppa, the California god issuing its blessings, the California god saying, *Yes, my daughters.* I thought about kissing her, right there on the street, licking the bow of her upper lip, sucking on her underlip, that word echoing in my mind, *daughters daughters daughters daughters.* Instead, I did her lipstick. I did it quickly, then stepped away, out of the light, and said, "There."

CHAPTER 27

"Twizzlers are kosher," Miriam said as we stood in line to buy our candy at the movie theater. "M&M's too, though they're dairy, so technically I should wait an hour after dinner to eat them, because we had meat, but I won't."

"I'm sure god will forgive you. God loves M&M's."

We'd reached the front of the line, and we were at the counter.

"What's god's favorite flavor of M&M?" I asked the boy who was helping us. He looked about twelve, and very confused.

"Uh?"

"Pretzel," I said.

"Obviously," said Miriam, giggling.

"We don't have pretzel," he said. "Only peanut and plain."

"Well, darn," I said.

"It'll have to be peanut, then," said Miriam. "And an extra-large Cherry Coke."

"So, this is what it's like to be an adult?" I asked her as I collected the candy from the counter.

"What do you mean?"

"Just, like, you can do whatever you want?"

She picked up the gigantic soda, wrapped her wild mouth around the straw.

"Well, yeah," she said, as though it were the most obvious thing in the world.

"Oh."

"Why? Don't you do what you want?"

She was so cute standing there, Cupid's buxom sister, all pinks and creams and honeys and golds, pure and indecent.

"No," I said. "Not often."

As we watched the movie, I ruminated on a question, and the question was: Did I want to fuck Audrey Hepburn? I realized I didn't. I coveted her black mesh veil, the red suit, the white trench. But I had no desire to kiss those lips. When I imagined her tiny titties, I thought, *Okay, if requested, I would lick them. I'd give the nipples a little flick. And if I put my face between those concave thighs and stuck my mouth in her little pussy with the black hair, straight like an arrow, it could be nice—a Givenchy fuck, swank and lovely. But compared to Miriam, it would be nothing.*

When the movie was over, Miriam and I stood together in the lobby of the theater by the exit doors. We were both silent, looking down at the blue rug, which was covered in a pattern of shooting stars and popcorn clusters. I didn't know what I was supposed to do, if I was supposed to do anything at all, but I knew I wanted to stay in Miriam's presence as long as possible. I kept opening my mouth to speak and then closing it again.

"Well," she said, breaking the silence.

"Well?"

"There's three left," she said, handing me the bag of Twizzlers and grinning. "You take them. Okay. Bye."

"Bye," I said.

She walked out the doors.

As I drove home, I felt high.

"Wasn't that a beautiful rug in the lobby?" I said out loud. "In all my life, I don't think I've seen such a beautiful rug, Miri. Can I call you that? Oh, Miri. Miri, Miri, Miri."

I kept touching the almost-empty bag she had given me and smiling. At a stoplight, I took out the last remaining Twizzlers and whipped them gently over my eyes.

CHAPTER 28

My mother had stopped calling. She was no longer sending family emissaries, weather warnings, or a narrative history of my upbringing. Now what I received daily was a lone text. The text simply said: *Hi.*

On Friday it was: *Hi.*

Saturday: *Hi.*

Sunday: *Hi.*

Monday: *I mailed you two coupons for Bed Bath & Beyond. 20% off WHOLE PURCHASE and 20% off one item!! Use in good health and prosperity!!!*

Tuesday: *Please make sure you use coupons fpr big item. Maybe a vacuum?? Do you have a cacuum??*

Wednesday: *Hi.*

The *Hi* was alluring. I wanted desperately to respond to the *Hi*. What was wrong with writing back a little *How are you?* or *Hey* or even *I miss you?* The *Hi* was so simple, so casual. The *Hi* made it seem like I could have an easy relationship with my mother—as though it were not a trapdoor to an emotional onslaught, a bombardment, a PowerPoint presentation of guilt—as though my mother and I were friends, great friends, as though I were one of those daughters who said, *Oh yeah, my mother is my best friend.* Those women were upsetting.

Mothers who doted on their baby daughters also killed me.

I couldn't be involved in their attempts to get me to cosign a child's cuteness. I'd see a mother walking down the street with her little toddler, the toddler babbling on about something or other, the mother smiling at the toddler, then looking at me, expecting me to celebrate her precious little one. I couldn't smile back.

When I met Ana for teatime the day after the movies, I felt like weeping.

"I'm sorry," I wanted to say as she handed me my hot cup of Harney & Sons, our fingers touching. "I'm sorry," and also, "Please help me."

I couldn't not want it: the approval, that feeling at afternoon teas past when my stomach rumbled and I was proud of its rumbling, when I knew exactly what was in me. It seemed now that in those calculated hollows there had been total security, even though I knew I was never really safe. The hollows staved off another kind of emptiness, thick with terror and mystery. Now the unknown was sitting on me.

"What do you think?" she asked.

"About what?" I grinned.

I was hoping we were about to evaluate Andrew's new haircut. The indie-rocker shag had sprouted bangs overnight.

"The tea," she said. "Darjeeling. I usually do Earl Grey."

I noticed that she said *I* and not *We*. I blew on the cup and took a sip, letting the warm liquid melt the piece of nicotine gum I had parked between my molar and my cheek.

"Great," I said.

It was going to have to be me who initiated the shit-talk.

"So," I said. "Having carefully read Ofer's e-mail on internalized misogyny and safe spaces, I've reached the conclusion that no space is safe . . . from him."

"Didn't read it," she said. "I saw *sensitivity* in the first line and deleted immediately."

"Do you think it was your internalized misogyny that did the deleting?"

"It was my internalized something."

"He's become a real bro-choice activist," I said.

"Mmmm."

Was I losing her? Did she no longer like me? I could never tell how other people saw me. Most of the time I felt like I was riding around in a car with a fogged windshield that made it difficult to decipher the perceptions of others. They were all just kind of pantomiming outside, grunting, while I ran the wipers over and over. No matter how fast I wiped, I couldn't clear the fog.

Still, I was pretty sure there was something about me that Ana was now rejecting. I was on the way out, no longer a fit for inclusion in her joyful exclusion of others. A *them*-ing had happened to our *us*. She could sense that I was becoming—what?

There was, growing within me, a great Fuck-You-ness. I didn't know if this feeling was surrender, freedom, or a total delusion that was ultimately going to hurt me. Miriam had transmitted the feeling to me, like an infusion—or a disease. It was exciting. But at the same time, it scared me.

I googled *How to stop the golem*.

> According to several Jewish tales, a golem came alive out of clay or soil when its creator walked around it reciting a combination of letters from the alphabet and god's secret name. To stop the golem, its creator must circle it in the opposite direction and recite everything backward.

"Mairim Mairim Mairim Mairim," I whispered. "Lehcar Lehcar Lehcar Lehcar. Ana Ana Ana Ana. Rehtom Rehtom Rehtom Rehtom."

I felt no less gone.

CHAPTER 29

"I'm totally down to die in a mudslide," I said into the microphone. "Like, as long as it kills me instantaneously, I'm available."

It was Thursday night, and almost-me was up and running with a darker twist to my *East Coasters care more about our weather than we do* bit.

"Am I emotionally available for a mudslide? No. But if the mudslide is down for a quickie, I'm in."

The laughter was decent. Then I heard a "woo" from the audience. The voice was familiar. When I looked out into the lights to try and decipher who the woo-er was, I saw Jace Evans.

"Hey, thanks," I said, pointing to him. "I'll be here all week."

When I got offstage, he followed me through the crowd.

"Hey!" he said.

"Oh, hi. Shouldn't you be in the dystopic future, wrangling zombies?"

"I do exist off camera."

"I'm just surprised to see you here, that's all."

"My friend Paul from Akron is one of the comics."

"Oh, right," I said. "The guy who did the whole set about jerking off into a family heirloom. He thinks my shit is too pedestrian."

"You were really funny. Definitely funnier than Paul."

"Thanks," I said.

He fumbled with the beads on his faux rosaries.

"Fred Segal?" I asked.

"What?"

"I was just wondering where you got those."

"Oh, my grandma gave them to me for luck. She's super Catholic. I never take them off."

I was being pelted with religious people.

"Well," he said. "Except when my fucking stylist makes me."

"Did your stylist pick out those?" I asked, pointing to his bracelets.

"No," he said proudly. "Those are all me."

I noticed a table of four young women looking at him. They must have been from out of town, because they weren't trying to hide their staring at all.

I asked myself again if I was attracted to him. The floof, unfortunately, was still floofing. But under the floof he had a pair of very earnest-looking brown eyes, round, like the embarrassed emoji, framed with very long, dark lashes. His voice was soft, something of a murmur, and it made me want to move closer to him. I noticed that I was disproportionately happy when he said I was funny. There were definitely flurries in my stomach. But it wasn't what I felt when I looked at Miriam, not that lustful trance I had with her at the restaurant. Still, I wanted him to want me. If he didn't think I was attractive, it negated the fact that he found me funny. I wished it was enough that he found me funny.

"Yo, I'm starving," he said. "You hungry?"

Of course I was hungry. But that would be taken care of shortly, upon return home to my allotted 150-calorie diet ice cream and 80 calories of cereal.

"Not really," I said.

"There's a great hot dog place around here."

"Hot dogs?"

"Yeah," he said. "Really good chili dogs and stuff."

I looked at him, all jaw, so casually trumpeting chili dogs. He was safe from judgment in his body, this naturally skinny, handsome actor. He had an armor to protect him from any consequences to his own hunger. In Miriam, it was different. She wore the fruits of her hunger on her body at all times.

"How good?" I asked.

CHAPTER 30

"You don't know how nice it is to hang out with a woman who eats," said Jace, as we downed our second hot dogs. I'd copied his order: one dog with chili and cheese and one dog with ketchup, mustard, relish, and onions. The cashier was a fan of *Breathers* and gave us the dogs on the house. She'd been the one who suggested onions. The fact that Jace took her up on it made me certain that he liked me as nothing more than a friend. Clearly, he didn't care what happened to his breath.

"The women you know don't eat?" I asked, playing totally dumb.

"Not the actresses on *Breathers*. I think they exist on charcoal lemonade."

Oh, the fucking naïveté of this asshole. Did he really think the average woman could be skinny enough for TV and also eat? Whenever an actress in *InStyle* or *Marie Claire* or *People* said, "I have fries every day," we all knew she was fucking lying. I wondered what Jace would think of Miriam if he saw her.

"Well, their job is to play the dead," I said.

"The *un*dead," he corrected me.

"What exactly are the undead?"

"You don't watch the show?"

"I do," I lied. "I just want to hear your perspective."

"Wow. Well, my take is kind of out there."

"That's fine."

"Okay. So, traditionally, a zombie is a bad dude. He's back from the grave, he's empty, and he wants to eat your brains—"

"Like Frankenstein."

"No, not at all," he said very seriously. "Frankenstein is *not* a zombie. He's a monster."

"Oh."

"But what's so special about *Breathers* is that the zombies are, like, less dead than the three main characters. It's like the zombies reflect the emptiness of our culture. They're forcing us to wake up from it. They still want to eat our brains, but they're giving us a gift, because with the threat of death, they're making us become more alive than ever. That's the emotional reality I'm trying to bring to Liam."

I watched him finish the hot dog with gusto, his strong jaw pumping up and down. He squinted every time he took a bite, and I wondered if that was a studied move—something he'd learned in acting class. He was using the hot dog like a prop. I felt a sudden urge to knock it out of his hands.

CHAPTER 31

In the morning I woke up with a microwave pizza in bed next to me, half-eaten. I was acidic, burping sour. I shoved down a handful of Frosted Flakes from a box on my nightstand.

On my way home from hot dogs with Jace, I'd stopped at 7-Eleven and bought a bunch of junk. I was only going to give myself until midnight to eat everything. I didn't want the food to permeate another day. But at 12:02 a.m., I was still chewing, so I'd decided to give myself another full 24 hours of limitless consumption. Maybe if I ate for 24 hours straight it would cure me of my bingeing problem.

I had 18 hours and 34 minutes left. Anything I wanted for breakfast could be mine. I decided I would stop and get a dozen donuts on my way to work, keep them hidden in my car. Throughout the day, I could sneak out to the garage and gradually eat the whole dozen. I would also buy an extra box for the office. Everyone would love that.

At Dunkin' Donuts, I selected two Boston cream, two chocolate glazed, two chocolate crème-filled, a cruller, a blueberry, two chocolate frosted, a plain cake donut, and a cinnamon for my box. For the office dozen, I told them just to pick out a variety, what normal office people ate. I only managed to gag down two and a half of my donuts on the drive in: the blueberry, the cruller, and the pudding from the Boston cream, which I dug out with my hand and licked in traffic. The rest of my box I shoved under the seat.

Everyone was excited to see the donuts. As with all office food, they went quickly. Only a pink iced donut and a coffee cake thingy remained. Around 11:30, I made my way into the kitchen to snatch up the pink. When Ana came in, I felt like I'd been caught masturbating.

"The receptionist just left," she said. "Her kid ate a fun-size Snickers. Peanut allergy. Now I'm answering the phones alone all day."

I was glad her focus was on a deadly Snickers and not my donut.

"At least it wasn't king-size," I said. "She'd be out the whole week."

"These allergies seem a little too trendy," she said. "Before 9/11, I don't remember a peanut ever hurting anybody."

"Jace Evans came to my show last night," I said.

I hadn't planned on telling her. But now that it was out, I wanted her to be impressed.

"To see you perform?"

"No. He just happened to be there. But he said he liked my set."

"Really?"

"Yeah. Then he asked me to go get dinner with him after. I didn't go."

"Good," said Ana, washing her hands in the sink. "You'll be the only woman this side of the 405 he doesn't sleep with."

I figured that she meant this as a compliment. She was saying I was strong, sharp, not easily fooled. But it didn't feel like a compliment, not entirely. It was a reminder that I wasn't special. She was saying he flirted with everybody. I should not consider myself a prize just because he'd paid attention to me.

I wanted more acknowledgment from her. I wanted her to

say, *Of course he was into you. Of course he was, my beautiful daughter. My thin and beautiful daughter. My funny, thin, beautiful, smart, and talented daughter.*

"I don't think he would have tried anything with me," I said. "He probably knows I'd get in trouble if I hooked up with a client."

Now I was trying to change the tone of the story—from braggy to skeptical—as if to say, *I knew all along he didn't want me.*

"I don't see what the big deal is about him," I went on. "He's not even that good-looking."

"Oh, he's good-looking," said Ana, turning off the sink. "At least until he starts talking."

CHAPTER 32

At lunchtime, I went over to Yo!Good to see if Miriam might be working. There was no way I could eat any yogurt, or any more food at all. I realized that this meant I was only going there to see her.

"Hi," she said. "I was wondering if I was going to see you again."

"Hi." I grinned.

"Do you want me to make you something special?"

"No," I said. "I just came here to see you."

"Ah," she said, smiling and tapping a plastic spoon against the counter.

I couldn't tell if this was a nervous gesture or if she was drumming out a celebratory beat—*tap tap, tap tap! I am glad you have come to see me Rachel! Here is my staccato indication of that!* And what did *glad* even mean? There was such a wide range of *glad*s, from platonic amusement to amorous hysteria. Would I ever decipher the precise timbre of her gladness, the origin from which it sprang, whether it was an *I think you're cool*, or, if I were blessed, an *I want you so bad*? I felt like I would die if I didn't find out soon. I also wasn't sure what I would do if I did find out. I knew that I wanted to be around her—a lot. I knew that I wanted to taste each of her moles: the caramel one on her cheek, the dark chocolate drop on her Adam's apple, the two milk chocolate drops on the left.

"What song is that?" I asked her.

"What?"

"The spoon," I said.

"Oh."

She hadn't known she was drumming. She put the spoon down on the counter. Then she picked it up and threw it in the trash. The store was empty except for the two of us.

"I'd love a smoke," she said. "Want to go out back for a clove?"

I nodded.

She squinted in the sun as she tried to light her cigarette. I offered her my sunglasses, and she accepted them. They were Ray-Bans, Blues Brothers–style, and they looked ridiculous on her. She looked like she was in a wedding band. She handed me the clove she had lit, then she lit one for herself, inhaling deeply. When she exhaled, it looked like she was blowing loop-de-loops. They were beautiful, actually, a series of perfect circles in a ray of sun.

"You blow rings?" I asked her.

"What?"

"Smoke rings," I said.

I held up my hand and poked through the center of one of the rings. But just as I made contact, the ring dissipated into a lazy cloud. She laughed at me from behind the sunglasses. They were too boxy on her, and I tried to imagine what kind of sunglasses would look better. I pictured her in round, mirrored shades. They would match the shape of her face and also lend her a bohemian air: Miriam as Mama Cass, Miriam as goddess of the canyon. Or she could go pure early '60s nostalgia—Hollywood beehive Miriam with a cat-eye frame in white or checkerboard or cherry red. I decided that I would definitely buy her a pair and bring them to her as a present. Then she could smoke in the sun whenever she wanted—in style.

I wanted to buy her all kinds of gifts. I pretended that my

generosity came from gratitude, fondness, but there was definitely a deeper motivation behind my desire to give. I wanted to "improve her" like a project, make her more fashionable. It was not so much about goodwill as it was about my own fear.

People in LA were always recommending things that were more about themselves than the recipient. They recommended obsessively—films, Netflix series—as though their association with a piece of media imbued them with sex appeal, intelligence, an irresistible whimsy. When I felt a recommendation coming on, I'd lie and say I'd already seen the thing: just so I didn't have to hear the plot explained. Did anyone genuinely like anything? So much art was bad. I preferred the work of dead people. At least the dead weren't on Twitter.

But in my desire to curate Miriam, I'd become just another version of an obsessive recommender. I wanted to show the world how beautiful she was, to present a different type of beauty, and in doing so, to own part of her. I felt that if the world embraced Miriam, I'd be healing something in me—making amends with young Rachel. But I didn't entirely trust the world to grasp her beauty. So I sweetened the pot with little aesthetic upgrades.

"I know you're not doing anything for Shabbat," she said. "You must come over to my family's house this evening for dinner. I insist. You will love it."

Now she wanted to introduce me to her family? This seemed very intimate, kind of fast. Or was it just an abundance of platonic friendliness in her, a kind and generous nature, nothing to do with romance? She was doing a mitzvah: reaching out to a fellow Jewish woman who was without family. It was Semitic sympathy, diasporic decorum. It was the right thing to do.

"I can't," I said.

"Why not?"

"Okay," I said. "I can."

"Fabulous."

She was so cute, exhaling the last of her cigarette, stubbing it out under her foot and clapping her hands together as if to say, *That's that*. When she clapped, her left hand cast a shadow inside her right hand. The shadow was ovular. It looked like an eye.

For a moment, I really wondered if I was seeing an eye in the palm of her right hand. The eye winked. I blinked. Then it was gone.

CHAPTER 33

I didn't know what I was supposed to wear to Shabbat. I didn't want Miriam's family to think I was being disrespectful, so I cut out of work early and popped over to Saks Off Fifth, where I bought a long black cotton dress that buttoned at the wrist and came down to my ankles. I had always felt culturally Jewish, even though I wasn't religious. But now in my ignorance of Orthodox customs I felt like a straight-up WASP. In some ways I liked that feeling: streamlined, self-contained.

I stopped at Schwartz Bakery and picked up a cinnamon ring, then parked my car and walked the rest of the way to Miriam's house on Formosa. I didn't want them to know that I was driving on Shabbat, because I knew this was considered work—even though the sun hadn't yet set. There was something nice about being forced to be done with everything by sunset, to be excused from life. It was like a teacher's note from the ultimate authority.

The house was one of those large two-story LA mishmashes on a small lot that looked like it had been built before the 1940s, renovated in the '60s, and then neglected since the '80s. It was made of stucco *and* brick *and* siding *and* stone, with wrought-iron detailing—some painted black and some painted white. Next to the front door was, of course, a mezuzah, and on the door hung a wooden cutout of an owl that said THE SCHWEBELS. So that was her last name: Miriam Schwebel. I smelled something roasting, some kind of meat, and immediately thought, *Turn around. Run.* The intimacy of it, the smell of another family's life, was terrifying.

Miriam must have been waiting. Before I even knocked, she opened the door and corralled me inside. I was the guest of honor. She'd lined up·most of her family in the entrance. Eitan was fifteen, and Noah was nine—and both of them had payos. Her father had payos too, but I was surprised he didn't have a beard. I reached out to shake his hand, and he didn't move. I remembered that he wasn't allowed to touch me. Miriam had a younger sister, Ayala, three years her junior, who she said was upstairs. There was also a toddler clinging to Miriam's foot.

"She's so cute," I said of the toddler.

"Ezra is a he," whispered Miriam.

"Oh," I said. "I'm sorry!"

"It's fine, of course," said Miriam's mother, smiling. "We don't cut their hair until they are three."

I liked Mrs. Schwebel for not judging me—and for acting like anyone could easily make that mistake. She looked so much like Miriam. They both had the same roundness: the large belly, the big ass, the plumpness under the chin. Her mother wore no makeup but was more stylish than I imagined. She had on a pretty long black dress and red loafers that looked like they could be Gucci. Her wig was a Rita Hayworth red, shoulder-length, and parted on the side.

"We've lived here since I was two," Miriam explained as she took me on a tour of the house, which was huge, but also a little cruddy.

"Oh," I said. "Where were you born?"

"Monsey," she said, as we entered the living room. "New York. My parents came here so my father could get into commercial real estate with my uncle Lavie."

The living room was done in '60s Flintstones chic, with avocado-green carpeting and furniture, and a faux-stone fireplace. I recognized it as the same faux stone from the exterior of my apartment building. But while this room was filled with what looked to be a whole century's worth of knickknacks—three shofars, two menorahs, a grandfather clock, a cuckoo clock, a broken Ms. Pac-Man arcade game, a collection of rabbi statuettes—my apartment was newly renovated, painted white, and existed in a timeless vacuum of nothingness. I had only my white Ikea bed, my white Ikea night table, my black Ikea sofa, and that was it. I'd thought about getting a rug, but I couldn't commit. I felt that committing to a rug would mean I existed on the planet more than I actually wanted to exist.

"When did your family get into yogurt?" I asked Miriam.

"Later. I was twelve when they started with the yogurt."

"Oh."

"It was my mother's idea, actually," she said, leading me into the dining room, which was older and more antique-looking than the living room, with dark wood paneling and white molding. "If we were still in Monsey, she never would have come up with it probably. Women don't really work there—or, like, they definitely aren't supposed to be the ideas people when it comes to business. Both of my parents come from ultra-ultra-Orthodox families. But here we're just modern Orthodox. Uncle Lavie is barely observant at all. He's my father's younger brother. He quit yeshiva to move out here and marry an Israeli woman. They only have two kids. They're Reform, or something."

"Who's Reform?" asked a young woman, entering the dining room. She was beautiful, with dark hair, sleek and shiny, and eyes that were almost black. Her ankles were slim in her flats, her face shaped like a doe's.

"Uncle Lavie," said Miriam.

"They're Conservadox."

"Oh," said Miriam. "Conservadox. Rachel, this is my sister, Ayala."

"Hi," I said.

Ayala held her hand up coolly in a sort of wave but didn't say another word. I disliked her immediately. I was glad when she left the room, just as promptly as she had entered. Her beauty was a reminder of the outside world, the type I had considered most valuable. I wished she weren't there at all.

The kitchen was a '60s wood-paneling affair, with a linoleum floor, yellow countertops, and every inch of wall space covered in oak cabinets.

"Can I help you with anything?" I asked Mrs. Schwebel.

"*Nisht*," she said. "Everything is done."

Noah and Ezra were seated at a small kitchen table with a box of Little Debbie honey buns.

"If you're going to open them, open them now," said Mrs. Schwebel. "I don't want to hear a single wrapper crinkling after sunset."

Then she turned to me to explain, "Opening the wrappers is considered work. Once night falls, that's it. No opening, no buns."

She turned her back to the stove. Noah and Ezra began pulling out every bun, opening all the wrappers.

"How many are you opening?" she scolded them playfully, with her back still turned. "At this rate, we'll need a Shabbos goy."

"We plan to eat all of them, *Mama!*" said Ezra.

Hearing Ezra use the word *mama* made me feel a pang of longing. I was not really longing for my mother, who certainly was no mama. I wanted another mama, a fictional one. I thought about what my dream mama would look and feel like. Would she be like Mrs. Schwebel? Would she be like Ana? If it were possible to create the mama I'd wished for, I wasn't even sure who she would be. My wish for that mama had always been a response to an absence. I didn't know how to think about a mama in terms of presence. In my fantasies, I'd cobbled together scraps—

fragments of women who'd crossed my path. I'd never come up with a mama from scratch.

"We're going to help them with these buns," said Miriam, picking up a honey bun and taking a bite.

"Ah," said Mrs. Schwebel. "I guess you're not starting your diet this Shabbos."

Mrs. Schwebel's tone was playful, not cruel or accusatory. But I felt sickened by her comment, panicked, like I needed to quarantine Miriam from the word *diet*, or the word *diet* from Miriam, lest it contaminate her.

"I am starting a diet," Miriam said, casually taking another bite. "The cake diet. It's very hot right now, very popular."

"A cake diet, really?" asked Mrs. Schwebel.

"Yes," said Miriam, chewing thoughtfully. "Honey buns, Swiss rolls, brownies, cupcakes, fruit pies. But not Twinkies."

"Why not Twinkies?" I asked.

"Not kosher," she said.

"Well, share some with Rachel at least," said Mrs. Schwebel. "She's so nice and lean."

Miriam offered me half the honey bun, and I took it, though I felt like a traitor. We'd never discussed weight between the two of us. I didn't like her being compared to me, or to anyone.

But then Mrs. Schwebel came over, kissed her on the cheek, and said, "All of my children are beautiful."

"Open up," said Miriam, holding the last piece of honey bun to her mother's mouth.

"Mmmm," said Mrs. Schwebel. "The cake diet."

Mr. Schwebel was already seated at the dining table. He wore a yarmulke, and I saw *tzitzit* dangling from his pocket. He smiled at me and nodded softly but didn't say a word. Even once everyone had sat down around the table, he just looked at us all with amused eyes. He seemed to defer to Mrs. Schwebel on everything.

He would open his prayer book and then she would send him into the kitchen to gather a missing condiment. When he returned, she sent him back for another set of candles to replace the current pair, because she wasn't happy with them.

"Hurry," she said to him. "It's sundown in seven minutes."

When Mrs. Schwebel was finally satisfied, she signaled that we were ready to begin. Then she stopped again and turned to Miriam.

"Oh shoot," she said. "I forgot. Miriam, before the sun goes down, take Rachel downstairs and turn on the light in the basement."

Then she turned to me.

"It's on a timer and will turn off by itself at eleven p.m. But we want to make sure that there is enough light for you to get changed into pajamas tonight and settled."

"Oh," I said. "I wasn't planning on staying over."

"She's not staying over?" Mrs. Schwebel asked Miriam.

"Of course you are," said Miriam. "How are you going to get plastered and drive home?"

Her mother laughed but didn't disagree with her.

"Tomorrow we can sleep in while the boys go to synagogue," Miriam said, rising. "Then we'll all have a nice lunch and you can meet some of our friends who will be coming by. It's a beautiful two days. It's not Shabbat without Saturday."

"Well, I don't have a change of clothes or anything, because I hadn't thought about that—staying over."

"You can borrow some of Ayala's," said Mrs. Schwebel. Then she turned to Ayala.

"Rachel is going to borrow some of your clothes, okay?"

Ayala gave her a dirty look.

I ordinarily hated sleeping at anyone else's house, mostly because it meant I had less control over what I ate, but also because I liked privacy in general. I preferred to be sequestered

in sleep. But what could it mean for Miriam and me to get plastered together and then for me to sleep over? I felt anxious, but
in an exciting way.

"So it's settled," said Mrs. Schwebel. "Girls, hurry up. It's three
minutes to sundown."

CHAPTER 34

The basement was already prepared for me. A sofa bed had been pulled out and made up with a soft pink-and-green blanket, old but comfortable. Everything was like that in this house: soft, old, and comfortable. It reminded me that for some people life was about the tactile, about relaxation, about feeling good. This could be the Schwebels' rhetorical motto: *Why wouldn't you take three pillows? Why wouldn't you use an extra blanket? Why wouldn't you just be comfortable?*

"I'm going to turn the space heater on too," said Miriam. "I'll just set it to low. If you need to adjust it in the middle of the night, it's fine."

"God's okay with it?" I asked.

"God wants you to be snug."

We returned to the table and sat down. Then Mrs. Schwebel stood up and lit the candles to signal the beginning of Shabbat. She waved her hands in front of her eyes, as though she were conducting a symphony.

"*Shekhinah*," she said, smiling. "Divine light."

She began to sing the blessing over the candles, and the rest of the family joined in. It dawned on me, with delight, that I knew the blessing she was singing. It was the old "Baruch atah" song I had learned in Hebrew school. I knew the blessing over the wine and the blessing of the bread too. They were just alternate "Baruch atah" iterations.

They sang the blessings to a slightly different tune than I had learned. As they broke into other songs, I realized this was the case for most of the melodies. I knew a lot of words, but the tunes varied. Then they sang "Oseh Shalom," and I suddenly felt very lonely. "Oseh Shalom" had been my grandmother's favorite song. Now they were singing it in a completely different tune, and I wanted to say, *No! You've got the tune all wrong! This is not how you do it!* Or, at least, I wanted to teach them my grandmother's melody.

But I wondered if perhaps it was my grandmother's melody that was wrong. Maybe that was the melody they gave to lesser Jews and nonbelievers. I felt sad that my grandmother had thought she was singing it correctly her whole life.

"Where do you go to *schul*?" asked Eitan, after we finished "Oseh Shalom."

"I don't go to school anymore. I work."

"*Schul*. It means synagogue, not school," said Mrs. Schwebel gently to me.

"Oh," I said. "Well, I'm not currently attending a *schul* either."

I felt around in my skirt pocket for one of the five pieces of nicotine gum I'd let loose in there.

"What other songs do you know?" asked Miriam quickly.

It was hard for me to think up what I knew. I remembered one that I really liked, a song I learned just prior to my bat mitzvah. The song had a beautiful tune, one that had really transported me and made me feel filled with a gentle bliss. But I was scared to sing it, because it was in English—not Hebrew.

"Come on," Miriam said. "If you know 'Oseh Shalom,' you must know some others."

"Fine," I said.

I took a breath. Then I sang.

"It is a tree of life to them that hold fast to it, and all its supporters are happyyy! It is a tree of life to them that hold fast to it, and all its supporters are happyyy!"

"Interesting," said Mr. Schwebel. "That's a line from Mishle, actually. The book of proverbs. 'She is a tree of life to them that lay hold upon her; and blessed is everyone that holdeth her fast.'"

"Oh," I said. "Cool."

"I didn't know it was a song," he continued. "Must be a Reform tradition. But the Hebrew is *Etz chayim hi lamachazikim ba, vetomecheha me'ushar*. If you want to sing it that way."

And so I found myself teaching them that sweet melody I had known and loved, pairing it with the Hebrew, which Mr. Schwebel repeated, patiently, until I got it.

CHAPTER 35

A fter we sang, we ate and drank. Mrs. Schwebel had cooked
an incredible dinner: roast chicken with a crisp and but-
tery skin on the outside, juicy meat inside. The chicken had
been filled with a salty stuffing—crunchy and full of celery. She
served some kind of apple compote that tasted like it was its own
apple pie. There were braised carrots with cinnamon, a terrine of
sweet-and-sour meatballs with raisins in the sauce, and challah
with margarine.

I imagined trying to eat here if I were counting calories. A few
glasses of wine were already more than what my intake would be
for a regular dinner. I thanked god I wasn't counting as I ate the
challah—sweet and flaky on the outside, cakey on the inside. I
felt like I was putting an exquisite bed in my mouth.

I watched Ayala eat. Miriam and her mother, father, and
brothers each took second helpings of every dish, eating with fer-
vor, but Ayala picked at her food. This made me self-conscious,
as though I should be doing the same. But everything was too
delicious for me to hold back. I told Mrs. Schwebel three times
how good her food was, which made her glow. She said that
her kids were used to her cooking by now, and they no longer
complimented her on her talent with cuisine. She smiled when I
took second helpings of everything.

"Such a good eater you are," she said.

I was reminded of the pride my grandfather had shown when we would go to the Second Avenue Deli and he would say, "There's a pickle with your name on it."

"Isn't she?" asked Miriam.

"Yes. Such a good eater for someone so slender."

I beamed like a hero. In the light of the candles, the warmth of the wine, and the happy, easy chatter of the family, I pretended it was the truth. When I stood up to help put some dishes in the kitchen, Mrs. Schwebel tutted me to sit back down, saying, "No, you are our special guest."

I felt a natural belonging. Was it only because I was Jewish that they were so warm to me? I was barely Jewish like they were Jewish. And yet they treated me like I belonged. I loved that their welcome took no account of other facets of my identity: what I did for a living, my interests, any achievements. I didn't need to be or do anything more than simply exist for them to love me. It was as though they loved my naked soul, some inner essence, with an unconditional love. But at the same time, that love was conditional. It was dependent on my being Jewish.

"Adiv sent me a photograph this morning," said Mrs. Schwebel, wiping her mouth and then passing around a blurry pic printed on a piece of computer paper. "Look at that *punim*."

I thought it was funny that she'd gone to the trouble to print out the pic, rather than just forwarding it or showing us on the computer. But the photo made me uncomfortable. I did not like seeing Adiv in army clothes, holding a gun.

"Poor Adiv," said Miriam.

"What do you mean? It was his decision," said Ayala.

"I know. But I think he's homesick."

"Too late now," said Ayala. "He enlisted."

"It's good for him," said Mrs. Schwebel. "It's good to believe in something."

Then she turned to me and said, "You've been to the Holy Land, right, Rachel?"

"No," I said. "I haven't."

"You must go!" said Mrs. Schwebel, and the whole family proceeded to describe the beauty of the place to me: the Dead Sea and Masada, the olive trees and the walls of Jerusalem, kibbutzim and the feeling of homecoming. They spoke of it the way my grandparents had spoken of the place, with wonder and awe.

I remembered, years ago, when Gaza and the West Bank were going to be returned to the Palestinians—an event that never really happened anyway—my grandmother reading the newspaper out loud to me. I remembered her looking up and whispering sadly, "Now Israel will only be this tiny strip."

Miriam and her family made no mention of settlements, nothing political. They spoke only of Adiv, the Negev, the blessing of the nation's existence. The way they spoke of this blessing, the land of milk and honey, you would not have known that people had been exiled from their homes. Their joy made me wish I could block that out too. Could you will the darkness away? Could you banish it and say, *No, this does not exist for me*? Was it okay to dissolve in the beauty of fantasy if you found yourself able?

I opened my mouth to ask them what they thought of the other side of things. But I heard my grandmother's voice inside me say, *Rachel, you actually know nothing*.

Miriam was right. I had gotten drunk, too drunk to drive home. We sat at the table for a long time after dinner and ate figs, nuts, and the cinnamon ring I'd brought. I wanted to hold Miriam's hand under the table. I wanted to thank her for bringing me here, the most comfortable family dinner I could ever remember. The word *hospitality* ran through my mind, and I saw now what it meant and what an art it was. I never liked having people in my space, but Miriam's family made it seem effortless. It was their joy to welcome me. They refilled my glass with wine. They complimented my cinnamon ring, which was very sweet and dry.

I heard my grandmother's voice again.

I can never resist a dry piece of cake, she said.

You'd be so glad I'm here, I thought, and took a last bite.

CHAPTER 36

At 10, Mr. Schwebel said, "Time for bed." Noah had fallen asleep at the table, and Ezra was playing beneath it. Ayala had already been excused to go upstairs so she could get some sleep for synagogue in the morning. I wondered why she was going to go to synagogue while Miriam, Mrs. Schwebel, and I would be staying home. When everyone had gotten up from the table, I asked Miriam what the deal was with that.

"My mom and I are lazy." Miriam laughed. "No, really, I don't know why we do it like that. Sometimes I go. But I think Ayala likes going better than me because, well, she likes looking down off the balcony to the ground where the boys are praying to look for a future husband."

"You don't do that?"

"I'm not really that interested."

I wanted to press her, but I didn't. Why wasn't she interested? Did she not like boys? Did she know why she didn't like boys? Did she like girls? Was she going to have an arranged marriage? Did they still do arranged marriages? Had any of this been discussed with her family? I tried to imagine what it must be like, trying to come out to a family like this. Maybe it was no harder than coming out to my own mother. The Schwebels would have religious misgivings, but I had a feeling that they would still accept Miriam for who she was.

Only once, in college, had I ever told my mother anything about my being into girls. It was right after I started dating Cait. My mother called me to harass me about some guy on campus named Ben Buber who she wanted to set me up with, the son of a woman she'd met at a bat mitzvah. She hated when I was single. If I wasn't in a relationship, she feared that I wasn't doing enough to find someone, that I was lazing in a fool's paradise, imagining a man would just fall from the clouds with the next Wisconsin snow. She believed it was up to her to bring me back to reality, to procure me a man via a sustained hunting-and-gathering effort at any social events she attended.

I told her I couldn't go out with Ben Buber.

"It won't kill you."

"I can't."

"Why?"

"I just can't."

"I think I at least deserve to know why."

I was silent.

"Are you seeing someone else?" she asked.

"I am, actually," I said. "And it's a woman."

I thought that my mother would be surprised at first. I imagined her reaction would be puzzled, maybe confused, but definitely not rageful or sad. She wasn't exactly radical, but she voted Democrat, watched Rachel Maddow nightly. She gave money to Planned Parenthood. In spite of her obsession with me finding a mate, she had always been concerned with women's rights. I was not prepared at all for the way she came at me.

She began sobbing. She said that I was doing this to spite her. She told me that I was confused, and she should never have let me major in theater. She said that my grandfather had not worked his whole life so that his granddaughter could be a fucking lesbian.

"Bisexual," I said, and hung up the phone.

I was filled with guilt. I wondered if all of this was even necessary: not only the admission to my mother that I was with a woman, but the act of being with a woman in the first place. I was being asked to defend a position when I didn't even know what my position was.

I told Cait how my mother had responded, and she hugged me.

"Your mother sounds like a real fucking cunt," she said. "I'm going to be here for you no matter what."

I'd never heard her use the word *cunt* before. I knew that she meant it. But I no longer wanted her to be there for me. I felt resistant to her touch, smothered. She was finally mine, and I didn't know what I was going to do with her.

Then came the phone call from my dad.

"Your mother is a mess," he said.

I was silent.

"She won't stop crying on the phone to me."

"Sorry."

"Let me ask you something. How important to you is your relationship with this . . . girl?"

"I don't know," I said.

"Well, here's a thought. Unless you are marrying her, may I suggest that you take back what you said to your mother."

"How?"

"Just retract it," he said. "I mean, to tell you the truth, I'm not exactly thrilled about this either."

"Fine," I said. "No problem."

"And what about Ben?" he asked.

"Who?"

"The boy she wants to set you up with."

"Oh god," I said.

Ben Buber looked like a giant infant: a baby on steroids. He expounded loudly on the importance of creatine supplements.

137

He kind of yelled when I told him I only did the elliptical machine, never weights. I got drunk on an empty stomach, vomited wine on both of us. Then I started crying.

"I don't think my mother will ever accept me," I said.

This freaked Ben out more than cardio. He paid quickly and left.

After the date, I called my mother.

"He's a weight-lifting preemie!" I yelled.

Then I texted Cait to end things. She'd already been sending heart emojis into the void for days.

CHAPTER 37

Miriam had bungled the light timer. Now the Schwebels' basement was pitch-black. Ayala said that she left me some clothes down there, and I felt around on the bed until I found a pair of soft wool pajamas. I wondered if I should go back up and try to find a flashlight, or if you were even allowed to use flashlights on Shabbat.

I thought about turning on the bathroom light. But I didn't want to break Shabbat in their house. I figured light was more of a big deal than heat, since it was the first thing god did in the Bible, or whatever. I felt my way in the dark to the toilet and peed in the blackness. I wasn't going to be able to brush my teeth. On my way out, I stepped on one of Ezra's toys and it squeaked noisily. After the squeak, I heard a giggle. Then Miriam's voice called down from upstairs.

"Rachel, is that you?"

I saw a light beaming from the top of the stairs.

"What are you doing down there in the dark?" she called. "Let me bring you a candle."

I heard her tiptoe down the stairs. Then I saw her white feet in the dark. She was wearing a pair of baby-blue cotton pajamas and was holding a pair of tea light candles in small glass jars. She had no bra on, and her breasts and belly heaved up and down.

"Here," she said, handing me the candles. "Sorry, I'm bad with the timer."

"Thanks," I said.

"Is this bed all right? And Ayala's pajamas?"

"Everything is great," I said. "So comfortable."

"Good," she said. "I want you to feel at home here."

I put the candles on top of the nightstand, which was really an end table that had been pulled next to the sofa bed. I sat down on the bed but did not invite her to come sit with me. I felt nervous and strange, but also excited to have her so close and unbound, near me in the candlelight. She was wearing underwear, and I could see them through her pajamas. I could tell that they were full underwear, like granny panties, and I couldn't help but think about what her pussy smelled like under there. I wondered if she was wet. Then I felt guilty for wondering that.

"You're sure you're not creeped out down here?" she asked.

"No," I said.

"Well, why don't I stay a bit, just in case, until you fall asleep." She sat down on a cushiony chair across from the sofa bed.

"Okay," I said, but I didn't get under the covers. I imagined going over to the chair, facing her and rubbing up against her body like a cat. I imagined grabbing the back of her head and kissing her forcefully, our teeth clicking together, her gorgeous tongue in my mouth. I imagined opening her pajama top and seeing those tremendous breasts, sucking each of them.

"Why don't you get into bed?" she asked.

"Okay," I said.

I lifted up the sheets and blankets, crawled under them. Miriam did not stand up or make any effort to tuck me in, and yet I felt as though she were somehow tucking me in from across the room. I watched her body moving gently up and down with each breath, her pale blue eyes so clear in the candlelight, like glass. I could hear her breathing too, as though she were trying to lull me to sleep with the rhythm.

"Comfy?" she asked.

"Mmmm."

"Good," she said.

"Tell me a story," I said.

"Really?" She laughed.

I hoped I wasn't pushing it. But I was in such a blissful space, and if I couldn't touch her, then I wanted the room filled with her words.

"Yes," I said.

"Okay. Do you want a story about animals or a story about plants?"

"Animals," I said.

What I really wanted was to slide my hand under my waistband and rest it there, to comfort myself, help myself drift off. But I was afraid that she would see the bump in the sheet where my hand was and be disturbed by it. Also, I didn't trust myself to simply cocoon my vagina with my hand without rubbing. I was wet and would have loved to gently rub my clit, light and fast. Instead, I settled for wrapping my arms around my upper body—like Dracula in his coffin, only sweet and soft. It felt nice, the warmth of a hug. I sucked my nicotine gum.

"There was a woman who lived in a village," she began. "She was about our age. It was a village outside of Los Angeles, but not in Orange County or the Valley. It was a village that had all palm trees and no other kind of tree. It was the only one in Southern California without any other kind of tree or bush except palm trees."

She stopped for a second.

"Sorry, I veered into plants. I'll get to the animals in a minute," she said.

"That's okay," I said.

"This woman was looking to bring some other types of trees to the village, particularly, what are those trees? Oh yes, evergreens. But none of the other villagers wanted them there. They didn't understand why she wanted any other kind of tree when palm trees were so beautiful. In fact, one or two other kinds of shrubs had started to grow there over the years, and the people had gone so far as to rip them out. This woman reminded the rest of the people that other kinds of trees, including evergreens, were native to Los Angeles, whereas palm trees had been brought over from somewhere else. But that didn't matter to them."

I heard her swallow.

"Also, this woman couldn't figure out why she even cared so much about other kinds of trees. The only thing she could come up with was that when she looked at a palm tree, she always felt like it was laughing at her. But when she looked at an evergreen tree, she felt that it was on her side. Uh-oh . . ."

"What?"

"Maybe this *is* going to be about plants. Sorry. Anyway, one night this woman went to see her aunt. Her aunt was the only person who didn't shut her down entirely when she said that she wanted to go to another town and get a baby sapling evergreen tree and bring it to this village, which, by the way, was illegal according to town ordinances. Her aunt didn't understand her fascination with evergreens, but she understood what it was like to really want something, because when the aunt was younger, she had wanted to marry a person but had been forced by her parents to marry someone else. So her aunt tried to be compassionate toward her. At the same time, she didn't want this woman to go to jail for bringing in another kind of tree."

"Jail?"

"It was serious business."

"Okay. Keep going."

"The aunt's name was Puah, by the way."

"Puah?"

"Yes. Puah Feinstein."

"What about the tree woman's name?" I asked, laughing.

"I don't know," said Miriam. "How about Esther?"

"Okay. One more question. Why didn't Esther just move? To a place where evergreens were allowed and she felt more comfortable?"

"She didn't want to move. It's hard for a woman to move, to just separate from her family, stuff like that."

"Yeah, I guess so. But I mean, how badly did Esther want these evergreens? Maybe rather than risking going to jail, or always being upset that she couldn't have the evergreens, she could just go somewhere else, to another town, and be amongst them there."

"Maybe it wouldn't have made her happy to move to another town, you know?"

"I get it," I said.

"Anyway, so Aunt Puah decided that she was going to have to find a way to stall Esther on her plan. So she told Esther that she should wait for a sign before she went and dug up a tree and brought it over. Aunt Puah instructed her to go to sleep each night and wait until, in her dreams, there appeared a bull. Okay, I think this is where the animals come in!"

"Okay."

"Aunt Puah told Esther that if she saw a bull in a dream, and the bull was gentle and kind to her, then it was probably safe to go steal a sapling and bring it back. But if she dreamt that the bull was cruel and vicious, or tried to attack her in any way, that meant it was a bad omen. If the bull was violent, then she should in no way attempt to bring an evergreen tree into the town, or she would surely be punished terribly."

"Shit."

"Aunt Puah thought that she was being clever. After all, everyone knows that bulls are never gentle and are always charging at you, on the attack. So she figured that the dream would never come. What were the chances of Esther dreaming of a bull anyway?"

"Probably fairly slim."

"Yes. Like a fifteen percent chance, maximum."

"More like ten percent."

"Right. And you know what? Aunt Puah was correct. Not only did Esther never dream about a bull being nice to her, but she never ended up dreaming about a bull at all. Every night she waited for a bull to come to her in her dream, and it never did. And actually, in doing this, in waiting for the bull, Esther's interest shifted from evergreens to bulls. And she was set free! She was no longer haunted by the need to have an evergreen. Okay, what do you think?"

"What do you mean?"

"About the story?"

"Wait. That's it?"

"Yes."

"That's how it ends? Esther never goes to get her evergreen?"

"Right," she said.

"What kind of story is that? I mean, how passionate was Esther about the evergreens if she ended up just forgetting about them?"

"Pretty passionate," she said. "I mean, she really loved them."

"She obviously didn't love them that much."

"No, she did, it's just that, you know, she didn't want to ruin her life for the evergreens."

"Oh," I said. "Okay."

"You seem upset," she said.

"No, I'm not. It's just, I don't know, I was kind of expecting it to end with like her planting an evergreen and everyone in the town eventually coming to love it. Or at least Aunt Puah would see its appeal."

"The town was never going to love it. Or Aunt Puah."

"Fine, so Esther should have just left and stayed away."

"I told you, there was no way she was going to do that."

"Well, it's kind of a sad story, then."

"Not as sad as if she had gone to jail. Or never seen her family again."

"I guess not."

"It's a good ending. Esther has her family and she doesn't get punished. Oh! And since she isn't so in love with the evergreens anymore, it's not like she's suffering. She got over it. She has bulls now. She can become a bull-ologist if she wants. The town has no problem with bulls."

"Fine," I said.

I felt angry. Was I annoyed that Miriam couldn't tell a good story? Or was I pissed off by the story itself?

"Well, I'm gonna go upstairs," she said.

"Okay," I said.

"Sleep well."

"You too," I murmured.

After she went back upstairs, I rolled over onto my side and put my hand down my pants. I was still wet. Some of the anger was maybe desire, trapped in there without anywhere to go. I rubbed my clit and the opening of my vulva quickly, not thinking about any images, only the anger and the feeling down there. Then I imagined Miriam, not from the front but from the back, lying fully nude on a bed with her hair wet. No, I would not allow myself to fantasize about her. Instead, I imagined another woman, one I'd never seen before, who had the same body as Miriam's but with very dark hair. Yes, I would create a woman right there in the Schwebels' basement. Esther! I was going to fuck Esther.

I rolled over onto my stomach and put one of the pillows between my legs. I was the Rabbi Judah Loew ben Bezalel of that fucking pillow. I was Adam, and the pillow was my rib, or whatever. From that pillow, I could create my dream woman.

I imagined how Esther's ass would look: how big and round,

like two gibbous moons. I imagined rubbing my pussy against each of her ass cheeks, humping and riding them. I imagined biting at her back fat and sucking on the rolls there as I fucked her ass cheeks. I realized that in my fantasy, Esther was not saying a word (it figured since she'd been so passive with the evergreens). Did I want Esther to speak? No, I liked it like this, her silence, her passivity, allowing me to move freely and have my way with her body. I felt no judgment from Esther, totally free to do what I wished. It was probably because I could not see her face or hear her voice. Also, Aunt Puah was dead.

CHAPTER 38

When I woke up the next morning, I had no idea where I was. Then I remembered. I felt strangely safe and relaxed. The basement had a window, and the sun shone white through the glass. It was 11:30, and I realized I'd slept late because of all the wine. Someone had brought down clean clothing for me—a long skirt and a long-sleeve shirt—but I decided to put back on what I had been wearing the day before. I didn't take a shower, but I fixed my hair as well as possible with sink water.

I went upstairs and found Miriam and Mrs. Schwebel sprawled on the avocado-green sofas in the living room. They were drinking tea, and both of them had little plates of crumbs —the remnants of what looked like challah. There was also a plate with a half stick of margarine on it and a bowl of dried fruits and nuts. At this point I didn't know where I stood with food at all.

"Well, you're finally up, sleepyhead," said Miriam.

She looked so happy to see me. But what did she even know about me: that I was Jewish, ate frozen yogurt every day for lunch, and lived far away from my family? Was that enough to make a person like you? I supposed it was.

I could only look at her and grin. Her mouth was wet with tea. I wished I could go over and pull her close to me, give her a big warm kiss. I wondered how she would kiss, if she'd know what to do from studying old movies or find her way intuitively. How would she react when my tongue entered her mouth? Would she prefer me just to suck on her lips lightly, or would she follow my lead and put her tongue inside my mouth? I wanted her tongue in my mouth. I wanted to swallow her tongue right there in the living room.

"Would you like some tea?" Mrs. Schwebel asked.

Of course I did. I wanted to be part of their little party, whatever they were talking about. They'd been gossiping, I could tell from the tinkle of laughter as I approached.

"We will be having lunch, but not until one o'clock," said Mrs. Schwebel. "You must be famished. Let me fix you some challah with margarine like we had for breakfast."

"Okay," I said.

It was amusing to think of an hour and a half as too long to go without food. In my old life, I'd considered anything less than four hours easy. Four hours meant that food was on the horizon, and it was the idea of forthcoming food that mattered most: an edible future. I'd subsisted on ideas, fantasies. But in this house, an hour and a half of hunger was not to be suffered.

The three of us talked while I drank my tea and ate the challah. The tea was sugared and nondairy creamed, and the challah sweet.

"In my day, in Monsey, you would never have thought of staying home from synagogue," said Mrs. Schwebel. "Everyone was up in everyone else's business. The women were always secretly taking attendance."

"More nosy than here in Los Angeles?" asked Miriam.

"You think the community gossips here? It is nothing compared to Monsey. You could not do anything as a child, good, bad, or otherwise, without someone else sniffing around you and reporting it back to your parents. And I'm not even talking about having a drink, but something as simple as lifting your skirt above your ankles for a moment on a hot day. You are lucky, Miriam, that we are so liberal."

I wondered if Mrs. Schwebel ever desired to be even less religious than she was now. Did she ever want to lift her skirt even higher? Above her knee? What would she have done with her life if she hadn't been religious at all? She might have gone to college, gotten an MBA. I could see her as the CEO of a nationwide chain of restaurants, rebranding Dairy Queen, infusing the Blizzard with lactobacillus and other friendly bacteria. Mrs. Schwebel as industry renegade, Mrs. Schwebel profiled in *Forbes* magazine, arms bared, no wig. I wasn't sure that was necessarily any better or more important than what she was doing right now.

"Whatever, Mom," said Miriam. "Everyone here is up in each other's business too. Like when Chaya Spielvogel started secretly dating a goy. Everyone knew in about four seconds what was going on, because Tali Diamond gossiped about it to a bunch of other people. Tali was supposed to be her best friend!"

"Oh, that's different," said Mrs. Schwebel. "I mean, that is something of major interest, you know? If I were the Spielvogels, I would be very ashamed."

So that was her official stance: no non-Jews for her kids. Was this how the Jews had stayed around for so long? We didn't recruit or attempt to convert anyone. We didn't go on pilgrimages, and we had no missionaries. But those who were already Jewish—we wanted to keep them Jewish at all costs.

In the living room, the sun was warming everything, warming me too. I couldn't imagine anything as delicious as sitting here with Miriam and her mother, gently filled with challah, sipping hot tea, so languid. What would Mrs. Schwebel think about the fact that I wanted to date her daughter? On the one hand I was Jewish; on the other hand I was a woman.

I watched Mrs. Schwebel smooth her red wig. I imagined that my mother would see the wig as archaic. My mother ate shrimp, ignored Shabbat, and hadn't been in a synagogue since my bat mitzvah. She referred to Orthodox Jews as "Oy, those people."

But I was sure that she and Mrs. Schwebel shared some of the same prejudices when it came to their daughters. In this regard, neither of them had come very far from the shtetl.

I thought about the *mikvah*, the ritual bath where women would go together after their periods. Warm women, wet women, women together, women taking care of one another, women naked in the same hothouse. Some of them must have secretly gotten it on.

When the rest of the family returned from synagogue, I felt like it was my family returning from synagogue, but a family I liked. It was as though they knew me well by now, despite knowing barely anything about me. It was as though you could know a person without knowing the details of their life. You could know their light, because you shared the same light, the way I'd known the prayers the night before without knowing I knew them. I had never imagined this kind of warmth could be so safe, abundant. I'd spent so much time cutting and carving away at myself, worshipping cold. I feared that light and warmth were a trick, a tease, false offerings that lured you into relaxing, and just when you made yourself vulnerable, they would be seized. Better to adapt to the cold. Better to thrust the cold on oneself. Be prepared.

Yet with the Schwebels it was so easy. The light was sustained, plentiful. It wasn't going anywhere. And so I ate what I wanted, when I wanted, maybe even overindulged compared to what a normal person would eat. I wasn't sure exactly what that was yet, to eat normally. But I feasted on the food and the warmth, the cozy togetherness, and I realized that the food itself was only one part of what a person needed in order to be sustained.

Mrs. Schwebel served a one-dish lunch, *cholent*, a stew of warm beef, carrots, beans, and potatoes that had been simmering on the stove all night. I thought of all the parts of the stew as I ate it: the carrots, the onions, the beef, the gravy. I imagined the vegetables growing in the ground. I imagined the cows grazing. Each element was nourishing in its own right, but even juicier and better when they came together as a whole. It was meant to be savored. Life could be savored. I was surprised to think for a moment that if there was a god, this could be god's wish for us.

Later that day, when the sun finally went down, I didn't want to leave and go back to my real life. Forget work, I didn't even want to go back to my apartment. No one was kicking me out, but I didn't want to overstay. I kept testing them, making sure they weren't sick of me yet. But each time I would say, "Okay, I'm gonna be leaving soon," they would all say, "No! Rachel, stay! Stay until sundown at least!"

When I finally got in my car, it seemed strange to be inside it, alone. I couldn't believe it was the same car or that it belonged to me. I looked at my hands and they didn't even look like my hands. I felt in that moment that I did not know myself at all, that the Schwebels, who knew nothing about me, somehow knew more about me than I did. What was a person supposed to do with herself in life? Maybe we did need spiritual guidance. No wonder I'd turned to the elliptical machine.

Miriam had traveled fewer places than I had. She still lived with her family and had no grand plans for any kind of career. Yet somehow, she seemed to be moving forward more freely than I was, or if not forward, then deeper and higher, in a series of infinite crescendos. While I was aggressively pedaling nowhere, she was orbiting peacefully.

I had thought that I was the sculptor and she was the golem. But now I considered that she might be the sculptor, the maestro, the creatrix, expanding and improving me, giving life to my dead parts, laughter to my breath. Maybe she was remaking me in her image. Maybe we were remaking each other.

CHAPTER 39

I wanted to text my mother and tell her about Shabbat, how happy my grandparents would have been that I was there. Instead, I went to 7-Eleven.

I bought a container of nachos that I microwaved right in the store and ate in line, plus a bag of Swedish Fish, a package of Hostess cupcakes, four little tubs of rice pudding, a box of Golden Grahams, and a jug of milk. This was how it was done. This was me taking care of myself the best I could. On another day, maybe tomorrow, I would assess the carnage and figure out exactly how I was going to live. But for the moment, life was between 7-Eleven and my intestinal tract.

That night, with my belly stuffed, I dreamt I was walking on a long, grassy path, like the one beside Santa Monica Boulevard in Beverly Hills. As I walked, I saw, to the left and the right of me, two sets of trees. On the left were evergreens, fluffy and emerald green, a small forest growing up in peaks. On the right was a row of palms, tall and elegant, with fronds that billowed lightly in the sunlight. When I'd moved to Los Angeles, I couldn't get over the presence of the palm trees, the way people were just living their lives against such an exotic backdrop. But in the dream, I found both sets of trees absolutely delicious.

Squirrels and chipmunks flitted around in the grass. They were having a feast, eating tons of nuts. I wasn't sure if someone had fed them the nuts or if they had dropped from the trees, but there were so many nuts—more nuts than I had ever seen in one place. I saw peanuts, almonds, hazelnuts, walnuts, cashews, acorns, and pistachios. It was like the grass was nature's infinite toppings bar of nuts.

But even though there were plenty of nuts to go around, more than the animals could possibly eat, the squirrels kept stealing the chipmunks' nuts right out of their hands. The chipmunks were bigger than the squirrels. They could have easily retaliated. But none of them seemed to get angry or upset by the theft. When a squirrel snuck up behind a chipmunk and grabbed a nut, the chipmunk would simply surrender the nut—then go pick up another nut off the ground and nibble through its shell.

Under the evergreens I saw one chipmunk that looked a lot like Miriam. The chipmunk had three white spots on its brown, furry neck. A shower of nuts rained down gently on its head, as though it were in a cartoon and being followed by a nut cloud. When I looked up to see where the nuts were coming from, I saw a gigantic wood-carved elephant—as tall as the tops of the evergreens—towering over the chipmunk. Seated on the elephant's back, tossing out nuts from a blue-and-yellow cloth bag, was Rabbi Judah Loew ben Bezalel.

"Shalom!" called the rabbi.

His beard was long and gray like in the picture I'd seen online, and he was wearing a flowy robe. The robe was made out of the comforter from the Schwebels' basement.

"Shalom," I said.

"Care for a nut?" he asked.

"No, thank you," I said.

"Would it kill you to have a cashew?" he asked, smiling.

"It might," I said, smiling back.

"Little Rachel," he said. "Tell me. How are your roots feeling? Have you been going deep?"

He tossed a pistachio my way.

"To be honest, Rabbi, I feel scared," I said, catching it.

"What's to be scared of?" he asked.

I opened the pistachio like a tiny door. But it was empty, no nut, just a shell. I tossed the shell onto the grass.

"Spreading," I said. "Not so much vertically but horizontally."

"What's so scary about the horizontal?" he asked, chucking me another pistachio.

I caught it and opened it, like a second door. This one was empty too. Now I really wanted a pistachio.

"I don't want to spread out into some crazy far outer reaches," I said. "What if I can't get back?"

"Eh," he said. "What's to get back to?"

It was a good question. I didn't know what to say.

The rabbi, clearly pleased with himself, winked and tossed me a third pistachio. This shell was tighter than the first two, and I had to open it with my teeth, like a squirrel or a chipmunk might. When I cracked open the shell, I found, inside, a lovely nut—perfectly ovular, glowing green, almost chartreuse. I put the nut on my tongue and sucked. It was creamy, salty, exquisite. I chewed it up and swallowed.

"Just because it feels good doesn't mean it's wrong," said the rabbi.

CHAPTER 40

M onday at work felt like hell. I'd packed my gym bag and my breakfast: the yogurt and the low-calorie muffin, though it all seemed futile now. My pants were tight on my ass and dug into my butt crack. They rubbed a pink ring around my stomach. I craved an alternate universe, to be some other Rachel who only wore clothing with elastic waistbands, sweatpants and parachute pants. In that world, I could inhale and exhale freely. In that world, I would cut my hair short, wear red Air Jordans and custom gold Air Force 1s, hooded sweatshirts, blazers and skinny ties, backward baseball caps. I would reflect casual confidence and power, a bit of nastiness, still Jewy. I'd be like a Beastie Boy circa 1989.

At noon, I looked up from an Internet image search of King Ad-Rock and was surprised to see Jace Evans walking toward my desk.

"What are you doing?" asked Jace, touching the floof part of his hair and then scratching the skinhead part, a one-two aesthetic check.

"Working," I said. "You?"

"I need to talk to Ofer about some problems I'm having with the writers of the show. They want to put Liam in a coma."

"Oh," I said.

Across from me, NPR Andrew was pretending to code Ofer's

client newsletter—this week's topic: *Auditions and Toxic Masculinity*. I could see him peeping out from behind his computer. Jace was too commercial for NPR Andrew's tastes, but fame was fame. Jace's attention had to make me more intriguing in Andrew's eyes.

I still disliked NPR Andrew and his eyes. But they were eyes. Any gaze that increased in its esteem of me made me feel validated: like I was earning my existence. What I didn't want was for Ofer to see Jace and me talking.

"I had a burger the other day at Cassell's," said Jace. "Best one I've had in LA. It's a definite must for late night after This Show Sucks."

Did Jace want to be my pal? I didn't need a pal. Maybe he just felt sorry for me, seeing me once again in my inferior position, the assistant, "the help." Our power differential was fucking with his Ohio value system. He had to pretend we were on equal footing, that we really had something in common. And it seemed the thing he thought we had in common was beef.

"I found it rather intriguing that he came to your desk," said Ana at teatime. "It's interested behavior."

I couldn't tell if she was fucking with me. Her words had become confusing. She'd started gossiping to me again, but I felt paranoid that the things she said had a double edge—as though they were also directed at me. When she called Kayla "fat and blundering," I wasn't sure if she was really talking about Kayla or about me. Sometimes I felt like she was laughing at me right to my face, like she and herself had become the "us" and I was the "them," and the joke was that I didn't know who was who. I figured that her comment was some kind of setup. She was trying to get me excited so she could deflate me again.

"He's an actor," I said. "He always looks interested."

"Well, why wouldn't he be interested in you?" she asked, giving me a gentle knock on my shoulder and giggling. "You're interesting."

The giggle was ambiguous. She could just as easily be showing girly camaraderie as making fun of me. But the shoulder knock was sportsmanlike: celebratory and chummy. It made me feel like we were on the same team. She seemed to earnestly be commending me. But for what exactly?

Ana always made it appear like she looked down on actors, the whole Hollywood scene. She earned money working in the industry, but otherwise declared that she was far above it intellectually. She may have been idealistic long ago, but when her husband left her, she'd abandoned any investment in Hollywood mythology so she could write the whole thing off as "stupid."

I hadn't considered that underneath her bravado was a feeling of weakness, loss, the fear that she was less than. I never imagined she might still be secretly smitten with celebrity. She was rejecting that world before it rejected her again. But that didn't mean she didn't secretly want to live there.

CHAPTER 41

After work, I had no energy for the gym. I chewed two pieces of nicotine gum at once and went anyway. When I changed into my workout clothes, I discovered that my spandex shorts were now so tight they gave me cameltoe—chronic cameltoe. Every time I fixed the toe, it emerged again, somehow deeper.

On the elliptical machine, I let the shorts rub against me, feeling horny. It was some new kind of horniness, or maybe a very old kind, raw lust, like when I first discovered masturbation and indulged in it daily. The horniness felt like hunger itself. I was fully famished, and I didn't know whether it was food or sex I wanted. Maybe I wanted both. All of this eating seemed to have made me more sexually charged, awake. But what was waking up, exactly: my pussy or my soul? I was scared of my soul. What if my soul was monstrous? If a person had a monstrous soul, should she still follow it?

I switched to the stationary bike. As I pedaled, my pussy rubbed against the black leather seat, and I felt a delicious warmth spread throughout my pelvis. The front of the bike seat was horn-shaped. It poked out in front of me like a cock. I took to this right away, having my own thick cock. I wanted to make the cock come alive, to say a blessing over it—Frankencock!—a bike-seat dick. I began reciting quietly any Hebrew I could remember.

"*Nun, gimmel, hay, shin, nun, gimmel, hay, shin*," I whispered, intoning the letters on the dreidel to the rhythm of my pedaling.

"*Oseh shalom bimromav, hu ya'aseh shalom aleinu*," I sang to myself, using the old tune I knew. But I felt guilty using my grandmother's favorite song to animate a penis.

Etz chayim hi lamachazikim ba, vetomecheha me'ushar! I crooned internally, delivering a captivating performance of the tree of life song.

Suddenly, I felt incredibly powerful—as though my cock were really coming alive. I imagined, as I pedaled, that Ana was sucking me. For the first time, I felt no hesitance in fantasizing about her sexually. It was as though the cock protected me from judgment.

I had total power over Ana. She looked up at me as I teased her face. She begged me to let her lick it. When I finally let her have it, grunting, "All right, suck," I acted like I was doing her a favor. She licked and sucked me, and I felt stimulated by two things: her mouth and my newfound dominance. I felt like another kind of creature altogether—some new being I had invoked. If I was a woman, I was not me as I'd known myself, but a woman with more courage than I thought I'd had. I was a woman of impulse, a woman of instinct. I was a woman of pleasure and a woman of confidence. I was a woman of appetites, a growling beast. I was a person.

I continued to pedal, closing my eyes, rubbing against the seat. I imagined Ana sliding my cock between her tits, rubbing me on her nipples, gasping, as though she could come from that contact alone. It was like her nipples were two clits. I whipped her nipples with my dick, then whipped her face with it. Her expression grew serious, ardent. She begged me to put it inside her.

At this point in the fantasy, I hit something of a choose-your-own-adventure. One choice was to lick her pussy. I wanted to taste her so badly. Another was to deprive her. I didn't want to give her any help in getting wet. I wanted to know that her wet-ness was effortless, spontaneous, a reaction to the sight and feel of me. I wanted her to be so intoxicated by my presence that she became a river.

In the end, I went with option A: lick it. Why should I rob myself of the taste of her elixir? I ate her dripping-wet pussy, ate it good, but I kept my reaction very self-contained. No reason for her to know how much pleasure it gave me. On the outside, I was a haughty daughter, then an impenetrable soldier just doing her job gruffly. But on the inside, I reveled in Ana's taste: coppery, like a shipwrecked chalice at the bottom of the ocean.

Now she was crying for my cock. I decided that I would fuck her from behind. I turned her around and bit her gently on the ass, which was ample but saggy with age. The sagginess turned me on even more. I massaged her ass cheeks, opened them like a book, and aimed straight for her pussy hole (a lovely shade of purple: seedless grape). I parked my cock right there at the entrance. She moaned, but not out of pain.

"Please," she said. "Please."

When I felt she had begged long enough, I activated Frank-encock. She groaned with delight and began moving back and forth on the length of me, so that I barely had to thrust. But I wanted to thrust. I grabbed her hips and steadied her.

"Stop fucking moving," I said.

Then I used the power of my own hips to thrust deeper into her.

I could go as long as I wanted. But while my phantom cock was made out of a seat, I could still feel all the pleasure in my organ. I felt a surge of tenderness for her as I came.

Do not go there, I said to myself. *No heart.*

I rode out the orgasm with the pleasure between my legs alone. It felt so good that I gave a little yelp out loud.

I looked over at the man on the bike to my right. He was an

older man, maybe seventy, with white hair. He had headphones on and seemed totally absorbed in what he was listening to. I got the feeling it was an audiobook, David Baldacci or Clive Cussler.

I laughed and closed my eyes again. Then I pedaled out the last waves of my orgasm.

CHAPTER 42

I sat in my car in the gym parking garage with the engine on. I put the heat on blast, then turned it off and cranked up the air instead. My vision was blurry, as though there were a veil of water between me and the world, probably from all the exertion. I felt blood pulsing behind my forehead—not a bad sensation at all. I felt high. I thought of the words *Variety Pack*. I began repeating them in my mind like a mantra to the rhythm of my pulse: *Variety Pack. Variety Pack. Variety Pack. Variety Pack.*

I reached for my phone, pulled up my father's number.

Hi Dad, I typed. Then I deleted it.

I pulled up my mother's number.

I typed three emojis: llama, tulip, hand wave. Then I deleted them.

I pulled up the number at Miriam's house. I called it.

CHAPTER 43

Miriam picked up the phone.

"Oh, good, it's you," I said. "I didn't want your family to think I was a stalker. Anyway, I'm just calling to say thank you for such a lovely Shabbat."

"It's Ayala," said the voice on the other end.

"Oops," I said. "Hi, is Miriam there?"

I didn't tell her who I was, though of course she knew.

"One second," she said.

She didn't say hello or ask how I was doing.

I heard the shuffle of her laying down the receiver, then her voice calling, "Miriam! Phone!"

"Hello?" said Miriam.

"Hi. It's Rachel," I said.

"Hi!" she said, sounding happy.

"I wanted to thank you so much for a lovely weekend," I said. "Please tell your parents I said thank you as well."

"Of course. It was our pleasure."

I didn't know what to say to her next.

"Did you work today?" I asked.

"Yes," she said. "But only from two to seven. A cousin covered the morning shift. Dov—he's a lazy schlemiel, and he should."

I liked how arrogant she was. Usually, I didn't like people who always thought they were right, but her belief in her own common sense was endearing.

She didn't ask about my day, which was a relief because I didn't feel like talking about it. But there was silence on the line. I wondered if she felt as awkward about it as I did. She probably didn't. Miriam was most likely fine with leaving moments unfilled, peaceful with silent space, existing in it, letting it exist. I tried to pretend like I was fine with it, as though this was just what everyone did: sat around on the phone in silence. Then I heard people talking in the background.

"Is that your family? I don't want to keep you."

"Oh no," she said. "I'm in my room actually. I'm watching a movie. Clark Gable and Jean Harlow. Something about a boat, I'm not sure. I turned it on in the middle."

"Is it good?"

"It's okay."

"Oh," I said.

I googled the movie theater on my phone where we had gone to see *Charade*. This week was *12 Angry Men* and *All About Eve*.

"Do you know what's playing?" I asked. "*All about Eve.*"

She didn't say anything.

"Do you like Bette Davis?"

"Not really. But I would go see it if you wanted to," she said.

"Well, there's also *12 Angry Men*."

"No, no angry men." She laughed. "*All About Eve.* That one's fine."

"Great!" I said. "Would you want to go to the Golden Dragon again?"

"Sure," she said. "I also know another place, great kosher Thai, that's not far."

"We could go there," I said hesitantly.

I was trying to re-create the magic of our first outing precisely!

"No. If you want the Dragon, we'll do the Dragon," she said.

"Okay! What night would you like to go?"

"I don't know. You decide. You're the one asking me on the date, right?"

Then she laughed. I swallowed hard. We both got silent.

"Thursday?" she asked finally. "Six o'clock?"

"Great," I said. I would have to skip This Show Sucks. I didn't care.

When we got off the phone, I considered her choice of words. I wanted her to mean what she'd said, that we really were going on a date. But she was probably just using the language of classic romance films in jest. And the reason she could do this comfortably, easily, was because there was no way we could possibly be romantic. It was friendship, that was it.

CHAPTER 44

Miriam was already seated at the bamboo bar, sipping her drink under the colored lights. It wasn't a Scorpion Bowl, but some other kind of tropical thing in a coconut with an umbrella and a bunch of fruit.

"Sorry," she said. "I would've ordered something for you, but I just didn't feel like a Scorpion Bowl tonight, and I wasn't sure what you would want. The mai tai is good and also the Blue Hawaii."

"What are you drinking?" I asked.

"A piña colada."

"Looks creamy."

"No cream, only coconut milk. If it was cream, they couldn't serve it with the meat."

"I'll have one too," I said.

She was avoiding the Scorpion Bowl. She didn't want to get drunk. This meant she was trying to stay on guard, afraid of what might happen if she let herself relax. But wait, there were more layers at play here. If she were really afraid of what might happen between us, she wouldn't have come at all. Secretly, she did want something to happen. Also, not at all. She was me, walking into a bakery and trying not to binge. Or I was just being hyperanalytical and the drink had nothing to do with her feelings about me.

"You smell good," she said.

I grinned at her, and my mind began racing again. Was this the kind of lingering little compliment a person would give if they didn't want to encourage another person to make advances toward them? I was a cobra, slithering behind her every word.

Stop fucking thinking for one second and try to have a good time, I said to myself.

Never in my life have I had a good time, I replied.

It was true: I had a bad relationship with the tree of life. I didn't water it properly, pruned too much. I needed to fertilize it, or something, find joy. I'd just begun admonishing myself when Miriam said, "Listen, I'm not super hungry."

"Oh," I said.

I must have looked devastated.

"Sorry," she said guiltily. "You should order whatever you want, and I will eat some of it."

This was heresy! She was just going to leave me out here to creep my way through the menu all alone? What about our chopstick games? What about our sauce play? I needed her confidence, her culinary wisdom, also her protection from the judgment of the waiter. I couldn't order too much. But you couldn't come to Golden Dragon and not order too much. So much for trying to reenact our last visit. She'd veered off script, and I did not want to improvise.

Then I noticed that she was wearing the Ruský Rouge. She was giving me a sign! Or did it mean nothing? I was having heart palpitations, and everything was unanswerable.

"The lipstick looks pretty on you," I said.

"Thanks," she said. "I figured out how to put it on good, and it only took four botched attempts."

"I like that you're wearing it. I like giving you things."

"Why?"

I couldn't bring myself to say what I wanted to say, which was, *Because you make me feel so good just to be around you.*

So I said, "I don't know. I just do."

I decided I would pray for a sign. But I didn't really know how to pray, another of the inadequacies in my Hebrew school education. I could remember building a miniature sukkah out of graham crackers, icing, and candy, stealing half of the supplies and shoving them in my backpack to binge on in my bedroom at home later. But nothing about how to really talk to god.

I imagined googling, *How to make a golem fall in love with you*. Maybe that's all that prayer was anyway—a cosmic google. In that case, any iPhone could be a synagogue. I wished I could FaceTime with Rabbi Judah.

The waiter came over, and I ordered a pu pu platter and the same sesame chicken dish, hoping she would eat it with me.

"Have you ever had a boyfriend?" asked Miriam, when the waiter walked away.

"Yes, of course!" I said, laughing, as though it were obvious. Then I softened. It was an honest question, and for Miriam, it was totally possible that I hadn't.

"Oh," she said.

"You haven't had one, right?" I asked. "I am going to assume that's correct."

"No," she said. "Of course not."

"What about a girlfriend?" I asked.

"What do you mean?" she said.

"I mean, have you ever had a girlfriend?"

She blushed. I could tell she knew exactly what I meant.

"I've had girls who are friends, of course. But never anything like *that*."

And that was all she said. She didn't say *I'm not gay* or *I'm not a lesbian*. She didn't say that it was something she could never have in the future. I didn't dare press her further.

When they served the pu pu platter, she told me to go ahead and eat first if I was hungry, that she was only going to eat a little.

The situation was growing tragic. The whole point was to share!

"Well, I'm not eating both egg rolls," I said. "So you might as well have one."

"Okay," she said, and picked up an egg roll. As she bit into it, she seemed to relax a little. Then she filled her plate with more of the platter.

I loved watching her eat, the way she licked a little bit of sauce off her lip, the way she licked her fingers. She ate like a woman for whom food possessed no dilemma, turbulence, or hardship. But as I watched her grow calmer with every bite, I realized it was not delight alone that compelled her to eat that way.

"So, boys and girls are not allowed to touch amongst the Orthodox, even modern Orthodox, is that right?" I asked her.

"That's right," she said.

"So kissing is definitely off-limits, but also hugging or holding hands."

"Yeah, I definitely don't hold hands with boys."

"What about girls? Are girls allowed to hug?"

"Girls are allowed to hug."

"And hold hands?"

"Of course, girl friends could hold hands if they want to."

She narrowed her eyes, put down her chopsticks.

"I was just curious," I said. "You don't mind if I ask you these questions, do you?"

"No," she said, looking me in the eye.

I wanted to know if girls could kiss each other. But I didn't say anything. Instead, I took a bite of chicken. It felt tough in my mouth, and I wasn't sure how I was going to swallow it. I chewed and chewed. I chewed it past the point where chewing it still seemed possible. Then I chewed it some more.

CHAPTER 45

"I might like Bette better than Audrey," I whispered to Miriam in the glow of the theater.

We were about fifteen minutes into *All About Eve*. She was sucking on a Twizzler from the big bag we were sharing. We also had a bag of Peanut M&M's and had parked them both in the cup holder between us.

"I've thought about this," she whispered, Twizzler dangling from the side of her mouth. "Bette is tough on the inside and the outside, right? Which is fine. Great. Audrey seems a little fragile on the outside, but inside you know she's tough. Like a Peanut M&M. She's more special."

"But isn't a Peanut M&M supposed to melt in your mouth, not in your hand, or whatever?"

"Everyone knows that isn't true."

"Oh, right."

We continued to snack and watch the movie. Then I whispered another question.

"What about holding hands in a movie theater?"

"What?" she whispered back.

"What about holding hands in a movie theater? Can girls hold hands in a movie theater?"

She didn't say anything for a long time. I wondered if she was just going to ignore the question. Now I felt embarrassed for asking it—like I had crossed some kind of line. I was pretending to be innocent and naïve, not knowing what Orthodox girls could do. But people didn't hold hands at the movies without romance. Everybody knew that.

Etz chayim hi lamachazikim ba, vetomecheha me'ushar, I thought to myself.

On-screen, a black-and-white Anne Baxter sat on a staircase with a black-and-white Marilyn Monroe and purred to a black-and-white Gary Merrill, "If there's nothing else, there's applause. I've listened backstage to people applaud. It's like . . . like waves of love coming over the footlights and wrapping you up."

Suddenly, Miriam turned to me. I felt her head move, her breath close to my ear.

"Yes," she whispered. "Girls can hold hands in a movie theater."

I stared straight ahead at the screen and did not dare stir. I tried to look at her out of the corner of my eye, and it seemed that maybe she was smiling in profile. I couldn't be sure. I didn't know what to do. Should I make a move like dudes had made moves on me—that whole arm-stretching thing? Should I pretend to be going for an M&M, then just drop my hand on hers?

Counting backward from ten, I edged my hand toward the M&M's. But when I hit three, I botched my mission. Instead of circumventing the bag and rerouting to my true target, I panicked and ended up with my hand in the candy. I took a few and shoved them into my mouth. Then I returned my hand to base camp on my lap.

"Why?" whispered Miriam suddenly.

"Why what?"

"Why do you want to know that?"

I looked at her face in the glow of the movie screen, swaths of light and shadow flickering on and off her pale skin. She was like a moon cycling through all its phases in rapid-fire.

"Oh," I said. "Because—I wanted to hold yours."

And just like that I took her hand.

It was so exciting to hold her hand. With this simple gesture, I felt nearer to her than anyone. Her hand in my hand was a deeper intimacy than any sexual act, all my past performances of pleasure. I felt brave, princely, thrilled in my bones, electric in my toes. I was holding her hand and she was letting me. I felt lucky; also, protective of her in the darkness of the theater. I remained very still. I was so quiet and aware of our being there together, like that, that any micromovement either of us made became a loud broadcast: the twitch of her finger, the sound of her swallowing. I swore I could hear my own blood. The movie was no longer on the screen but between us.

Then, suddenly, she let go. My arm dropped to my chair. A wave of disappointment welled up inside me. The hand-holding had felt like an arrival, an answer to a question, a resounding yes. But the dropping of my hand seemed like another, more final answer.

Oh well, I thought. *That's that, I guess.*

I watched her hand fumble in the Twizzler bag. Had she only dropped my hand because she was reaching for a Twizzler? She placed the end of the candy in her mouth, chomped on it. Then she reached for my hand again. I gave Miriam's hand a little squeeze, and the sparks lit up in me again, every inch of my skin, every hair on my head, thrilled.

We sat like that for a long time, very still, Miriam's hand in my hand, only letting go every now and then to grab a piece of candy. Neither of us looked over at the other. The only acknowledgment of separate personhood was when one of us would briefly release the other's hand to grab a piece of candy or adjust our bodies. The first time I dropped her hand to scratch my forehead, I was terrified. What if, while my hand was gone, the rules changed and her hand became suddenly off-limits? What if it wasn't where I'd left it? I scratched my head quickly, then snatched her hand again, relieved to have it back. Each time our hands reunited, I felt bliss newly restored.

I hoped my hand wasn't too damp. Hers never got sweaty. Her skin was soft and powdery, and the texture of her skin evoked old-time blotter papers, violet pastille candies, the petal of a tea rose. The shape of the webbing between her thumb and pointer finger was the tubey mouth of a calla lily. Ever so gently, I took my pointer finger and slowly traced the lip of that tubey mouth. I traced it cautiously and lightly, as though I were gathering a bit of pollen that was dusted upon it. Then, after I had gathered enough pollen from the lip, I dipped my fingers delicately into the space where her thumb and pointer finger curled onto each other atop the webbing. Slowly, I entered the throat of that flower, as though to carefully excavate more pollen from the inside.

I remembered, just as I entered the flower, that it was not a flower at all. It was Miriam's hand. And not only had I just stroked her hand, but I'd moved inside of it—in a gentle way, a comforting way, yet also in an undeniably sexual way. I stopped moving and just kept my finger resting inside that flower opening of hers, that sweet little hole, without thrusting, just leaving my finger there so she could feel some of that fullness. I noticed that I was flicking my tongue back and forth against the backs of my teeth like a hummingbird wing—as though my tongue wanted to be my finger and I wanted her hand to be her elsewhere. My tongue felt irritated. I wondered how long I had been doing it.

The next time she reached for a Twizzler, she changed the direction of our hands. Now instead of her hand forming a little floral opening, it was my hand that was opened in a circle and hers that was the fingers, the penetrating object. I was surprised by how cock-like her hand felt resting in mine: fat, hard, content, warm. When the cock shifted, I wondered for a moment if it would try to fuck my hand. But her hand flattened into a hand again, and mine did too, and each of her fingers began to search the skin of my palm.

When she found my lifeline, she gently rubbed it with one finger—more of a tickle actually, up and down, as though it were something she was doing mindlessly or haphazardly. She did it in the softest possible way—like a ghost haunting a place, elusive, felt only in flutters. The tickling stimulated me so much that I wondered if I was wet through my clothes, if I had gotten some of me on the movie theater seat.

Etz chayim hi lamachazikim ba, vetomecheha me'ushar, I thought.

With every sensation of her moving finger, I felt it down there, so that when she approached the top of my lifeline, she was slipping her finger ever so lightly over my clit. And then as she reached the bottom of my palm, she was tracing my inner lips, up and down, almost entering me, but never fully entering me at all. No, she was not even almost entering me. It was not even that close, not nearly.

CHAPTER 46

W hen the movie ended, she dropped my hand. We both sat there silently in the dark as the credits rolled until we were the only ones left in our seats. I was glad she wasn't speaking or getting up to go, and I wasn't going to be the one to break the silence. I didn't want to leave the dark theater.

Finally, she turned to me and raised an eyebrow.

"Wow," she said. "That movie was better than I remembered."

Then she stood up, and I stood up, and we filed out into the harsh light of the lobby, the smell of popcorn, people no longer in profile: three teens in heavy eyeliner laughing in the corner, a man pushing an older woman with oily hair in a wheelchair. I told Miriam that I had to use the bathroom before we left. She said that she didn't have to go and would wait for me.

I peed, and when I wiped myself I was shocked by how slick my vagina was.

"Goodbye to the dregs of bitterness," I whispered, though I had no idea what that meant.

I felt feverish, delirious. My face in the mirror was pink, my eyes bloodshot. A faint rash crept up my neck. We were just two girls holding hands and eating candy in a movie theater, that was all. But my desire: I was sick with it. Sweet sick. Good sick. With trembling hands, I turned on the faucet, splashed cold water on my face. It gave me a moment's relief. Then, still dripping, my temperature rose again.

In the lobby, Miriam didn't say anything about the hand-holding. We left the theater and walked silently together down the street. When we came to the furniture storefront where I'd applied her lipstick on our last outing, she stopped us under the awning so she could light a clove.

"You know, I think I realize what Bette Davis is lacking," she said.

I didn't want to hear any more about Bette Davis.

"What?"

"It's the way she moves. Her motions aren't distinct. If you saw Audrey's shadow—if you just could see a silhouette moving—you'd know immediately that it was her. But it's not the same with Bette. Bette Davis, the way she moves, she could be so many women."

She exhaled hard and handed me the cigarette. Her exhales weren't coming out in any magical shapes, at least as far as I could see. Now they were just exhales.

"What about kissing?" I blurted out.

"Their kissing styles?"

"No," I said, taking a drag of the cigarette. "I mean what about Orthodox girls kissing other girls? Is that allowed?"

"Oh yes," she said. "I mean I kiss my girl friends on the cheek sometimes. And Ayala and my mother. So yeah, that's okay."

"No, I mean on the mouth," I said. "What about girls kissing each other on the mouth? Is that okay?"

A shadow crossed her face. She looked scared.

"I don't know," she said.

"Interesting," I said, taking a final drag of the cigarette. "Interesting."

I flicked the cigarette to the ground and stamped it out underneath my foot. Then, without another sound, I put my hands on her shoulders and brought her in close to me. She was breathing deeply, and her eyes widened, but she didn't pull back.

I put my hand on the back of her head and moved her face into mine. I kissed her softly: first on the upper lip, then the lower. I didn't bring her into the moisture of my mouth, but stayed on the soft surface. I felt so much in each of her lips, like I could dwell there forever, tracing her cupid's bow, the plumpness.

She pulled away. I opened my eyes, but hers were still closed. Then she kissed me, and I was shocked to have her initiate it. I introduced my tongue into her mouth and felt her whole body shudder. Now it was clear. We sucked at each other hungrily, mouths wet and pressed hard together. I knew this could not be mistaken for any kind of kiss between friends.

I wanted to fuck her right there, our tongues in each other's mouths. I wanted to ride her every last shudder, and as though she could feel what I wanted, she pulled away again. This time she did not come back.

"No," she said. "We are not allowed to kiss other girls. At least, not like that."

She took a step backward, then pulled out another cigarette and lit it. We were both silent.

"I'm sorry," I said.

She shook her head as if to say, *No, no, no, it's my fault*, and waved her hand in the air to dismiss me, the cigarette making loops of smoke around itself.

I wanted to say, *But did you like it?*

The way her body shook suggested that she did.

I wanted to say, *If you weren't Orthodox, then would you want to continue kissing me? Oh, Miriam, maybe that was enough, just that you wanted to. I wondered if you wanted me, and you did!*

But I didn't say another word. I had already said and done too much. I'd crossed a line—multiple lines. Now she looked upset.

"I should go home," she said. "It's late."

"Okay," I said. "Where are you parked? Do you want me to walk you to your car?"

"No," she said suddenly and loudly. "That's fine. You should just go home too. Goodbye, Rachel."

"Bye," I said, still standing there as she turned and walked away.

CHAPTER 47

O n the way to work, I made a detour to Bed Bath & Beyond so I could use one of their scales and get an accurate assessment of what was happening to me—at least from a numerical perspective.

In the bathroom accessories aisle, I took out three scales—two digitals and an analog—and arranged them on the floor. I took off my shoes for accuracy. A bald man with a toilet plunger and a StackEms T-Shirt Organizing System in his cart cleared his throat as he tried to get by. I glared at him, like, *What?* until he was forced to back up and use the next aisle. Then I took a deep breath and stepped onto the first scale: a chrome one, sleek, one of the digitals.

The scale took a second to think, then delivered me the news in red digits. I had gained 13.5 pounds. I felt a cold sweat rise to the surface of my skin. I stepped off the scale, then got back on again. 13.5 pounds—still the same. The numbers were so absolute, so certain and unyielding.

I moved over to scale number two, another digital. This one was black and cheaper than the first one, and I liked it better immediately. I inched my foot out and tapped the scale ever so slightly, letting the numbers go to zero. Then I stepped on.

But the news was even worse: I'd gained 14 pounds.

"What the fuck?" I said out loud.

I stepped off and let the numbers disappear, then stepped back on.

14.5 pounds!

I got on the analog scale. Its wheel spun and shook, struggling to decide my fate. But the analog scale said I'd lost 28 pounds.

I began moving from scale to scale, doing a kind of body dysmorphic waltz. 13.5 pounds. 14 pounds. 13.5 pounds. 13.5 pounds. 14.5 pounds. 13.5 pounds. A woman deliberating over a fake-gold vanity set looked at me strangely. She had her toddler and a Shark Lift-Away vacuum cleaner in her cart. I thought about my mother's coupons. They had expired.

What was I expecting the scales would say? Did I think all that food was just going to vanish like poof? This was science! From now on there would be a very strict regime: no breakfast for me, two protein bars for lunch, and then we would see about dinner. I might even have to start doing laxatives again, or at least that herbal dieter's tea that made you shit.

I didn't know how I would face the day, living inside my body, a conscious being. I only wanted to sleep until all the weight came off. It was Friday; just one more day of work and then I could try to sleep through the weekend—or some combination of gym and sleep—a bare-bones death march. It was what I deserved. I felt disgusting.

Driving to work, I pressed the gas pedal down as hard as it would go, taking out my anger and disappointment on the car. On the side streets, I swerved back and forth from side to side. So what if I crashed? At least I'd get to be unconscious.

I lingered in the parking garage, walking up and down the aisles, not wanting to face anybody at the office. I timed myself as I walked, trying to get up to ten minutes of exercise. I prayed some kind of truck would come zooming around a turn and just take me away, right there, one hit, so I wouldn't have to feel. All of this suffering over a 13.5-pound weight gain! If Miriam had kept kissing me, I wouldn't have weighed myself at all.

It was better that things had ended between us now, not some unknown time in the future when I would wake up suddenly and find my body blown up big as hell, orbiting the Earth like a wild balloon, my mind all the way out there too, no longer of this planet, no longer able to decipher the real from the not-real. I didn't want to reach that point, did I? I needed to cut the thought of her out of me completely—cut me out of me too—chunks of my thighs and hips and arms and the rest of my exploding body.

I pulled out my phone and googled *How to kill a golem.*

> *In some tales, the creature has the word* emet *carved on its head.* Emet *means* truth. *In order to kill the Golem, its creator removes the* e *from* emet *so that the word spells* met. Met *means* dead. *This is how the golem dies.*

It was strange that truth and death were so close to each other. I pulled up Dr. Mahjoub's number.

I need to see you, I wrote.

CHAPTER 48

T he following afternoon at Mahjoub's office, I noticed she'd acquired a new elephant: a three-foot rust-colored wire statue thing by the door. I was grateful that she was willing to see me on a Saturday, but the fact that she could fit me in so quickly made me suspicious of her skills, as usual.

"I'm sorry, Rachel," she said, flipping through my file. "I used the last of the Theraputticals for some trauma work with another patient last week. But it should be easy enough for you to order online. Or maybe you want to consider taking ceramics classes—"

"Whatever," I said. "You should just know that your little art therapy exercise has totally destroyed my life."

"Do you want to talk about how or why you feel that it has been . . . less than beneficial?"

"No, I don't," I said.

I didn't want to give her the satisfaction of knowing how many binges deep I was. This was what she'd wanted, right? I wondered if she could see it on me: 13.5 pounds of challah and egg rolls and cholent and noodles. We stared at each other silently.

Finally, I blurted out: "I was doing such a good job with my mother! I'm still doing a good job. It's been thirty-seven days of total boundary holding."

My mother's texts had stopped entirely. If she was trying to smoke me out, it was working. The absence of contact made me want to reach out to her more than when she stalked me every day. I was scared she'd given up on me. All I'd ever wanted was to be left alone. Now I wanted to reach out and say, *Wait!*

"That's amazing," said Dr. Mahjoub. "I'm so pleased."

"I know! But you had to push it. You had to push it with the body stuff. I told you I was well enough. What does it even mean to be well anyway? Is there some plateau of wellness—some place we are supposed to get to where we are, like, fine forever? Because to me that sounds like death!"

"Well—"

"Is death the best we can aim for? I'm starting to think it might be."

I was feeling reckless. I wanted to fuck with her. But also, I was curious.

"Rachel, if you're thinking of harming yourself or someone else, I'm required by law to report it. Are you thinking of harming yourself or someone else?"

I thought about how I wanted to take a knife and cut myself out of me. I thought about how I'd been praying for a truck to just hit me. I thought about death and truth and how, in some languages, they were just one letter apart. I wanted to ask her if she knew that.

"I'm fine," I said. "I'm not thinking of harming myself or someone else."

CHAPTER 49

W hen I got home that night, I pulled up to the curb of my apartment building and there was Miriam standing out front on the small, dirty lawn. I had told her I lived in the building with the fake-stone front across from Doughy's Bagels, one of her favorite bagel shops, on the other side of Pico. I had not expected that she would materialize.

"Uh, hi?" I called out from the car.

She stood there not smiling, Coach bag over her shoulder, and gave a little wave.

"Shit," I muttered, and put the car in reverse and parked.

Was she here seeking an apology for the way I had behaved? Now she was looking down at the ground, as though there were something fascinating happening there. As I got out of the car and walked toward her, I noticed that she had clasped her hands in front of her and they were trembling. It was not the trembling of a supernatural creature, but the trembling of a human being. This made me very uncomfortable.

"Hello," I said, swallowing dryly.

"Hello," she said, still looking down at the ground.

"Went to Doughy's?"

"No," she said. "I came . . . to say I'm sorry."

"*You're* sorry?" I asked, surprised. "Why are *you* sorry?"

"Because I didn't tell you the whole truth," she said.

It felt like my lungs had forgotten what to do, that my inhalations were no longer automatic, and I had to force myself to breathe intentionally. To distract myself from my impending suffocation, I came up with a movie plot. Miriam was about to confess to me that we were living in some surreal Jewish fable. Rabbi Judah Loew ben Bezalel was being played by Uncle Lavie's wife's dead great-uncle, an actor from the Yiddish theater. The rabbi and Miriam had both been sent by my dead grandparents to instill in me some Zionist pride, by way of clove cigarettes, hot cholent, and a stolen kiss. I was Cary Grant and Miriam was Eva Marie Saint, the honey trap—or, in this case, the milk-and-honey trap.

"When you asked if girls could kiss, I knew what you were saying," she continued. "And when we were talking about whether or not I'd ever kissed anyone, I guess I wasn't completely honest."

"Oh?"

"There was a girl in my high school named Bluma Sternberg. We were good friends, actually, for a long time, since elementary school. In high school we would sneak out to the movies because her parents were more strict than mine and she wasn't supposed to be watching films that weren't religious. But I got her into the classic movies, and she was hooked."

"Uh-huh . . ." I said.

"I used to go over to her house, because she wasn't allowed to come over to mine. Her parents were afraid we weren't kosher enough—that something might slip in terms of our dishes, brisket in the *milchik* bowl, I honestly don't know. Maybe they thought we were unclean."

"Bastards. As though your mother isn't running an impeccable household."

"I know! Anyway, so I would always be at her house. I would sneak over a bottle of something from my parents' house, something they would never notice was missing, crappy wine. She loved to drink! Or at least, she learned to drink with me and seemed to really love it. In fact, she may have even liked it more than she liked me. She didn't really have many other friends at the high school, because it wasn't the most religious one in the city. I'm really not even sure why her parents sent her there. But anyway, I would hang out in her room and we would drink there together. One time she asked me if I would want to do some romantic things like we saw in the movies. If we would maybe want to practice for when we were married."

"Whoa!"

"I got really scared when she asked me that. But I was also excited, because, well, I really liked her a lot. So I asked her how we would practice. She said just by hugging for the first week, so that's what we did, just hugged. Then she said we could also kiss if I wanted, and I said yes I did want to. So we kissed. And then we really started making out."

I was surprised she knew what making out was. I mean, of course she knew what it was, with all the classic movies and stuff. But still it surprised me to hear her say the words.

"I started going over there more and more often," Miriam said. "I would always bring something to drink, and we would always make out in her room."

"Just kiss each other?"

"Yeah mostly," she said. "And we would rub—you know—we would rub each other's bodies, but only over our clothes, never underneath. I think we both felt that as long as we had our clothes on then we weren't doing anything really bad, you know?"

"Right," I said.

I was jealous of this Bluma Sternberg—jealous that she'd gotten to be with Miriam in this way. It felt like a different jealousy than I'd ever experienced. Usually, I compared myself to a woman and felt jealous of her body or her boyfriend. This was more of an ache—a hard ache in my chest, and also, I noticed, in my groin. I didn't like that someone else had been with her first. I didn't like that I hadn't been the one to uncover this side of her.

"Bluma didn't have a lock on her bedroom door, which meant we always had to sneak around and be on the alert. At least she had her own bedroom, which is rare in Orthodox families. But her parents must have gotten suspicious, or figured out what was going on, because one day her mother snuck up to the door and just burst in on us."

"Oh god, what happened?"

"She immediately started beating Bluma. Just—beating her up with her hands. Then I tried to stop her and she hit me too."

"That's horrible!"

"She screamed at her—partly in Yiddish, which I couldn't understand, because my parents didn't speak it in our house. But the part in English was terrible."

"I'm so sorry," I said.

"She called her a slut. She called her a . . . dyke. And me a dyke too. Her mother threatened that she was going to tell my parents, which terrified me. For days I waited for that hammer to drop. But she never did."

"Why do you think she threatened but didn't say anything?"

"The more people who knew, the more chance there was of gossip spreading. She did not want what had happened to leave that room. But a few days later, after school, she found me and pulled me aside. She said that if I ever went near her daughter again, she would kill me. And then she took Bluma out of my school."

"Shit!"

"Yeah."

"I'm surprised you didn't tell your parents that she beat you."

"They'd want to know the reason why!"

"You couldn't tell them?"

"You must be kidding. I would be disowned."

"Really?"

As the word left my mouth, it sounded judgmental. But I wasn't judging her at all. I thought of my own mother, not religious, and how terribly she had reacted to my own admission. I had wished, because they seemed so kind, that the Schwebels could be different.

"If they thought I liked a girl, it would be unacceptable," said Miriam.

"Oh," I said.

It was getting cold out.

"All of that is to say I'm sorry if I gave you the wrong idea or anything, but . . . I was embarrassed to tell you that story. I knew what you were asking about the kiss. I just—anyway, I would like us to stay friends."

"Yeah," I said. "I'd like that too."

So she'd had an experience with a girl. And she'd enjoyed it. Now I was convinced that she'd known what she was doing with me all along, this kosher coquette. Well, I wasn't about to drag her over any thresholds.

"It's getting late," I said. "I should probably go upstairs."

"Yes, I should go home," she said.

I wanted to say, *Come upstairs with me, please. Just come up with me to my stupid, nothing apartment with its white walls and vacant fridge and bare wood floors and so much emptiness.*

Instead, I said, "Good night."

CHAPTER 50

That night I dreamt about white lilies. I was starving. I was in a field of them, licking rainwater off the petals to try to fill my stomach. As I licked, I had to avoid getting any pollen or petals in my mouth, because the lilies were poisonous. But I was so hungry! At one point, while I sucked the droplets off one of the petals, I found myself biting into the petal itself—chewing that up and sucking out the juice from inside. It felt exciting to be doing something I shouldn't do. It felt good to be nursing myself on the earthy, vegetal flavor. I ate it all the way to the stem. "I'm not dying," I said. "I'm not dying."

"Of course you're not," came a voice. "Nobody brings flowers to a Jewish funeral."

It was Rabbi Judah Loew ben Bezalel. He was standing inside a tall, white calla lily, the one calla lily amongst all the other regular lilies, which thrust skyward like an upturned trumpet.

"Hi Rabbi," I said, wiping pollen off my lower lip.

"Hello, Rachel," he said, his long beard hanging over the edge of the flower, as though he were Rapunzel. "Nice to see you noshing. It's a mitzvah, you know."

"They're delicious."

"That's what I'm told. I abstain. Not kosher. I can only do the calla lilies."

"Oh."

"Which is interesting, because, if you'll notice, the lilies of the field are shaped like the Star of David. But god has a sense of humor."

"Totally," I said, now biting into the stem of my lily. "Okay if I eat this in front of you?"

"Please, go ahead," he said, waving his hand. "I don't want to interrupt your nosh. I just came to let you know that it's nice to see you trusting your kishkas."

"My kishkas?"

"Your guts! Your intuition."

"Is that what I'm doing?" I asked.

"You are!" he said. "You did it. I mean, you didn't *do it* do it . . . with Miriam, which would also be a mitzvah, by the way, but you were right about one thing. She likes you."

I heard a loud buzzing sound. It was like the end-of-period buzzer in a basketball game, except it was coming from above.

"God really enjoys basketball," said the rabbi, laughing.

But he looked scared. Then the buzzer sounded again. The rabbi's eyes widened. I had a terrible feeling that this was it. This was the end of the game. I had poisoned myself after all. The buzzer was letting me know I would soon be dead.

I opened my eyes and blinked. I saw the clock. It said 1:15. There was still 1 minute and 15 seconds left of the game. Then I realized I was in my apartment. What I was hearing was not the buzz of death. It was the buzzer on my intercom. I was scared. I ignored the buzzer and inched down farther under my blanket. Then it rang again—this time a little longer.

I threw the blankets off, got up, slipping and sliding around the floor in my wool socks, and made my way to the intercom.

"Hello?" I said, annoyed.

"It's Miriam. Hi."

Had I summoned her?

"One second!" I said.

I fixed my socks and raced down the hallway. Then I had a better idea. I made a U-turn and went back into my apartment. Kishkas. I pressed the intercom again.

"Want to just come upstairs?" I asked.

CHAPTER 51

When Miriam came to the door of my apartment, she was crying. There was a teardrop welling in her left eye and one on her right cheek. They reminded me of the water droplets from the lilies.

"What's wrong?" I asked. "You okay?"

I saw her struggle with words, unsure of what to say. I hated seeing her weeping, and I felt the urge to wipe her tears and comfort her.

"I don't know," she said finally, wiping her dripping eyelids. "I'm a faucet."

"Do you want to come inside and have something to drink?"

"I'm fine," she said.

"Do you want me to just stand in the doorway with you for a while?"

"All right," she said, laughing.

She moved her hands up the doorframe. I reached out and touched her left hand with my right hand. Then I brought her hand down and held it with both of my hands.

This could be enough, I thought. *Just hold the fucking lily.*

But I found myself leading her inside, closing the door quietly and gently behind her. I didn't want to frighten her with any loud sounds or sudden movements that might imply I was expecting anything. I went to the sofa and sat down. She followed and sat beside me.

"So," I said.

Then I took her hand in mine again and gently tickled the inside of her palm, just as she had allowed me to do at the movies. This time, we weren't in the dark, so I could watch her reaction to everything I was doing. Her face grew flushed, and I noticed a sheen of perspiration on her forehead and dotted on her upper lip. I went even slower, gentler.

"You can smoke in here if you want," I said.

"I'm out of cigarettes," she said.

"I've got some nicotine gum we can burn."

She laughed with a noise that sounded like a sob. Then she put her other hand on my other hand.

"Well," she said. "Maybe we *can* kiss."

I moved closer to her, our lips almost touching. I could feel her warmth, and I stayed there for what felt like a very long time. Her breath smelled sweet. I kissed her. She made an "oh" sound into my mouth as she took a breath, then slowly introduced her tongue. I sucked it like a piece of liver she was kind enough to feed me. She moaned into my mouth. Her throat clicked a little, and I drank up all the sounds.

Gently, I kissed her lower lip, the side of her mouth, her chin, and then the plump white area under her chin. I began to suck on her there, not hard, just enough to nurse for a moment like a calf drinking of its mother. Then I moved my mouth to where her Adam's apple was, just underneath all that flesh, and sucked there for a while. I was hungry to taste each of her moles, but I took it slow and teased myself like I was just beginning a big feast.

I moved first to the milk chocolate drops on the side of her neck, then made my way to the dark chocolate drop, right at the center of her throat. She made new sounds as I tongued at them, as though they each mapped a different locus of pleasure on her body. As I sucked, it was as though they were the phantom moles cut from my body years ago, and I was sucking myself. Only instead of my inner arm, they resonated in my pleasure points: my throat, my chest, my pussy.

I longed to take off Miriam's shirt and enjoy those heavy breasts of hers. I wanted to lick her down her belly, all the way to her cunt, taste all of her. But I didn't dare go past that center mole, no lower, although I was wet, then wetter, and my pulse beat hard. I felt queasy with desire, weakened by it. But I could also keep going. I kept my mouth on her neck, slowly moved my hands to her breasts, cupping all that I could over her shirt. She was in my hands and spilling out. It was touch heaven.

She was an infinite planet with so many different territories on which to set up camp and play. If I had eons, I'd still never finish exploring her. I sensed that I could feel what she was feeling. She shivered at my every touch, and I wanted to make her feel even more. I wanted us both to go even higher.

Without removing any clothing, I pinched her nipples through the fabric and squeezed her breasts harder, circling my fingers around her areolae, gently milking her with my hands. I swore that I could smell her pussy now, earthy and creamy, like a cool basement, wafting up from between her thighs. Then, suddenly, she pulled away.

"It's getting late," she said, my spit still on her upper lip. "I'm going to have to go."

I wanted to say, *Stay! Sleep over!*

But instead I kissed her on the forehead and on each of her eyelids.

"You're going to come back, aren't you?" I asked.

"Oh, Rachel," she said in a way that sounded sad.

She paused for a moment.

"Yes," she said finally. "I will come back."

"When?" I asked. "Tomorrow! Come back tomorrow!"

Her face lit up at the possibility.

"Yes!" she said. "I guess I could come back tomorrow!"

"Good," I said, stroking her hair.

I walked her to the door and put my mouth on her mouth a final time.

I love you, I mouthed silently into her mouth.

If I did not love Miriam, if it was purely attraction, then I felt that I would never know what love was—and I did not care to know. And when she left, I got down on my knees and touched my face to the ground.

"Thank you, thank you, thank you," I said to who knew what.

I wasn't even sure if Jews prayed on their knees. But I was so grateful.

CHAPTER 52

I was drinking Lipton in the office kitchen, because Ana hadn't offered me Harney & Sons. The Lipton was fucking good. I'd forgotten how much I loved Lipton.

"You seem happy," she said suspiciously, blowing on her tea.

"Oh god, that's a terrible thing to say to a person," I said.

"I'm serious."

But it was true. I couldn't hide my joy. The change was obvious. I was putting milk in my Lipton with regular sugar, lots of it, stirring it into a sort of milkshake-type concoction with a jaunty yet circular motion. There were some leftover shortbread cookies from a meeting that had taken place earlier in the day. I picked one up, dunked it in the tea, and bit it.

"Are those good?" Ana asked me, scrunching her nose.

"They aren't bad," I said.

"You're happy," she said. "Now tell me why."

"No real reason," I said.

"Oh, come on. This wouldn't have to do with a certain some-one?"

"Jace?" I whispered. "No, I haven't seen him."

She looked disappointed.

I was afraid to say a word about Miriam. I had never told her that I liked women. I suspected that she wouldn't take it well. She would laugh and say I was just going through a phase. She might even say mean things about Miriam. But I wished I could tell her what was happening. I wanted her to know me.

My mother had never known me either, though it wasn't because I hadn't given her a chance. I'd given her a lot of chances. What was saddest was that she didn't seem to want to know me, not as I was on the inside. I wasn't even sure if she could grasp that I had an inside, that I was real. Sometimes it seemed impossible that she had ever given birth to me at all. Other times, it made perfect sense that I had lived inside her for so long. It explained why she could only see me as an extension of herself.

There was total silence now on my mother's end, no communication. Still, I carried her inside me: her voice, her feelings, her fears, her ideas of food, bodies, the world, women and men. She had long ago implanted herself in me at the cellular level, spread into my organs—my brain, my heart—until what was hers and what was mine were indistinguishable.

I wondered whether there was a deadline for when a person had to finally stop blaming her mother for her own thoughts. I thought I'd hit that age, then hit it again. At nineteen, twenty, I decided: *Okay, this is enough. You are a grown-up. Time to take responsibility for your own mind.* At twenty-one, *I am over it.* At twenty-two, *I understand why she did what she did.* At twenty-three, *I forgive.* At twenty-four, this imposed silence. But now what?

Declaring myself liberated was one thing. Putting freedom into action was another. Even the idea of freedom made me feel nauseous, spun out, vertiginous, lost in a vast limitlessness, zero walls. I was scared to just float, free but alone. My mathematics, no matter how isolating, had given me companionship. In that restricted life I had rules, a border, a system for certainty—even if the very idea of human certitude, within the boundless mystery of existence, was, itself, false. I wanted walls. I wanted them soft and womblike, but I settled for a frigid vault. My mother had helped me build the vault. But now it was my own.

CHAPTER 53

I wanted to look effortlessly pretty for Miriam. I put on a little black skirt and tank top, blotted makeup, no shoes, as though I were just lounging casually in my apartment after work. I shrouded my lust in softer feelings of romance, giddiness, which made me feel less guilty about wanting her. At its core, though, the feeling was undeniably lust. It was all wet.

I still didn't know exactly how to be the seducer, the one who moves assertively toward another person or teases them fearlessly to the point of action. In my seduction fantasy of Ana, it had been so easy. She was a ghost, and ghosts were static. It was much scarier to be confident when engaging with the warm, vacillating body of another human being who could reject me at any moment.

I'd worn the skirt and tank on purpose, because I knew that I looked thin in the outfit. I wanted to accentuate this feature, to remind Miriam of what I was and what she was in that old competition between women. I felt more comfortable seducing from this place. If I was going to be vulnerable, express that I wanted her, then I needed to already be some kind of victor. I needed to win elsewhere in order to be vulnerable here.

But when Miriam walked into my apartment and told me that I looked "really good," I regretted my little competition. I felt admiration for her then, for the courage it took her to say that.

I'd wanted to hurt her with my body, with our differences. Now I just wanted to help her feel comfortable.

I offered her some kosher wine, something called Baron Herzog California chardonnay, which the tag at the wine store said was "sure to titillate." Then we sat side by side on my sofa and she told me about her day at Yo!Good.

"It was slow. I spent most of the time out back smoking cloves," she said. "Oh, but of course we ran out of s'mores yogurt because the schlemiel cousin forgot to place the order."

"You're a s'more," I said, kissing her on the cheek.

I felt strangely protective of her—motherly, even.

She surprised me by taking my face in both of her hands and kissing me on the lips. She looked me in the eyes just before she did it. We kissed slowly, making tiny smacking sounds. I let my tongue wander into her mouth, heard her swallow. Then her hands drifted from my face to the back of my head. She pulled me to her harder, and I felt like I was now the daughter—protected—and she was the mother. No, we were both daughters, equals, and I liked being equals. Together we had power. I felt that our kissing could sustain the ritual of women loving women for eons to come.

I went to her breasts and rubbed my face over her blouse, firmly, so she could really feel me. Her nipples hardened beneath the cotton. She didn't stop me when I unbuttoned the top button, then the next and the next until her blouse was open and I could see her body, full of gravity, pale and momentous. Her bra, a modest beige, strained to contain her breasts. Below that rolled the waves of her belly, her navel wide and deep, moving up and down with her breath. I was so grateful for everything I got to see, that she was letting me gaze at her like this.

I hugged her and we swayed a little. Then I climbed on her lap so that I was straddling her, my legs spread wide, feeling strong and powerful in my thighs as I kissed her wet mouth, unhooked her bra from behind. I took off her bra slowly, and her breasts spilled out: magnificent, weighty pendulums, nothing like mine. Her nipples were as big as silver dollars, tinted the palest pink. Beneath her areolae were a network of veins, blue and purple, bringing forth the blood that sustained her.

I sucked on one nipple, tickling, squeezing, and giving little pinches to the other, wishing I had two mouths with which to suck her. No, I wished I had more than that: one for each breast, one for her neck, one for her navel, her mouth, her pussy, her eyelids. At any moment I thought that something wondrous might come out, deeply sweet: butterscotch topping, warm caramel, honey. I moved to her other nipple, kissed it, then lapped there ever so gently, as though it were her clit. I got overexcited and nibbled a little, and she gave a squeal. But when I looked at her face, she was smiling.

Everything was pink. I slid down and came face-to-face with her belly, kissing her there all over, gentle little kisses, tiny soft love bites. There were three rolls of fat, and I covered all of them with kisses, imagining the rolls as big lips, my upper lip falling between two of them at a time, my tongue extended just enough to taste what was inside. Then the space between her rolls became like pussies to me, and I thought, *How incredible, she has so many pussies, so many places to explore.*

She moaned, giving off deep sighs with quickened breath, no self-consciousness, as though she knew each part of her was worthy of pleasure. I wanted to hump her calf, right between my legs, but I was scared to rub against her, so I rubbed against the air in front of her, imagining feeling her leg between my thighs, fucking her psychically.

She reached down and put her hands on my chest, rubbing my sternum and clavicle, the way Ava Gardner might do to Clark Gable. She did not touch my breasts, only stroked the bones above them. I tried to move up, so my breasts were in her hands, but she stayed at my chest, then migrated to my shoulders.

"Strong," she said.

"Not really," I said.

"Do you want me to do anything to your tummy?" she asked suddenly.

"My tummy?"

"Kiss it? Like you did mine."

"Okay," I said, laughing.

"Lie down on the sofa," she said.

We switched positions, and I lay down on the sofa and closed my eyes.

She lifted up my tank a little, exposing only my stomach. My abdominals were no longer flat, but I still had muscle. She kissed me there, up and down. Then she nuzzled me in a circle, nipping the top of my skirt, the sweetest torture. My pelvis jerked. Her kisses slowed. My nipples got hard. I put my hand on hers, guided it to my breast. She moved away quickly.

"I'm sorry," I said. "Was that too much?"

Of course, I knew that it was.

CHAPTER 54

I was afraid that Miriam would stay away from me, that I wouldn't hear from her again. I imagined I would have to go to Yo!Good and beg her to come over between bites of strawberry sundae flecked with Heath bar pieces, standing out back in a puff of clove smoke by the dumpster. But she returned the following night, and every night that week: the seven nights of Miriam.

It was our own creation myth of sorts—seven days and nights commenced by a rabbi in a calla lily and god's cosmic buzzer. I felt as though a new calendar had begun. I stopped counting the days of the mother detox and started counting the nights of Miriam.

On the third night, I humped her over her skirt, rubbing myself wildly on the meaty dome between her belly button and her pussy. I almost came on top of her, but I wanted to make her come first. Clothes still on, I positioned myself between her thick legs. I used what I had: my pelvic bone, my thigh. I undulated against her. She rose and fell beneath me. Then she gasped. I kissed her lips to drink her sounds. She moaned loudly in my mouth.

"Did you have enough?" I asked her, touching her hair as we sprawled together on my sofa after, legs still entwined.

She nodded. We were both quiet for a while.

"Crickets," she said finally.

"What?"

"There're crickets outside. In the grass."

I had never noticed them before. But now that she'd pointed them out, they were all I could hear. I felt enveloped by their chirping. The sound filled my ear canals and skull. It covered me like a soft, minty blanket.

CHAPTER 55

On the fourth night, we went on a proper date. At the Golden Dragon, we sat across from each other at a back corner booth and shared a Scorpion Bowl and a Blue Hawaii.

"Open your mouth," she said, giggling over her straw.

"What?"

"Just open."

I obliged. She fished a cherry out of the Scorpion Bowl, then placed it in my mouth.

"Mmmm," I said. "Cherrylicious."

"And?"

"Cherrytacular. With subtle notes of cherry."

"Yes," she said. "It's the best part."

But when I went to hold her sticky hand, she pulled it away and said, "No, it's a bad idea. Someone might see."

"Of course," I said quickly.

I felt hurt—and surprised that I was hurt. But I didn't want to ruin our date by sulking. So I focused on the strands of lights twinkling over the bar. One was made of pink flamingos, another of green palm trees. Then there was a long strand of shooting stars and crescent moons, space blue and banana yellow. The lights were reflected in our Scorpion Bowl, as though the whole solar system were in there.

"By the way, just so you know, I think I kind of believe in god now," I said to Miriam.

"Really," she said, grinning. "And how did this shocking turn of events come to pass?"

"Okay, maybe *believe* is a strong word," I said. "But I definitely like god. I'm down with it."

"What's not to like?"

I reached under the table and found her knee. I expected her to bat my hand away, but she didn't, so I parked there for a while. Then I inched my hand up just a little, to the zone that was not quite knee and not quite thigh. She crunched aggressively on a handful of noodles. She did not evict me. I wanted to go higher. But from where I was sitting, I couldn't quite reach my desired territory. I slipped off my shoe, then tiptoed my foot under her skirt, up her leg.

"Rachel," she said.

"Yes, Miri?"

I continued to tiptoe until I reached her underpants.

She took a sip of the galaxy from the Scorpion Bowl and closed her lids. Softly I rubbed my foot over her undies, finding her crease. I tickled and kneaded. She cleared her throat but did not open her eyes. Her undies were warm and moist.

"You're the wettest," I whispered.

She gritted her teeth at me. Then the food arrived. For a moment, she looked like she couldn't eat, and I felt proud to have put her in a state where she only wanted me. I made my way back down her leg, out from under her skirt. Gradually, she started eating. I loved watching her slurp dumplings, so aroused by her appetite. I swore I could smell her on me now, the scent of dirt in rain coming up from under the table. I imagined her leaking through her skirt, leaving a wet mark on the pink banquette. I wanted it stained forever, as if to say, *We were here*.

CHAPTER 56

Miriam wore white cotton underpants, full coverage, the fullest of all the coverages, concealing every pubic hair, cordoning her from my wants. The underpants were basically bloomers, and I was on my knees on the floor of my bedroom, under her skirt, lapping at the cotton.

She was the one who took them off, then removed her skirt with a look of benevolence. Her pubic hair was reddish brown, and from thigh to thigh she was covered in thick, balmy swirls of it. She sat down on the edge of my bed, then stretched out on her back across my comforter, leaned her head on my pillow, stared at me.

"You are so fine," I murmured. "So very fine."

She closed her eyes. When she opened them again, she smiled.

"And?" she asked.

I smiled back at her.

"Gorgeous."

I lay down beside her and kissed her mouth. Then, as I kissed my way down her naked body, I spoke to her more.

"So lush. So pretty."

I put my face in her soft shtetl wool.

"Fucking delicious too."

When I tasted her brine, I was hit with a feeling of timelessness, as though this had all happened before, somewhere as far back as our ancestors in Russia or Lithuania or Poland or Moldova. We were two shtetl Jewish women reincarnated, two women who had known each other and been lovers in a past life. I felt that all that had ever happened before was happening right now—and that everything happening right now would happen forever. There was a love that had always existed between women. It would continue to exist. We were propagating that love. It was radiating out my apartment windows, through the city, across the canyons, over the hills, and into the night sky.

I ate her with empathy, the way that I would want to be eaten. I teased her clit with my tongue, letting her know that I knew where her pleasure locus was, and that I would get there, just not yet. As I teased, I smelled the faintest waft of shit coming up from underneath her. It smelled like fertile heaven: peat moss, soil, sod, loam. It smelled good because it was her. She had a perfume, and this was her base note. I wanted to work my tongue all the way down, taste the sludge of her, the deepest secrets. But I continued licking her as I would want to be licked: with tiny, fast strokes on her clit, as though my tongue had a vibrator in it. I was fast and gentle. I was a hummingbird, a cicada, a flickering eyelid.

Miriam began to groan and writhe. I tongued her harder. I spelled out the word L-O-V-E on her clit. I spelled B-A-R-U-C-H-H-A-S-H-E-M. I spelled E-M-E-T and M-E-T, T-R-U-T-H and D-E-A-T-H. Then I tongued her in my own language. The words meant nothing, but they made sense to both of us. She was enjoying the rhythm so much. I was fluent. I knew exactly what to do to keep her going. I took her clit fully in my mouth, sucked until she swelled. She became a juicy piece of pulp.

Then, for a moment, she stopped moving entirely. Her moans ceased. She got still and tense. She gripped her hands around my head, and I knew that she was going to come. I wanted to fuck her with my fingers. But I held back. I would penetrate her next time.

She bucked against my face. She shook as she came. It was a fucking wonder. She said my name.

"Rachel."

Then she moaned, "You feel so good!"

"*You* feel so good," I said.

"I feel so good," she cried.

"Good," I said.

CHAPTER 57

I found myself eating the way I imagined normal people ate: three squares, some snacks, whatever I wanted, really, with a feeling of impunity, and without bingeing to the point of illness. There were pancakes for breakfast at the diner, pizza for lunch on my break, burritos for dinner. My kitchen counter was full of junk—Reese's peanut butter cups, Doritos, frosted Donettes—all the food I'd fantasized about over years of deprivation. Only now I wasn't eating everything all at once. It felt like a miracle to be able to eat what I desired, not more or less than that. It was shocking, as though my body somehow knew what to do and what not to do—if only I let it.

It was as though I had a knowing person inside me, not the healthy, loving adult that Dr. Mahjoub had said I should try to cultivate in order to "reparent" young Rachel, but some kind of careless skater teen, the lovable scamp I'd never been, who ate what she wanted, when she wanted, and stopped when she was full.

Miriam had begun buying me presents: a black, tailored, menswear-inspired blazer from Nordstrom at The Grove that fit me perfectly, a pair of motorcycle boots. On the fifth night, she brought a boxy denim jacket with a pair of sparrows on the back, a fragrance redolent of whiskey and ambergris, and a sports bra.

"Why a sports bra?"

"I just thought it was cute."

"Cute?"

"Yeah. Cute."

"Oh. Well, I already have a ton of these, because I used to go to the gym a lot."

"Sorry," she said. "I didn't know you had them. I like the look of them."

"What is it about the look of them?"

"I don't know," she said. "I just think they are attractive."

"Well, I could wear it, I guess," I said, wanting to please her.

That night, with my breasts bound, I fucked her with my hand. As I was licking her clit, my tongue flattened the way I knew she liked, I introduced the tip of my middle finger inside her. I didn't go deep inside, just below the clit, where I knew there was sensitive tissue. She gasped and moved against my finger, trying to push me deeper inside of her. But I stood my ground and stayed at the entrance, just hinting at the fact that I could put a finger deeper in there if and when I wanted. I did it for a while like that until she was sopping, my hand covered in her juices, my tongue slick with her. Then I inched in a little farther and began to thrust.

"I'm so hard for you," I said. "Do you feel how fucking hard you make me?"

"Uh-huh." She sighed.

"I'm—I'm *bulging* for you."

She reached down and grabbed my hand, pushing it deeper inside her pussy. I began to thrust my finger in and out, fucking her there, slow but strong, with the same rhythm as I was moving my tongue.

She was drowning my finger. I made come-hither motions each time I penetrated her so that I could rub her G-spot, never taking my tongue off her clit. I put two more fingers inside her and felt that she was about to come.

"Do you feel how fucking hard you make me?" I asked again.

"I feel it," she said. "I feel it I feel it I feel it."

CHAPTER 58

The black blazer that Miriam got me made me feel debonair. I went to Nordstrom and bought a second one, also black but pin-striped, with matching pants for both. I wore them to work with my hair tied back tight in a low bun, the way a minimalist fashion person or a name-dropping aesthete might. I thought the suits hid my weight gain too. I felt sexy and protected, as though I had evolved to a more sophisticated realm of beauty.

"You're dressed differently," said Ana.

It wasn't teatime, but we had run into each other in the kitchen. She was putting green goddess dressing on a salad, preparing to take it back to her desk, and I was taking two leftover pieces of pizza out of the fridge to microwave them.

"Yeah," I said. "I'm experimenting with power clothes."

"Power clothes." She laughed. "What sort of power are you looking for? You want to be a Hollywood power player?"

I realized that she was making fun of me. I didn't know what to say. I took the pizza slices out of their foil and stuck them in the microwave, set it to 75 seconds.

"Oh, pizza power," she said. "Pizza power clothes."

"Yep, pizza power clothes," I said, though I had no idea what the hell she was talking about. I wasn't even sure if she knew.

I watched the microwave timer creep from 67 seconds to 63. I wanted it to move faster.

"You know, Rachel," she said, putting her dressing back in the fridge, "I don't want you to take this the wrong way. But I've noticed—well, is everything all right?"

"What have you noticed?" I asked.

"Never mind."

"No, tell me."

"I've noticed that you've . . . gained a little weight."

I felt, immediately, that her words would kill me. This was how it was going to end. I was going to die in a talent management office kitchen. The microwave timer was at 54 seconds. My pizza started to bubble.

"Everything is fine," I said, staring at a mushroom on the bubbling pizza.

I wanted to disappear under the mushroom, just tuck myself into the warm pizza cheese and drape the mushroom over me like a blanket.

"Are you eating differently?" she asked. "It seems like you are. I know you indulge in the snacks here at the office more now."

I felt tears come to my eyes. The timer was at 41 seconds.

"Do you think I look bad?" I asked.

"No, not bad," she said. "But I did notice."

I couldn't believe that I'd gotten to this place. I was angry at myself. I was angry at Ana too, for saying what she said. But I was most angry at Miriam. From the very first bite of the yogurt with the sprinkles, she had led me to this territory. At times I'd felt courageous on the journey, but it was borrowed courage. Now we were here, and neither of us had a plan. Was she going to abandon me, leave me stranded in my body? I'd be in exile with a stomach that demanded more of everything.

No one is abandoning anyone, I said to myself.

How do you know? I replied.

"Well, thanks for telling me," I said to Ana. "I appreciate it."

"Just looking after you," she said.

The timer on the microwave went to 2, then 1, then 0. It beeped three times. The light went out. My pizza was done.

CHAPTER 59

Miriam and I were lying in bed in my empty, white bedroom. It was the sixth day, the one where god created all the animals—the cattle and sheep and beasts of the Earth. It was the Adam and Eve day, the "be fruitful and multiply" one. She was on her back, smoking a clove, tapping the ashes out my window into the night. I was wearing leggings and a T-shirt, and I'd wrapped myself around the side of her thigh. She had just come. I traced the crease of her pussy and made little designs with her own moisture across the canvas of her belly.

"You know what I miss?" I asked, taking the clove from her hand.

"Hmmmm," she said.

"That challah," I said, taking a puff of the clove. "That Shabbat challah. The amazing one your mom served."

"It's delicious, isn't it? I know where she gets it. I'll bring you a loaf."

"Okay," I said, exhaling up to the ceiling and handing the clove back to her. "Although I wouldn't mind having it with some of that cholent too."

"That's a little bit harder to bring," she said. "Though if I come over this Sunday, I could put it in a Tupperware. It's meant to be eaten for a few days, and we always have extra."

"Okay," I said.

We were both silent. She took another puff of the clove, then stubbed it out in a bottle cap on the windowsill.

"I thought maybe I could come to Shabbat dinner tomorrow night," I said. "That is, if the invitation is still open."

"It is!" she said quickly, a little too quickly.

"Good," I said.

"I mean, you know my mother liked you. And you are always welcome."

"Great!"

"It's just. I mean. We can't do any of this," she said, gesturing to her naked body and my clothed one.

I took my hand off her belly.

"No, no," I said. "Of course not, not in your parents' house."

"Right, but I just mean—like, we can't even hint at the fact that this has gone on, you know?"

"Hint how?" I asked. "Like, I can't get you naked at the dinner table?"

"No." She laughed. "I just mean no kisses or anything."

"Of course not."

"No hand-holding."

"No hand-holding. I'll be a perfect gentleman."

She kissed my cheek.

"Hey, where do they think you are, anyway?" I asked. "All these nights. Where do they think you've been spending your time? Do they know you are always with me? What kind of friends spend every single night together? It would be a lot, wouldn't it?"

"Oh no," she said. "They don't know I'm with you. They think I'm interning at a movie theater."

I laughed out loud.

"Interning? At a movie theater?"

"Yes," she said. "Why is that funny?"

"I've just never heard of anyone getting an internship at the movies. Anyway. So tomorrow is good?"

"I don't know about tomorrow. Adiv is home visiting."

I didn't understand what Adiv being home had to do with it not being a good night for me to come.

"What's wrong?" she asked.

I didn't say anything.

"Do you really want to come over for Shabbat that badly? I didn't mean to hurt your feelings. It has nothing to do with you. I just thought the table might be a little too full."

I didn't want to have to push. I wanted to be wanted, as I had been in that first Shabbat incarnation, before anything physical had happened between us. Yet I felt I had to push, just to test and see what she was willing to do. I wished I was cool enough or strong enough not to test her. I didn't want to show that I wanted or needed anything from her. But the truth was I did want and need her. Why did it feel so much safer to be wanted or needed than to be the one who wanted or needed?

I was terrified of being rejected. I didn't want to be a loser. That was the word that came into my head whenever I ran the risk of caring about someone: *loser.* I couldn't remember my mother ever saying it to me. It was something I must have come up with all by myself. What did it mean, anyway? If Miriam hurt me, would that make me a loser?

Miriam was not the malicious sort. I knew she would never take pride or joy in hurting me. It was not about power or control for her at all. It was me who saw people and the world that way.

"Forget it," I said to her.

"No," she said. "I'm being silly. I just get nervous, I guess."

"It's all right," I said.

"Please," she said. "Will you come? I really want you to come."

She kissed the side of my face and then my neck. I closed my eyes and envisioned us again as the ancestral shtetl women. We were in a dark cottage that smelled of cholent. Everything stank like potatoes, chicken schmaltz, turnips, beef. The house was so tiny that we were forced to be intimate. Only now, in this vision, I was not a woman, but Miriam's husband. She was trying to convince me to do something or other—let her trade the mule for a new saucepan, maybe—by kissing me.

No, that was not right. Start again. We were in the dark cottage. It was still pungent with potatoes. But she was nobody's wife, and I was nobody's husband. I was a woman. We were daughters of the village. We were both beautiful. She was plumper than I was, but I was a well-fed beauty too. I suppose we were wealthy, then, even though the house we were in was so small. Was it my parents' house or her parents' house? Was it a house we had snuck into?

No, that was not right either. We were not in a house at all, but in the forest. We had snuck away with each other to an evergreen forest, two daughters of the shtetl, friends since childhood. We had snuck away in the dark of night so that we could have the whole forest floor to ourselves to make love. We had just fucked. We had fucked each other in our skirts. We had fucked each other in mutual desire and now we were lying on the forest floor curled up together, two girls in pine needles, under starlight. This was the definition of holy. Tell the village matchmaker not to bother with us. Here in the forest there was no potato smell, no pogroms. Only the scent of evergreens.

I opened my eyes. Miriam didn't seem worried about our future. I wondered if her faith in god made her believe that everything was going to work out for us. I decided that I would borrow some of her faith, siphon that solace of existing only here, in these sheets, because I didn't want to think about the alternative. I hugged her, kissed her mouth softly. She was very warm. We were safe for now.

CHAPTER 60

When Mrs. Schwebel opened the door, she gave me a big smile.

"Rachel!" she said.

Then she noticed my outfit, the pants and matching blazer, and her face changed. She looked me up and down. I wondered if it was bad that I'd worn pants on Shabbat.

"I brought you this," I said, handing her a bottle of kosher white wine.

"Wonderful," she said briskly.

In the hall, I pulled Miriam aside.

"Should I have worn a skirt?" I whispered. "I feel like your mother doesn't like that I'm wearing pants."

"No," she said. "We've had women come over for Shabbat wearing pants. Don't be self-conscious."

I followed behind her as she went into the kitchen to get some wineglasses.

"Grab me a napkin off the counter," she said.

I handed her a big stack. But instead of taking the whole pile, she only took one. When I opened my hand, the napkins fluttered to the floor.

"Oy," she said, laughing.

"I'll pick them up," I said, touching her on the arm.

When I turned around to grab the ones that landed behind

me, Mrs. Schwebel was standing in the entrance to the kitchen, watching us. Her eyes were narrowed. I wondered if it was something about this particular pair of pants that had bothered her. Maybe it was the full suit.

I told myself to stop obsessing about what was wrong with Mrs. Schwebel and focus on Adiv. When he saw me in the kitchen, he waved as though I were an old friend, which I guess I kind of was. But seeing him made me feel sad. He looked different—no longer pale and lanky, but tan and buffed up. He had lost his boyishness, his awkwardness. Now he had a confidence that bordered on arrogance.

"Try Rachel's wine," Miriam said to him at dinner.

"I don't like white," said Adiv.

"Since when?"

He didn't respond.

"Try this other one, then—cabernet," she said, bossing him around as usual.

"I'm fine," he said.

"You're not going to get drunk with me? Boring!"

She picked up a glass and began to pour. But just as she reached the halfway mark, he jutted his hand out against the bottle to stop it, and the red wine spilled onto her denim skirt.

"Adiv!" said Miriam.

Noah and Eitan laughed.

"Go get me some seltzer!" she said.

But Adiv just sat there and stared ahead calmly.

"I told you I was fine," he said.

CHAPTER 61

That night in the Schwebels' basement, I couldn't sleep. The sheets were very cold, and every time I tossed and turned, I felt like my feet were touching something wet. At 2 a.m., I finally kicked off the covers and tiptoed upstairs to Miriam's room. I knew that I shouldn't, but I couldn't help myself. I got into bed with her and put my arms around her big belly, pressed myself against her ass. Miriam stirred, then she put her hands on mine.

"Is it okay that I'm here?" I whispered into her ear.

She rolled over to face me.

"Shhhhh," she said.

She got up and locked the door. Then she came back into bed and began kissing me, rubbing her body against my body. Gladly I kissed her back, crawled on top of her. On the other side of the wall was Ayala's room, and I knew we could not make a sound. I kissed her very quietly all the way down to her pussy. She was wearing a nightgown to her ankles, and I pulled it up, exposing all of her pallor in the dark. But when I went to take the nightgown over her head, she said, "No, leave it on," and so it remained up around her neck like a funny scarf.

I buried my face in her soft pubic hair. Wetness was running out of her, and I wondered if she had been like that at dinner. Her pussy tasted different tonight, like pure water, spring water from a mountain in Austria or Switzerland. She tasted Alpine.

She tasted . . . *Christian?* I had never eaten her on Shabbat, and I tried not to laugh when I thought, *A Shabbos goy is running this pussy tonight.*

I put two of my fingers inside her and fucked her while I licked her clit. When she gasped, I shoved my other fingers in her mouth to quiet her down. She sucked on my hand and thrust herself in my face. Then I felt her come, contracting and surging with her usual brine. The Shabbos goy was gone. It was the seventh day.

CHAPTER 62

I sat in the avocado-green living room looking at a photo book called *Israel: An Introduction*. Miriam was still upstairs. Ezra crawled around at my feet. Mrs. Schwebel came in. She did not offer me any challah or tea. Instead, she looked at the sofa where I was seated, sighed, then walked out again. I wasn't sure if the sigh was for me or for Ezra. I was worried. The look on her face seemed troubled, even disgusted. The corners of her mouth turned down. It was like she was going to sneeze, then didn't. I wasn't sure whether I should go try to grovel, suss her out, or just sit there. I stayed put.

I looked at a photo of the Dome of the Rock, its intricate blue tiles and beaming golden dome. *Qubbat As-Sakhrah: Seventh-century Islamic edifice enshrining the rock from which Muhammad is said to have ascended to heaven*, read the caption. I thought about my grandparents, and I wondered how they felt about this beautiful old mosque. Did they love it like they loved the rest of Israel? Probably not.

What did it mean to love something so much and also be wrong about it? What did it mean to love a version of something that might not really exist—not as you saw it? Did this negate the love? Was the love still real?

Mrs. Schwebel came into the living room again.

"Rachel," she said, "would you please cover your arms when you're in our home?"

It was true, I was still wearing the T-shirt I'd worn to sleep, and it only came to my elbows.

"Oh shoot," I said, flailing. "I'm sorry."

"And Ezra, let's go," she said.

I stood up, followed her out of the living room, Ezra crawling behind me. Why was I such an idiot? In the hallway, we ran into Miriam coming down the stairs.

"Hi Mom," said Miriam.

Mrs. Schwebel looked at her.

"What?" she asked her daughter.

"Hi," said Miriam.

"Hi," she replied briskly.

When Mrs. Schwebel went into the kitchen, I made Miriam stay out with me in the hall.

"Hey," I whispered. "I hope everything is okay. Your mother seems—weird."

"Shhhh," she said. "You have to be quieter!"

Sorry! I mouthed.

It was the first time I could remember Miriam ever scolding me. She beckoned me to follow her farther down the hall, away from the kitchen.

"This is why I didn't want you here for Shabbat," she hissed.

"Why?"

"You know. You should not have come upstairs last night."

"You didn't exactly kick me out."

We were quiet.

"I'm sorry," I said finally. "I'm not trying to cause a rift between you and your mother."

"But you are!"

"Do you think she knows?" I asked.

"She may not know exactly. But something is up. She's a smart woman."

"And you care?"

"About what?"

"What she thinks."

"Of course I do," she said. "I love her."

This kind of love seemed strange to me. It was not out of love that I'd obeyed my mother, not really. It was out of fear, the way a person might placate a punishing god. Ultimately, I'd always been terrified that if I didn't please my mother, she would smite me. But I believed Miriam when she said that she cared out of love.

"Even if she is dead wrong?" I asked.

"Wrong about what?" asked Miriam.

"That two women together are . . . disgusting!"

"Yes, even if she's wrong," she whispered. "But she isn't."

I felt like she'd punched me in my throat. My tongue was thick and furry in my mouth.

"Do you want me to leave?" I asked.

"No!" she said. "That would look weird. You have to stay."

I thought about Rabbi Judah Loew ben Bezalel in the calla lily. He had said that Miriam and I were a mitzvah. I wanted to tell her that a famous rabbi from the sixteenth century, a mystical rabbi from Prague, had given us his blessing.

"Okay," I said.

CHAPTER 63

I wished I could enjoy Saturday's Shabbat lunch, all of the Schwebels gathered around the table. But the cholent tasted different this time, bland. I found it hard to swallow it down. I wondered if the dish had ever been flavorful at all.

"Look at my soldier," said Mrs. Schwebel, ruffling Adiv's hair. "Doing god's work. Spiritually and physically."

What did she imagine Adiv was doing in Israel? How could she be so sure of what god thought: about soldiers, the occupation?

"Do we really know?" I murmured.

Miriam, seated next to me, nudged my leg with hers under the table. But Mrs. Schwebel had heard me.

"Excuse me?" she asked.

"Nothing," I said.

Everyone at the table was silent. They all looked at me. I could feel my pulse beating in my temples.

"Please, Rachel," said Mrs. Schwebel calmly. "I'd like to know what you said."

I took a deep breath. A tiny piece of vegetable flew from my molar into my throat. I coughed it back out into my mouth, then swallowed it.

"I guess I was just wondering how we know," I said. "Like *know*, know. What god wants."

"God wants to see the state of Israel protected," she said. "Don't you think god wants to see Israel protected? Don't you think god wants Israel to flourish?"

What had I done?

"I just mean—I guess it's hard for me to believe that god is happy when people are suffering," I said. "You know. With the occupation and everything. The conditions in Gaza and everything."

"You've been to Gaza?" asked Mrs. Schwebel.

I shook my head no.

"No. I didn't think so. You told us you've never been to Israel."

"You're right," I said.

"Okay, then."

Satisfied, she began eating again.

Just keep your mouth shut, I said to myself.

Fine, I replied.

"But what about the history?" I heard myself say aloud. "What kind of god would be happy with seeing hundreds of thousands of people expelled from their homes?"

"Rachel!" said Miriam angrily.

She had her pointer finger in her mouth and was biting her nail. I noticed that her thumbnail and ring finger were bitten too, up past the skin. When had she started biting her nails?

It dawned on me then that Miriam might not know how the Palestinians had been expelled—that she might never have learned about it. I wasn't taught this in my Jewish education either.

Mr. Schwebel met my eyes. It seemed he was aware of what I was talking about. Then he looked back down at his plate quickly again and put his fork into a tender piece of beef.

"There's something that the Palestinians call the *Nakba*," I said. "It refers to when they were driven from their homes into exile—when Israel became a state. It sort of puts a different perspective on Israeli independence. I mean, I was taught that the Palestinians went to war with us. But I don't think that's true. If you're kicked out of your home, I don't think you're going to war if you retaliate. You're just defending your home."

There was silence at the table. Adiv got up and went to the bathroom. Miriam was still chewing on her pointer fingernail. I wondered if I had somehow transmitted the habit to her, if she'd caught it from me.

"That isn't true," said Mrs. Schwebel. "I don't know where you got that information, but it's wrong."

I'd never been a good debater, and I could not point to one place where I had gotten my information. The Internet, mostly. Students for a Free Palestine. Arguments between stoned people at college parties. Half an audiobook called *Disputed Yesterdays: The Israeli-Palestinian Conflict Made Simple*.

"What part?" I asked. "That they didn't live there first? That they weren't kicked off their land? That when someone attempts to reclaim what belongs to them, it's not an attack but a defense?"

"All of it," she said. "The land belonged to Britain. It didn't belong to anyone else. It did not belong to the Palestinians any more than it belonged to the Christians who lived there. The British gave it to us. It was given as a reparation for the Holocaust, because we had nowhere else to go and we should never have nowhere to go again."

"But there were Palestinians living there," I said.

"So they were relocated," said Mrs. Schwebel. "So what? That's history. It's just how it is."

"Is it?" I asked.

"They had plenty of time to make peace. They were given land in the separation, and they chose not to accept it. They chose to always stay and fight. They brought the rest of the Arab world into it with them. And that's the thing, if the Arab world cared so much about the Palestinians, why didn't they give them any of their own land? If they cared so much, why didn't Egypt just cut out a slice for them? Because Egypt didn't actually care about the Palestinians. It's purely anti-Semitism."

"Well, I don't know about that," I said.

"What don't you know? That history belongs to the victor? How about you give up your apartment right now? That land once belonged to the Native Americans, but I don't see anybody coming after that now. It's only when it's Israel and the Jews are involved that people raise a stink, because they like to have a reason to hate the Jews."

I didn't know what to say.

"The Arab world does not care about the Palestinians one bit or they would give up a cut of their land. Israel is only the size of New Jersey. Why should we be asked to give up what is rightfully ours?" she asked.

"But is it rightfully ours?"

She ignored my question.

"It's only because people hate the Jews that they take the side of the Palestinians. That is the truth. It's true of anyone who believes that Israel does not have a right to exist."

Now I was silent. Adiv was still in the bathroom. Miriam picked up her glass and took a sip of water. Her cuticle was bleeding. She wouldn't look at me.

"Let me ask you," Mrs. Schwebel continued, "do you hate yourself? Because that's the only reason why I could see picking a side against your own. My guess is that you do. You hate yourself. You must, or else why would you go against your own people?"

"I don't know," I said. "Maybe I do hate myself. But I know it's more complicated than that. I just—I want to know what is right, what is the truth about that part of the world. I feel like I have never known the truth."

"Do you hate our family? Do you hate us?"

"Of course not," I said. "Of course I don't hate your family. I really love being here. I'm grateful to be here. I love your cooking and the way that this house feels and the way that you welcomed me as a Jew."

"Maybe that was foolish of us," she said. "To have welcomed you with such open arms. You take the welcome you receive for granted. You think that Israel is just an idea that you can toy with and play with. But you don't know what it was like before it existed, when there was nowhere, no homeland for the Jews. What do you think it was like then? No, I think you must hate yourself—and more than that, you must hate us."

"I don't," I said. "It's not true. I don't hate you."

I took a deep breath. Then I put my hand on top of Miriam's, the one that was bleeding.

"I've liked you since the first day I met you," I said, looking Mrs. Schwebel right in the eye.

Miriam pulled her hand out from under mine. I immediately felt sorry I had done it.

This was not what I had planned. I was being brave, but it wasn't for me to be brave. I was being brave with someone else's family, someone else's territory, not my own. I was laying claim to someone who did not want to be claimed. I was being brave on false terms. I'd never once told my own mother anything about Miriam.

"I think you should leave," said Mrs. Schwebel.

"Please," I said. "Please, I'm sorry."

I felt like I was going to cry. Miriam didn't say a word in my defense, but I don't know what I would have expected her to say. If I were in her position, I don't know what I would've done. Mr. Schwebel got up from the table. Ayala followed him into the kitchen.

"You've ruined Shabbat," said Mrs. Schwebel. "I'm asking you again, nicely, to please leave."

Miriam finally met my eyes.

"I'm so sorry," I said to her, then looked down at my hands.

A tiny smear of blood, the size of an eyelash, had transferred from her finger to my palm.

"Just go," she said.

CHAPTER 64

On the way home from the Schwebels', I passed a barber-shop. I slowed down my car and looked in the window. Then I parked and got out.

"I want a very short haircut," I said to the barbers.

There were two of them, both handsome, with dark hair and eyes. One was tall with a muscular chest under a very low-cut black V-neck T-shirt. The other was just a few inches bigger than me with scruffy hair and a headband like a soccer player might wear. They smelled strongly of cologne, something with patchouli in it.

"Nooooo," said V-neck. "You're crazy! You're so pretty as you are."

"Just a trim, that's it," said the soccer player.

"Do you want my business or don't you?" I asked.

V-neck sniffed and cleared his throat.

"Well, then," he said. "Sit down."

He pointed to the barber chair in front of him and snapped his scissors twice.

"So what kind of cut are you looking for exactly?"

"Not like yours," I said.

He had a Caesar-looking thing, cut very short and combed forward into a bangs situation. He didn't crack a smile.

"Do you want me to leave it a little long?" he asked. "Let's do a lob. That's a long bob; it's very trendy."

"No," I said.

I pulled up a photo of the two remaining Beastie Boys on my phone and pointed to Ad-Rock.

"Can you do that?" I asked.

I imagined Miriam grabbing me by the back of my head, the way a rough buzz would feel in her fingers. I pictured her guiding me by the ears down to her cunt, then tousling my forelock as I licked.

"Of course I can do that," he said.

He didn't move.

"Okay," I said. "So do that."

I closed my eyes and felt him moving his hands through my hair, then parting it on the right and combing it. When I opened my eyes and looked in the mirror, nothing had happened yet. My hair was no different. But staring into my own eyes, I felt like I was already changing, that another person was looking at me. Then he moved the scissors around my head with a rapid motion, and I saw some of my long locks fall to the floor. As they fell, I felt that they were the locks of another person—not mine. I imagined they were the payos of Rabbi Judah Loew ben Bezalel. I closed my eyes again and listened to the buzz of the electric razor, humming along. I hummed "Oseh Shalom," the old version of the song I had known. I felt a wild rush.

I was still humming when I got into my car. It had been a few minutes since the barber had cut the last of it off, but I had no regrets. I looked in the mirror. I was handsome, foxy. I liked my long neck. Or did I look like a potato? No, I had a nice-shaped head. I started the car. Then I looked in the mirror again. I saw a flash of colors behind me: pink, blue, yellow, green.

I turned around and looked at the back seat.

"What the fuck?"

Lying there, as though it had been with me all along and was just coming for another ride, was the clay figure.

CHAPTER 65

I thought about throwing it out the car window. But that wasn't good enough. What if it came back again, like a zombie in *Breathers*?

I decided I would burn it. I bought a lighter at 7-Eleven, but Theraputticals was apparently nonflammable. I just kept singeing my hand.

I decided I would microwave it to death. But when I took it home, I brought it into bed with me instead. I lay there on my dirty sheets, crying next to it. It smelled like baby powder.

I wasn't sure if I was crying over Miriam or the strangeness of finding the figure again or because of my missing hair.

The heart gets wounded—so what? I thought. I'd seen all the plays. I should have been prepared. Love goes. But what I hadn't known was how good the love would feel when it was there, like a hymn moving through me all the time. Or if Jews didn't have hymns, then a rhythm. I'd moved my body in time to it the best I could. But I hadn't been able to hold on.

I touched my hands to my head. I noticed I could feel them more closely against my scalp. It felt good at least to be able to offer myself comfort in this way, so close, skin to skin.

I rubbed my head and cried for a long time. Then I stood up and went to the mirror, mussing my hair around, what was left of it, pushing it forward and back. It looked better like this, messy on purpose, not frozen stiff the way V-neck had gelled it. It was maybe even cute. It looked cool when I parted it on the right side and tousled the left and the back. There was a surfer iteration where I pushed all the hair forward and roughed up the front.

"Punk," I said out loud and gave myself the finger, kissing the air.

My stomach felt hollow. It made a little noise like it was crying. I called the fake '50s diner down the street and ordered a grilled cheese, french fries, a chocolate milkshake, and a Diet Coke. After I ordered, I played with my hair some more in the mirror.

"What do we think?" I asked the clay figure.

The clay figure said nothing.

"What good are you?" I asked.

I took the figure outside with me anyway. I walked down the street with it dangling from my hand, like a child holding her favorite dolly. People looked at me as I walked. I wondered if they were looking at me because of my new haircut or because I had been crying or because I was clutching a colorful clay figure. I didn't care whether they thought I looked good.

CHAPTER 66

"D amn, Rachel!" said Ofer when he saw my hair.

I wasn't sure if it was a good *damn* or a bad *damn*, but it seemed like a bad *damn*. Regardless, he caught himself quickly. I watched him flay himself internally, probably using the phrase *body shaming*.

"Cut your hair, I see," he said, trying again. "Looks— empowering! Great to see you empowering yourself."

Just shut the fuck up, I thought.

"Yep," I said, tucking the clay figure under my chair. "Feeling mighty."

I'd brought the figure into the office with me and kept it on my lap, touching it with my left hand while my right hand typed. I felt attached to it now—like a kid's blankie, or the way people talked about their relationship to crystals. As long as I was touching the figure, I felt like I could keep from crying.

NPR Andrew didn't address my hair directly. But I could see that it won me some points with him—made me look more indie, I guess.

"Ever seen *Salmon Jelly*?" he asked. "Danish youth movement film from the seventies. Watched it this weekend. Tragicomic exploration of pornography, melancholia, and nationalistic conformity."

Then Ana walked by.

"Rachel! What on *earth* have you done to your hair?" She made a noise that sounded like a cackle.

"Cut it," I said casually.

"I see," she said. "Well, it is a rather . . . interesting look."

"Interesting how?" I asked.

She moved closer to my desk.

"You look a little bit like—well, between the hair and the suit, it makes you look a little . . ." Her voice trailed off for a moment, then she whispered, "Gay."

I didn't say anything.

"Not that it's a bad thing. But is that the look you're going for?"

I wished I could cry to her. I wanted to be held by her, comforted, seated on her knee and rocked against her breast, transported into that white floral scent. I wanted kindness, wisdom, infinite understanding. I wanted to be mommied by a woman who was kind only to me. I wanted her to be a completely different woman than she was.

CHAPTER 67

"I feel okay about being intimacy avoidant when it comes to my death," I said into the microphone.

I'd returned to This Show Sucks to try to get a little serotonin going by way of natural disasters. The show was now being held two nights a week, and in my absence I'd been cordoned off into the inferior Wednesday slot. I hoped that if I could really nail the annihilation piece of my mudslide bit, I might be re-promoted to Thursdays. With the way I was feeling, I had plenty to say about obliteration.

"Anyone else here hoping for a quick and painless death?" I asked.

Only a few takers. A quick and painless death was less popular than asking if anyone came from the East Coast.

"I think it's fucked that there are mean people who get to die peacefully in their sleep and nice people who end up suffering for years," I said. "It's like, check your death privilege."

"Check your death privilege!" someone called out.

It was Jace.

Later, he found me at the bar. I was drinking a beer, a regular one—Guinness—not even light, when he tapped me on the shoulder.

"Oh, hello," I said.

"You were really great tonight," he said. "Best I've seen you."

"Thanks. It wasn't me up there. Just almost-me."

"What?"

"Nothing," I said. "I'm surprised you're here. I thought you were shooting the second season up in Vancouver."

"They put Liam in a coma," he said.

"Sorry to hear that."

"Nah, it's okay, just for two episodes. When did you cut your hair?"

"A few days ago."

"It's cool. I like it. You look really *intense* or something."

"Thanks?"

"No, I mean it really looks good. It's a totally different look for you. It's probably your *soul aesthetic*."

"My soul aesthetic?"

"Yeah, that's what my acting coach calls it. It's when your look and your soul align."

"Oh."

"Like this," he said, pointing to his leather jacket and his rosaries. "This is my soul aesthetic."

"Uh-huh."

"Of course, my stylist is trying to rebrand me. She thinks I need to go more nineties, like an early Luke Perry vibe, may he rest in peace. But I see myself as more of an . . . eclectic. A little James Dean, a little gothic, a little spiritual—that's me. A hybrid. That's my soul aesthetic."

"Right."

"Everyone is always trying to change you in this town."

"I think that's part of the job," I said. "It comes with celebrity and getting shit for free and making lots of money and getting to have people look at you all the time and tell you how great you are."

"I don't even care about people looking at me."

"If they weren't looking, you'd care."

"Maybe," he said. "But I'm just interested in making good art."

Was he really referring to *Breathers* as *art*?

"You're a real artist," he said. "I can tell."

He reached out and chucked me under the chin. Why was he touching me?

"It's all about the craft for you," he said. "Not that you aren't ridiculously adorable too. So cute."

He moved his hand to my left cheek, stroked it. I flinched.

"Sorry," he said, snapping his hand away. "I've wanted to do that for a long time."

I looked down the bar. There were four college kids, out-of-towners, gawking at us. I was excited that they'd seen him touch my cheek. The thought of it made me feel giddy, much giddier than the actual act of him touching my cheek.

"How long?" I asked.

"What?"

"How long have you wanted to do that? Did you want to do that when we ate the hot dogs?"

"Yeah," he said.

"Damn, I had no idea. What about at lunch with Ofer?"

"Definitely," he said. "Even when I caught you eating in the bathroom at the cast party."

"A defining moment," I said.

"But tonight. Tonight you've got the soul aesthetic!"

I burst out laughing.

Jace's friend Paul from Akron was onstage, newly bearded and wearing a checkered beanie. Apparently, he'd been demoted to Wednesdays too. He was making his way through a set about air travel.

"Every plane is stuck in 1997," he said. "Somewhere, embedded on every aircraft, is a secret room where Bill Clinton is always getting a blow job."

"Wanna get out of here?" I asked. "You can touch my other cheek."

CHAPTER 68

From a technical standpoint, Jace was a good kisser. But making out with him in my living room felt like being under slow siege. He moved gently and caringly and that was the problem. I couldn't tell what disgusted me more: him feigning tenderness, or the possibility that it might be real. I wished the out-of-towners were still watching. In my mind, I kept repeating, *Liam, Liam, Liam,* to remind myself that a lot of people out there would love to be in my position.

When he began to eat my pussy, I felt a murderous instinct well up within me. His tongue meandered leisurely in the neighborhood of my clit, without zooming in on the clit itself.

We got all night, his tongue was saying.

Can you just expedite? I wanted to cry.

He moaned a lot down there, as though he were having his own zombie apocalypse. I squeezed his head between my thighs to muffle the sounds, but he only took this as a sign that I was having an awesome time. He increased the speed of his casual crawl, tonguing harder, still circumventing the clit itself, moaning all the way.

"You wax your chest?" I asked when he took off his shirt.

His chest was bare, with some stubbly regrowth between his nipples.

"The stylist makes me," he groaned.

He had nice, thick pubes, though, and a perfectly lovely penis—clean, handsome, just above average—a penis that all the Liam lovers out there would be delighted to discover.

There really was nothing wrong with the aesthetic part of Jace's "soul aesthetic." It was the soul part that was missing. That was what was lacking in his pussy-eating. You had to be really smart about the way you handled the pussy, and not only smart, but intuitive. You had to listen to it. You had to follow the moisture. Jace looked good performing, but he wasn't intuiting.

"Let me get on top," I said.

I sat on his cock and began to ride him. I imagined I was the one with the cock, that I was Liam. But if I was Liam, who was he? He was still Jace. So I was Liam, played by me, fucking Jace with my psychic cock.

"Spread your legs wider," I said, wandering my hand down to the skin between his balls and his asshole.

With confidence, I inserted the tip of my finger into his ass as I fucked him. I felt his asshole twitch around my finger in pleasure. He moaned and writhed against me.

"Say my name," he said.

"Jace."

"No," he said. "My real name."

"What do you mean?"

"My name is Jason Blagojevich. Say it."

"Jason Blagojevich," I said.

"Louder."

"Jason Blagojevich!"

I said it with all the passion I could muster. My performance was strong, actually.

Acting is behaving truthfully under imaginary circumstances,

I thought, remembering my college textbooks. More like behaving imaginarily under truthful circumstances.

"Jason Blagojevich!" I laughed.

I was no longer Liam, I was just me. Jace's zombie moans rose to a crescendo. Then he came.

CHAPTER 69

I called an emergency morning tea with Ana in the kitchen. I was eager to share my news. I wanted a witness to help elevate the drab reality of sex with Jace into an intoxicating story. I wanted her camaraderie, and more than that, I wanted her approval.

Someone had left half an entire sheet cake, white with white frosting, just sitting on the counter, with a sign that said EAT ME! Eyeing the cake, I recounted to Ana everything that had happened the night before. I excluded nothing except the part where I'd invited him to come over. I wanted to make it seem as though he had initiated it, which he sort of had with the cheek-touching—but not fully. I wanted to seem wanted, to wow her, and give off zero whiffs of desperation. It had been confirmed: I was the object of Jace's affection. That was it. For good measure, I even told her that he'd begged me to stick the finger in his ass. That's how much he'd wanted me inside of him.

"So he's gay," she said, when I finished my story.

"No!" I said. "A finger up the ass has nothing to do with his sexual orientation."

I didn't like that she was coming up with her own interpretation of this detail of the story, the part where I had shined so bright. Did he have to be gay in order to agree to have sex with me—as though I were an afterthought, an accident, maybe even a beard? Why couldn't she see me as a person that he could genuinely like?

"Besides," I said. "It's twenty-first-century Los Angeles. If he were gay, he would just be gay."

"Not necessarily," she said. "I mean, he is a TV star. Don't forget, he has to maintain that heterosexual appeal."

"If he was looking for a beard, he would've chosen someone way more public, like one of his costars or something. There are a ton of women who would love to date him. No, he's just, like, kinda into me."

I hated that I felt the need to puff myself up. I also felt bad about all of the sexual details I'd revealed about Jace—particularly the ass play and his proclivity for having his birth certificate orated. This was not the way girl talk should go. I wanted giggling, encouragement, cheering—not skepticism. I wanted conspiratorial comradeship, a walking diary entry. Instead, Ana seemed almost angry.

"You obviously can't date him," she said firmly.

"Of course. I know that," I said.

I couldn't figure out what was making her mad. I wondered if it was sorrow from her past, or jealousy. Under her left eye, her skin was twitching. She tapped on her teacup with her pointer finger. I could practically feel her nerves, vibrating.

"Should I not have told you?" I asked.

"No," said Ana, without smiling. "I'm very glad you did."

I realized, as she took a sip of her tea, that we no longer looked as much alike. Where we'd once mirrored each other physically with our long, woolly hair, now we had less in common. If she was trying to experience Jace through me, it wouldn't be as easy. The weight gain, and now the hair, fucked with her conception of the way a woman was supposed to be—especially a woman who got the attention of a handsome man with a shitty TV show.

I hadn't spoken to my mother in forty-nine days, but she was still right in front of me.

CHAPTER 70

When I got back to my apartment, Jace had left a note on the fridge.

Went to go run lines. That was cool. Let's do it again really soon. Love, J

I wondered how long he'd hung around. I was surprised when he'd asked if he could sleep over. I'd said yes because it seemed easier than saying no. But in the early hours, he'd tried to come over to my side of the bed to snuggle and I had to let out three loud, fake snores so he'd retreat back to his side.

I popped a fresh piece of nicotine gum and used the note to dispose of my last one. When I was eating more, I chewed less. But now I was back in the chain-chewing game. I opened the cabinet and eyed my protein bar stash. Then the buzzer rang.

Great. Touch a dude's asshole once, and you could never get rid of him.

"Hello?" I said.

"Hi," came a voice.

But it wasn't Jace. It was Miriam.

I scurried around my apartment, looking for obvious signs that a C-list, maybe B-list actor had been fucked there. I found a telltale Yeezy sock on the floor. I threw it in the trash. There was a condom in the trash. I flushed it. Fortunately, Jace had stripped the sheets and remade the bed. His grandmother would have been proud of him.

I mussed up my new hair in the mirror, pushing it forward, then sideways. Then I buzzed her up.

When she got to my apartment, we just stood there outside the door.

"Hi," she said.

"Hi."

It was like the first time she had come over. Only this time, I didn't have to lead her into the living room. This time, she was the one who took my hand and led me inside. She was the one who kissed me.

"Your hair," she said, running her hands through it.

"Do you like it?"

"It's so—sexy."

I felt nervous. I let her do all of the leading. She took me into the bedroom and lay down on the bed, beckoning me to climb on top of her. But I only stood there. So she stood up again, then sat me down on the bed, kissing me ever so gently, mostly with her lips and just the tip of her tongue: my cheeks, my forehead, my neck, my shoulders. I felt her hands go up my shirt and under my bra, grabbing my tits as though she were picking apples, clumsily, not sensual. Then she caught herself and stopped for a moment. I wondered if she would take her hands away. But she only seemed to focus more on the way that she was touching, remembering, perhaps, to touch me how she would want to be touched. She grazed little circles around my areolae with each of her fingers, making her way to the very center to pinch at my nipples, which stood upright, hard for her, making me gasp.

I was even more surprised when she kissed her way down my belly, and then, looking up at me, said, "Can I?"

I said, "I want you to," though I was scared. I hoped that my pussy would not frighten her or make her run, as though she had been in some kind of trance that would be broken once she saw me fully naked.

But instead her eyes widened in the light as she softly stroked my crease with her finger, doing exactly what I'd done to her in the past. I felt some moisture leak out of me and grew embarrassed. *Just let yourself*, I thought, as I felt myself get more and more turned on. *It's okay.*

Gently, she spread my lips apart and ran her tongue lightly over my clit, teasing it. I'd never imagined she would do it. I wanted to thrust my pelvis in her face, say, *Suck me, please*, but I remained still because I wanted her to do everything.

I wondered what I tasted like to her, if I tasted like what she'd expected. But when she began to pant on my clit, I stopped thinking. I was overcome with electric goodness.

She thrust her middle finger up inside me, and I could no longer contain myself. I fucked her face to the rhythm of her sucking and came all over her, coming for a long time, longer than I had ever remembered coming.

I moved her face away quickly, too sensitive now. Then I lay back with my eyes closed, very peaceful. My head seemed to be filled with space, more space than I'd known it could hold. She lit a clove. I chewed a piece of nicotine gum. A breeze floated in through the window.

CHAPTER 71

In the morning, Miriam was Rubenesque in my bed—her hair spread out on my pillow, body placid in the sheets. I said, "Good morning," and she put her arms around me, whispered "Good morning" back, and pulled me on top of her.

I looked up at the clock.

"Oy," I said. "I have to get up and take a shower, get ready for work. But you stay here!"

"No! Don't go!" she said. "Stay here with me."

I looked at her rosy cheeks, her lips plump and pink. She could have anything she wanted from me.

"All right," I said.

I called the office to tell them I was sick. Strep sounded official. Ana picked up at the front desk, and while I delivered the sad news of my illness Miriam tried to kiss me slurpily.

"Stop!" I whispered to her.

"What's going on?" asked Ana.

"Nothing," I said. "I'm feverish, and it's making me loopy."

"Uh-huh," she said.

I knew she thought that I was in bed with Jace.

After I'd hung up the phone, Miriam said she wanted to go to Doughy's to get us a little feast.

"I'll come with you," I said.

"You stay in bed," she said. "Let me get it. I want to do it for you."

So I watched her get out of bed, savoring her naked figure from behind: the cascading flesh of her back, her ass its own planet. I would paint her if I could paint. I'd carve her in stone if I could really sculpt. I'd make all kinds of Miriam idols and I'd worship each one of them. But all I knew how to do was sit there grinning stupidly, thinking. I wanted to freeze time right here, in this moment when she was leaving, only to come right back to me.

When I heard the door close, I began projecting a slideshow in my mind of future Miriams and Rachels. There was Miriam on the toilet in the bathroom of a shared apartment, door not even closed, pee tinkling. Miriam and Rachel on vacation in the Russian forest gathering mushrooms. Miriam as nurse administering Jell-O, ice cream, tea with honey to a sick Rachel. I saw Miriam in a blue coat and matching hat, standing outside the mall, in the suburban New Jersey winter. Miriam, knife in hand, ready to deliver the verdict on my first attempt at cooking pepper steak. Miriam the mother clutching candlesticks at the head of a long dining table, though I could not picture our children. Miriam and Rachel as crones playing mah-jongg in Boca Raton and reading fortune cookies.

She returned with a feast: chocolate-covered cake donuts, bagels, cream cheese and lox. Also hot chocolate. I lay on the bed watching her unwrap all of the delicacies and thought, *Mama*. Then I thought, *No, sister*. Then I thought *lover* and *friend*, but none of those words felt completely right.

We ate breakfast in bed, naked. Miriam fed me and I fed her. I wondered if one day I would tell her what I had been like before, about the eating disorder, all the years with it. I wondered if she would understand. I felt there was a danger in sharing the real details of that sickness—that it would taint the lovely way we ate together. I wanted our throats to stay free, not clogged with diagnoses from my history. There were other words I didn't bring up for similar reasons. I didn't want to diagnose the relationship. I never used the word *girlfriend*, as in, *Are you my girlfriend?* I never asked, *What are we?*

She had barely finished eating when I climbed on top of her. I slid my way up and down so that our bare pussies were pressed against each other. I imagined our clitoral hoods conjoined, our clits giving each other kisses in the friction. I looked on the nightstand and saw the clay figure: the swirls of pink, blue, yellow and green. It had no eyes, but it winked at me. It had no mouth, but it smiled.

CHAPTER 72

All afternoon, we napped. I dreamt that I was as big as Miriam. We flew around together on the gold dragon as it exhaled light and steam. We sailed over the Hollywood sign, swooped past Griffith Park Observatory, two gorgeous fat women on display. We both wore the same long, black silky dress—like the yellow one she'd worn the first night we'd gone for Chinese food, but in black. We both wore the same Ruský Rouge lipstick. The lipstick was everywhere, smeared across all the straws and stars and forks and moons and Twizzlers and movie screens and televisions and buildings and money of the world. We swapped lipstick from mouth to mouth, totally open for all the world to see. We turned on men and women alike. The men wanted us, and the women wanted to be us. They envied our gorgeous freedom. We were a double mirror, reflecting their own deep desires. The mirror was framed in gilt bamboo.

We kissed each other between sips of Scorpion Bowl. We kissed each other between bites of sesame chicken. Rabbi Judah Loew ben Bezalel sat on a giant scallion pancake in the clouds. He nodded approvingly.

"So it's all real!" I said to the rabbi.

"Real, shmeal," he said. "Don't look a gift horse in the mouth. There are emanations of god we can't even see. What's important is that you feel it."

"But I want to know."

"You think anyone knows? A mother loves the way she sees her child. A people love their myth of a homeland. You love your Miriam."

I offered him the Ruský Rouge. He wrote the word *LIFE* in the sky. Then he playfully tossed a fortune cookie at my head.

"Remember," he said. "The spiritual world and the physical world go hand in hand."

CHAPTER 73

When I awoke, Miriam was playing with my shorn hair.

"It's almost sundown," she said. "I have to go home for Shabbat."

I had forgotten it was Friday. The clock said 4:27. I didn't want to let her leave. I took her hand for a moment, then I let it go. I couldn't ask to go with her. I was not welcome there. I wished there were a version of reality that could embrace us all: Mrs. Schwebel and candlelight and challah and song and wine and Miriam and me as we were. But it was better to stay in bed and dream of her than to be together in a realm where we had to pretend that physically we were strangers to each other.

"When will you be back?" I asked.

"Tomorrow night," she said. "As soon as the sun goes down again."

I was afraid. I had no control. I took the clay figure off my nightstand and held it, hoping it would make me feel more courageous. I still felt afraid. So I handed it to her.

"What's this?" she asked.

"It's a gift," I said. "A sculpture. Something I made."

"Is it supposed to be . . . me?" she asked.

I was surprised by the question. I sat there for a moment and wondered what I should say.

"Yes," I said finally. "It's you."

"The boobs are wrong." She laughed.

"I know," I said. "But the hair is right."

CHAPTER 74

On Saturday evening, I went to Doughy's and bought another incredible feast: bagels, cream cheese, whitefish salad, sliced tomatoes, Jordan almonds, chocolaty mints. It was the kind of dairy feast my grandparents used to make after Yom Kippur to break the fast, and I knew that Miriam would love it. I liked these echoes of the past, the way a food could rouse a memory from death. As I walked home it was still light outside. Then I waited in my apartment for the sun to set.

By 7:30, the sky was totally dark and Miriam had not arrived. I began to worry. Had she changed her mind about coming? Had her parents stopped her? In her temporary absence, I began to dread a more permanent absence. I could do nothing but lie on my bed and stare at the ceiling. It was strange how we traveled together in my mind so easily across space and time, but we couldn't just be here together. My vision of our future, the slides I'd allowed myself to play, were fading fainter. Soon, the only light would be my clock in the darkness, ticking.

I put my pillow on top of me, to try to conjure her. She was breath and moan and hips. I could replicate, to an extent, the feel of her breath by breathing on my own hand, the sounds of her moans by moaning into my pillow, but I could not fashion her hips: not with my pillow, or by touching my own hips, which

I had so feared were growing wider, but now realized were not wide enough at all.

I thought about the story of the trees, the woman who chose her family over the evergreens. But I had felt Miriam's blessed desire for me so clearly. I looked out the window and saw something moving on the lawn in the darkness. It was just a woman with a dog. Miriam would be here any minute.

At 9:15 I got up and made myself a bagel with cream cheese. At 10:08, I ate another one. At 11, I placed a piece of Saran Wrap over the giant block of cream cheese, wrapped it up, and put it in the fridge. As I closed the refrigerator door, I remembered being a little girl and asking my mother if I could taste sugar and cream cheese on the same spoon.

She had said I could try it in a few weeks if the weigh-in at my annual pediatrician checkup was good. But I was dying to try it, and so I snuck into the pantry and refrigerator while she was in the shower and made it for myself. It was like a small, beautifully granular cheesecake. I couldn't wait until I grew up and had my own apartment, all to myself, so I could eat cream cheese and sugar whenever I wanted.

A few days later, my mother noticed grains of sugar in the cream cheese container. Nothing escaped her.

"Do I have to put a lock on the pantry and the fridge?" she asked.

But now I had my own apartment and could do what I wanted. I took the cream cheese back out of the fridge and ripped off the wrap. Then I searched the kitchen cupboards for sugar. I didn't have any, but I did have packets of Splenda.

I kneeled down on the kitchen floor with the cream cheese and emptied out a few packets of the Splenda onto the big hunk. With my fingers, I scooped out chunks. I thought about kneading the chunks into shapes, like the putty at Dr. Mahjoub's office. Could I shape a woman out of cream cheese, say a prayer, and she would appear before me? Could I conjure Miriam out of dairy? I thought about singing "Etz Chayim." Instead, I said, "Amen," out loud and stuck the chunks in my mouth, one after the other, like I was taking the wafer—only Jewish. Miriam wasn't coming. It was over between us. I was on my knees. I was alone, but I still felt watched.

CHAPTER 75

O n Monday morning, as I headed to the office, I got a series of texts from Jace.

Yo can you call me?

Call me when u can

Call me

Did he understand that I had to work? Not all of us got paid to be in a post-apocalyptic coma.

When I got to my desk, there was a note on my computer from Ofer. The note said: *Rachel, come see me immediately.*

I stepped into Ofer's office, and he motioned that I should sit down. Then he got up, slammed his door shut, and began pacing around my chair.

"I just want to know," he said. "How little respect do you have for me?"

"I don't have little respect for you," I said.

"And how little respect do you have for what I've built? This family. Our office culture."

"I'm not sure what you're getting at," I said.

I was afraid I knew exactly what he was getting at.

"Don't fuck with me, Rachel!" he yelled. "Do you know how lucky you are? You could be working at Management180, where the only company values are packaging deals and agent reciprocity! You could be in a mailroom somewhere!"

A little fleck of spit flew from his mouth onto my hand. I wiped it on the sofa.

"Jace told me what happened," he said.

My stomach dropped. I knew then that I was fucked.

"You are terminated immediately, in breach of contract," said Ofer.

"But—"

"It's an ethics violation, no severance. You've completely disappointed me."

"Wait," I said. "You don't even want to hear my side of the story?"

The truth was, I didn't really have a side of the story. I had fucked Jace, and it was a breach of contract. I wondered what Jace's contract stipulated. He was probably allowed to fuck all of us. Of course, he wasn't going to get in any trouble.

"You have half an hour to get your things and go."

I felt humiliated. Tears filled my eyes. I stood up to leave.

"I really believed in your vision," said Ofer.

Then I almost laughed. What vision was it, exactly, that he had believed in? I hadn't even had a vision!

I wanted to say, *Way to uphold a hegemonic power structure within the matrix of fame privilege and the feminization of poverty, Ofer.*

Instead, I said, "I'm sorry."

CHAPTER 76

I called Jace from inside a stall in the office bathroom. He picked up his phone on the first ring.

"Asshole!" I said. "You must've known I would lose my job."

"Rachel. I can explain."

"You're worse than TMZ."

"Listen to me," he said. "When Ofer called, it was like eight this morning. I'd just woken up. I thought he was calling about the commercial I'm doing for American Express. I break character to charge a Taser—anyway, he asked me flat-out if we had slept together."

"He called you to ask if we slept together?"

"Yes! I was confused. I panicked. I figured you'd told him and that I was in trouble. So I told the truth."

"Why would I tell him we slept together?"

"I don't know. But he knew, so I just figured. Then, after I said yes, he said he hadn't talked to you yet and I was like, *Oh, shit.*"

"So some member of your asshole posse spilled the beans."

"No! I didn't tell anyone."

I wasn't sure whether to be insulted by his discretion or grateful for it. But I knew he was telling the truth. First of all, he wasn't that good of an actor. It was me who had been the dishonest one. I'd used him to elevate my status in the eyes of strangers, to prove to Ana that I was desirable. I'd gossiped to her about fucking him.

Then I realized. It was Ana who had told Ofer.

CHAPTER 77

Ana was on the phone with a client's assistant when I stopped by her desk. I was carrying a box with my cacti, my mugs, and the puffer jacket. I set the box down on the floor next to me and cleared my throat. But she didn't look up.

"They rescheduled the shoot for the twenty-seventh so it works with her schedule," she said. "Two thirty p.m., I'll send the call sheet."

I took a step closer to her.

"Full makeup and hair. But she should arrive prewashed, no product. There will be three parking passes—one for her, one for you, and one for the publicist. Everyone should bring ID."

I took another step closer.

"And they received the rider. Craft services will make sure to provide at least two keto options for lunch."

I took another step closer. I was practically in her lap. Finally, she looked up at me.

"I'm swamped," she whispered. "Can you come back later?"

"You fucking told him," I said.

CHAPTER 78

I t was day 53 of the detox when I broke down and called my mother.

I wondered if there was something significant about the number 53. I googled *53 Jewish number meaning* and found nothing, only information for the number 36:

> *The number 36 is a holy number, because it is twice the number 18. In Jewish numerology, the number 18 means* chai *or life. The number 36 is holy, because it is two lives.*

Great, had god wanted me to call my mother at 36 days?

My mother's phone rang until her voice mail picked up. It was after midnight on the East Coast, and I knew she would be asleep. I didn't tell her I'd been fired that day. I didn't tell her that my heart hurt. I didn't address the detox either.

I simply said, "Hi, it's your daughter. Just calling to say hello. I'll be around tomorrow."

Then I hung up.

Then I cried. More than anything, all I'd ever wanted was a total embrace, the embrace of an infinite mother, absolute and divine. I wanted to lose the edges of myself and blend with a woman, enter the amniotic sac and melt away. I wanted a love that was bottomless, unconditional, with zero repercussions. I wanted an infinite yogurt, a mystical and maternal yogurt, something of which I could have unlimited quantities that would not hurt me.

But nothing was unlimited. Every cup had a bottom. Miriam and I were done. Certainly, my time in the womb had ended, harsh and abrupt in the cold hospital, bright light, a stranger's pair of hands, searing consciousness. The woman who had carried me inside her for nine months had become a stranger. Even those women whose mothers loved them unconditionally, that love too had an end.

Still I wanted it. I wanted a love contingent on nothing finite. I wanted a love without end. Everyone was always saying you had to give it to yourself. Self-love, self-love. What did that even mean?

Dr. Mahjoub said it all the time: *Mother yourself, parent yourself.*

It seemed impossible. I had no idea how to be a mom, let alone my own mother. But what about daughterhood? Was it possible that I could be my own daughter?

This seemed more doable. I wondered if the universe, in its roundness, somehow already contained my daughterness. Perhaps I'd been being held there, a daughter all along, until I woke up to it. If I could not be my own mother—or at least not the kind of mother worth having—then maybe I could be my own daughter.

"Daughter daughter daughter daughter daughter," I heard myself saying, roughly from a place in my throat just below my Adam's apple.

"Daughter daughter daughter daughter daughter daughter daughter," I said again, and found that I had put my arms around myself.

I sat down on the wood floor and began to rock myself. Then I moved over to the sofa, because it was softer, and rocked myself there.

"I'm so sorry, daughter," I said, tears in my eyes. "I'm sorry that you felt I had abandoned you."

"That is okay, Mother," I said. "You were always here. I just didn't know how to find you."

I heard myself talking to myself. I wondered if I had finally lost it.

"Daughter daughter daughter daughter daughter," I said.

"Yes, Mother," I said. "Promise me you will never disappear from me again. Show me how I can always know you're here. Show me how to share my joy with you, that you will be happy to receive it."

"Oh, my daughter," I said. "You will forget that I am here. This is the way of human beings, to forget. But you found your way back to me once and so can find your way back again, because I am always here. The world will hurt you again and again. You will hurt yourself again and again. And when it does, and when you do, you will remember me again and again. You will drop to your knees. You will hold yourself. You will be your own daughter again."

CHAPTER 79

I saw Miriam one more time, three years later. I was walking down Fairfax, eating an ice-cream cone of all things—mint chocolate chip, no toppings—when I saw her coming toward me. She was pushing a double-wide stroller with two babies inside— twins, it looked like. Her hair was up under a beret.

It's not her, I thought. *You are hallucinating.*

But the closer we came, I realized it could be no one except her. I recognized the precise constellation of moles on her neck, unchanged. I knew them so well, first from my own body and then from hers. I would always know them.

Miriam recognized me too, of course. Our eyes met and locked on one another. When she stared for a moment, I felt tears spring to mine. Then my lips curled into a smile, and she smiled too. She nodded at me, not like a person she had known, but like someone who was a friendly passerby—looking at her and her babies in admiration. Neither of us stopped.

I wondered if Miriam had kept the clay figure, or if she'd thrown it away. I wondered who she was married to, if her parents had rushed to quickly find her a match because of what happened. But I also felt it wasn't part of our story for me to know. Maybe I was only supposed to know that she had two little ones and was happy to mother them, regardless of whether she loved the man she was with.

It was a warm day for fall, even in Los Angeles. I had gigs coming up all over the East Coast, and my mother would be coming to see my set in New York. She didn't like my hair, which was still short, but she was being quiet about my weight. I told her I would keep any mother jokes at bay.

Since Miriam, I'd dated one man and one woman. The man was a comic and the woman a minister at a Unitarian church in Pasadena. I'd told my mother about both of them. She was disappointed that the man had not worked out.

That night, Rabbi Judah Loew ben Bezalel came to me in a dream. I hadn't seen him in three years, and I told him I still didn't always know what was real—or wasn't. He said that the word *golem*, in English, means *shapeless mass*. But in Hebrew, it means *unfinished substance*.

"What ever happened to your golem?" I asked. "The famous one."

"Ah! For a little love, you pay all your life." He laughed. "The last I heard, he followed a woman to New York and into the Yiddish theater."

I asked the rabbi where I could find him again when I needed his wisdom. He reminded me that I was his creator.

ACKNOWLEDGMENTS

Love and thanks to Meredith Kaffel Simonoff, a real macher; to Tamar McCollom for editorial chutzpah, Nan Graham, Kara Watson, Jaya Miceli, Katie Monaghan, Brianna Yamashita, Zoey Cole, Sabrina Pyun, and the whole Scribner mishpocha; to Alexis Kirschbaum and Bloomsbury UK, and to Clément Ribes; to Petra Collins and Karah Preiss; to Stacey Silverman and Liz Tigelaar; to the shtarkers at Lighthouse and UTA; to Ruth and Stan Harris and Eve and Lou Broder; to my parents and sister; and to the mensch of mensches, chavrusa of chavrusas, Nicholas.

ABOUT THE AUTHOR

MELISSA BRODER is the author of the novels *Death Valley* and *The Pisces*, the essay collection *So Sad Today*, and five poetry collections, including *Superdoom: Selected Poems*. She has written for the *New York Times*, Elle.com, *Vice*, *Vogue Italia*, and *New York* magazine's The Cut. Her poems have appeared in *Poetry*, the *Iowa Review*, *Tin House*, and *Guernica*, and she is the winner of a Pushcart Prize for poetry. She lives in Los Angeles.

Milk Fed

MELISSA BRODER

*This reading group guide for Milk Fed includes an intro-
duction, discussion questions, and ideas for enhancing
your book club. The suggested questions are intended to help your
reading group find new and interesting angles and topics for your
discussion. We hope that these ideas will enrich your conversation
and increase your enjoyment of the book.*

INTRODUCTION

Rachel is a lapsed Jew and obsessive calorie-counter. She's overwhelmed by her attraction to Miriam, who works at the frozen yogurt shop Rachel frequents every day. Miriam begins to fall for Rachel too, but Miriam is Orthodox and takes great joy in eating. With a golem, an ancient mystic rabbi, a wicked mother, and some truly wild erotic fantasies, *Milk Fed* is a tender and riotously funny meditation on love, certitude, and the question of what we are all being fed.

TOPICS & QUESTIONS
FOR DISCUSSION

1. This book is partially about extreme dieting and disordered eating. As a group, discuss this phenomenon. Have you encountered other fiction about food? How has it affected you?

2. Before Rachel meets Miriam, how do you feel about her?

3. What is Ana's role in Rachel's life? What do you make of Rachel's mental state when you read about her fantasy involving Ana (pages 27–29)?

4. On page 18, Rachel refers to her mother "opening an emotional spreadsheet." What does this metaphor mean? How does it compare to Rachel's relationship with her father (chapter 13)?

5. What is Rachel's impression of Miriam when she meets her for the first time?

6. Take a moment to discuss the cadence of dialogue in *Milk Fed*. How does the author use it to reveal more about Rachel, Miriam, and the supporting cast?

7. On page 54, Rachel loses the sculpture her therapist asked her to create. What do you think is the significance of this?

8. In chapter 36, Rachel ponders how the Schwebels would react to Miriam coming out to them, and contrasts it with the way her own mother responded. What is the significance of the imagined differences in these parental responses?

9. Throughout *Milk Fed*, Rachel fantasizes about Miriam. Do you think there's a big difference between her fantasy of Miriam and the actual, real Miriam?

10. Discuss the various appearances of Rabbi Judah Loew ben Bezalel. What do they signal? What's happening to Rachel when she sees the rabbi in her subconscious?

11. How do Rachel and Miriam observe their Jewish faith differently? How does that layer of culture add to *Milk Fed*? Are there religious references that you were compelled to research?

12. How does her relationship with Miriam fundamentally change Rachel?

ENHANCE YOUR BOOK CLUB

1. Read more of Melissa Broder's books! Her first novel is *The Pisces*, another obsessive love story that's both sexy and hilarious, but this time involving a merman.

2. Have a Yo!Good-style sundae buffet—the host can provide the frozen yogurt, and everyone else can bring their favorite toppings to share (see who makes the most Miriam-like sundae).

3. As the moderator in your group, obtain a copy of Melissa Broder's poetry collection *Last Sext*. Have a reading party at the end of your book club and pass the collection around, each person reading a poem or two aloud. Nibble on some Twizzlers while you're at it!

TWIZZLER ON THE ROOF

A *MILK FED* RECIPE BOOK

BY MELISSA BRODER

LOW-SELF-ESTEEM SECRET SPLENDA PARFAIT

Rachel, our *Milk Fed* protagonist, consumes two breakfasts daily. Breakfast One is a piece of nicotine gum chased with a swig of warm shower water. Breakfast Two is a 0% fat Greek yogurt with two packets of Splenda mixed in, plus a 100-calorie diet chocolate muffin top that is essentially a cocoa-painted sponge—but to Rachel is a delicacy. Breakfast Two must be kept secret, hidden behind a blockade of file folders, because Rachel's nosy coworker judges her use of Splenda.

Like any good obsessive food ritualist, Rachel then repeats this indulgence again at night, using a variation of the recipe: a pint of low-cal diet ice cream, half a cup of Special K Red Berries cereal, and of course, more Splenda. This she consumes under the covers in bed, alone, which is way better than any kind of public eating.

INGREDIENTS

- 1 part dairy base: 1 cup nonfat yogurt or 1 pint light ice cream (Halo Top is tastier than its lower-calorie cousin, Arctic Zero, but depends how much you hate yourself)

- 1 part carb: A diet muffin top (VitaTops if you're blessed to find them, otherwise Veggies Made Great are passable) or cereal or crumbled rice cakes

- Splenda packets

DIRECTIONS:

If you're doing the yogurt version, open the yogurt. If you're doing the light ice cream version, open the pint and microwave it for 20 seconds until nice 'n soft. Then put the carb part into the dairy part and mush it around. Add Splenda to taste.

SERVING SUGGESTION:

Like all weird food rituals, the parfait is best prepared and enjoyed alone. And remember: low self-esteem is better than no self-esteem.

STORAGE:

Just eat it out of the container and finish it. Thanks.

YIELDS:

The judgment of others. Artificial sweeteners are very yesteryear—everyone uses stevia now because they don't want to die. Only the real punks among us still use artificial sweeteners. The author still uses artificial sweeteners. Her favorite is Equal.

MYSTIC PU PU PLATTER
OF DIVINE LIGHT

Rachel and our other protagonist, the gloriously zaftig Miriam, have their first real hangout at the Golden Dragon: a fictional kitschy-kosher neon American Chinese restaurant in the Fairfax district of Los Angeles. The Golden Dragon, which possesses beatific powers, is inspired by the now-defunct Yee's Village in Somerville, Massachusetts, as well as the close relationship between American Jews and American Chinese restaurants, and the author's own, private longing to eat eternal scallion pancakes.

At the Golden Dragon, Rachel has a spiritual experience involving the flame of the pu pu platter: an anxiety-inducing but ultimately transcendent vision that is part ego death, part egg roll.

It may be noted that the pu pu platter, a round tray of assorted American Chinese appetizers, possesses the qualities of variety and abundance. It may also be noted that the *Shekinah*—the holy flame or light—is considered, in Kabbalism, to be the embodiment of the divine feminine.

INGREDIENTS:

- 1 dimly lit American Chinese or Tiki-style Polynesian restaurant
- 1 pu pu platter with flame

—OR—

- Your kitchen
- A big plate with a candle in the middle
- Microwaveable bags of frozen appetizers, like dumplings, mini egg rolls, wontons. Don't be afraid to go full bar mitzvah and throw in some other shit like pigs in a blanket and mozzarella sticks. You could even do fondue. The point is that there is fire.

DIRECTIONS:

Eat the food. Stare at the flame. Maybe something cool will happen.

STORAGE:

It's not easy to integrate big, epiphanic experiences into our daily lives. The author has found that it's usually the smaller, deliberate changes that provide more lasting impact. Still, who doesn't love a peak experience? Good luck!

YIELDS:

Hopefully, a better life for you and humanity.

———————————

APHRODISIAC TWIZZLERS
À LA MIRIAM

On their multiple excursions to classic movies in a darkened LA theater, Rachel and Miriam hit the Twizzlers—and they hit them hard. As the tension between the two women grows, so too does their consumption of Twizzlers: served up in a king-size bag, room temperature, and always with a heaping side of Peanut M&Ms.

INGREDIENTS:

- Twizzlers (please see "Understanding Ingredients")

UNDERSTANDING INGREDIENTS:

The author is personally more aroused by Red Vines than Twizzlers. But Twizzlers are a frequent offering at movie theaters and, as Miriam notes, they're kosher. So for the sake of narrative accuracy, Twizzlers are "the chosen" candy of *Milk Fed*.

DIRECTIONS:

Eat the Twizzlers? You can also bite off both ends of a Twizzler and use it as a drinking straw, but that doesn't happen in this book.

STORAGE:

Traditionally, Twizzlers are packaged in a plastic wrapper and may be stored in that wrapper when not in use.

A NOTE ON KOSHER CANDY:

According to the Internet: Skittles are kosher. Red Vines are kosher. M&Ms are kosher. Hershey Kisses are kosher. Jelly Bellies are kosher. Kit Kats are kosher. Twix bars are kosher. Ring Pops are kosher. Laffy Taffy is kosher. Pez are kosher. Reese's Pieces are kosher. Milk Duds are Kosher. Starburst are *not* kosher. SweetTarts are *not* kosher. Circus Peanuts are *not* kosher. Haribo gummies are *not* kosher, although they do make a special line of kosher Gold-bears, Peaches, and Happy-Colas, which are . . . kosher.

RABBI JUDAH'S SAVORY NUTS FROM THE SKY

Would it kill you to eat a cashew?

Rabbi Judah Loew ben Bezalel was a late-sixteenth-century rabbi who constructed a golem—an animated being made of inanimate matter—to defend the Jews of Prague from anti-Semitic attacks. In *Milk Fed*, the rabbi is an ally and guide who appears to Rachel in dreams and visions.

In one dream, Rachel experiences Miriam as a kindly chipmunk who is continually showered with nuts from the heavens: pea-nuts, almonds, hazelnuts, walnuts, cashews, and pistachios. When Rachel looks up, she sees that it's Rabbi Judah tossing out the nuts from high atop a giant wooden elephant statue (Rachel's therapist is obsessed with elephant décor, so the elephant gets in her dream).

When Rabbi Judah peer pressures Rachel to have a pistachio, she discovers that the shell opens "like a tiny door" to a chartreuse realm of exquisite creaminess and saltiness. Beautiful things like this can happen when we let go of control (though it should be noted that surrendering control in a dream is often less challenging than letting go in real life).

INGREDIENTS:

- 1 deceased spiritual leader—be it rabbi, high priestess, rever-end, lama, mufti, or guru—with whom you feel connected

- 1 bed, or other place you enjoy sleeping

- 1 bowl of your favorite snack mix (mixed nuts are the time-honored snack, though the author enjoys creating a mix of dry cereals, like Golden Grahams, Cocoa Puffs, and Lucky Charms, which—in some cultures—is considered a blessed snack)

DIRECTIONS:

Dreams and visions are mysterious. Can we will a dream to happen? Lucid dreamers say yes. If you want to give it a go, place a bowl of your favorite snack mix on your nightstand and consume the snack in the dark before falling asleep. As you chew, imagine being held in the arms of your fave spiritual leader. If you don't like any spiritual leaders, then imagine being held by an angel or simply by the ambrosial aura of god. If you're an atheist, imagine being held by the void—but, like, a really loving void. Fall asleep eating. It's fine. You're not becoming a fundamentalist, you're just doing this for one night, so you don't need to brush your teeth.

SERVING SUGGESTION:

It's actually okay to eat all your meals in bed.

YIELDS:

A celestial experience and/or just a nice snack.

MOIST BLOCK OF CREAM CHEESE EATEN ALONE ON KITCHEN FLOOR IN REVELATORY EMOTIONAL CATHARSIS—A CLASSIC!

If you're going to experience a revelatory emotional catharsis, it's best to do so while eating compulsively by yourself on the kitchen floor.

For Rachel, this means consuming a large block of cream cheese with her hands.

But there's more than one way to do a cathartic food bender . . .

INGREDIENTS:

- Massive quantity of a soft food, one which would cause you great shame if someone were to bust you eating the whole thing alone on the kitchen floor with your hands. Peanut butter? Too safe. Mayonnaise? Closer. French onion dip? Nice. What's important here, maybe even more important than the food itself, is the shame, because it is only through getting naked and alone with our shame that we can . . . something.

- Shame

DIRECTIONS:

Your heart knows what to do.

SERVING SUGGESTION:

Go hard.

STORAGE:

Finish the whole thing.

YIELDS:

Technically serves a family of six to eight. But in the case of emotional crisis, it's just one serving. All for you.

Keep reading for a preview of
Melissa Broder's next novel,

Death Valley

Coming from Scribner September 2023

One

I pull into the desert town at sunset feeling empty. I felt empty the whole drive from Los Angeles and hoped that my arrival would alleviate the emptiness, so when the emptiness is not alleviated, not even momentarily (all emptiness-alleviators are temporary), I feel emptier.

"Help me not be empty," I say to god in the Best Western parking lot.

Since I don't turn to god very often, I feel self-conscious when I do. I'm not sure what I'm allowed to ask for, and I worry that I shouldn't want the things I want. Are my requests too specific? I should probably ask to simply be happy doing god's will, though I've heard it said that when you're doing god's will you feel like you're flowing with a great river, not against it, so it seems like the happy feeling should just come naturally.

Earlier today, a friend texted me a quote by Kierkegaard: "Life is not a problem to be solved, but a reality to be experienced."

Ordinarily, I'd do nothing more than mark this kind of text message with a heart, maybe respond with the word *yesss*, and move on. But because of the low place I've been in, I saw the quote as a life raft, as though I were a small version of me adrift in a bowl of milk and the quote was the lone Cheerio I had to grab onto.

Halfway between LA and the desert town, I stopped at a Circle

K to pee and get some beef jerky. On the public toilet, I tried to meditate using the Kierkegaard quote as a mantra, but the quote only made me feel worse. I realized that I was doing the exact opposite of what the quote suggested: trying to solve a problem, the problem of me and my mood, rather than just experiencing it. But how do you just experience things?

In addition to the beef jerky (Jack Link's brand, Sweet & Hot) I bought a large cup of black coffee and two cans of Red Bull Sugar Free—a decision that is now coming back to haunt me in the motel parking lot. Some bad electricity is going down in my nervous system, and I can't tell what's caffeine-induced sensitivity and what could be a real physical problem. When I look at the glowing blue WELCOME sign, it appears to be vibrating.

The Best Western is at the edge of town, and beyond it lies nothingness: a desolate stretch of sand and rock, peppered with dead brush, all the way to the hills. I play it fake cool to the dust, casually unloading my black duffel from the trunk. But my hands are trembling.

Am I dying?

This thought triggers an unexpected surge of tenderness, as though I am a child who needs comforting.

In the settling dusk, I try to think of a positive self-affirmation, the kind that one woman I know has written on Post-its stuck to her bathroom mirror (a behavior that makes me judge her as a person, though there's really nothing wrong with it and I wish I didn't).

What I come up with is: *You have a good reason to be depressed.*

The phrase serves as a soothing reminder that my doominess isn't baseless. I am going to clutch it like a blankie as I move through the gloom—deeper and more alarming than my typical sea levels.

My raison de depression, if I were to convey it briefly in an e-mail, is thus:

Hi!

Five months ago, my father was critically injured in a car accident. Unfortunately, he is still in the ICU. As a result, I am overextended and cannot fulfill your request at this time.

Best,
me

One nice thing about a tragic situation is having an excuse to say no to everything. Nothing says *Don't ask me for shit* like *ICU*. It's simple, effective, succinct. At the same time, my prevailing compulsion is to recount every stage of the whole ordeal—as though by omission, I'll fail to convey the prolonged awfulness of the situation, or worse, I'll lose some of the time in which my father and I have existed on Earth together.

When asked, "How are you?" (never a good question) I keep bursting into monologue: his accident, his broken neck, the aspiration, the sedation, the surgery, the failure to wean off the ventilator, the prolonged unconsciousness, the tracheotomy, the awakening, the bronchoscopy and five-second death, the second death, the Decision, the really awakening, the weaning success, the collar, the sound of his voice, the pneumonia, the falling unconscious again.

Sometimes, mid-monologue, I catch myself calling my father's tracheal tube a "trach" and his ventilator a "vent"—a breezy familiarity that disgusts me, as though the life-support machines are now my friends. For the sake of narrative clarity, I do my best to organize the flood of events into temporal subheadings like Unconsciousness One and Resuscitation Two.

During the period of Unconsciousness One, my younger sister and I went to visit our father in the ICU most evenings.

Through our tears we smiled at the nurses, feeling righteous and kind. What devoted children we were! What bringers of light! From our mouths burbled fountains of *I love you*s. We could not stop saying it if we tried.

We "tucked him in" each night, reading aloud from *Pat the Bunny*, *The Great Blueness*, and other bedtime classics from our faraway past. We sang "Puff the Magic Dragon" and "The Bear Went Over the Mountain," the ventilator swishing behind us for rhythm.

It is easier to have an intimate relationship with the unconscious than the conscious, the dead than the living. As my father slumbered, I created a fantasy version of him—resurrecting the man from my youth, before his depression set in. I re-entered a world of home-cooked stews, tobacco smells, cozy sweatshirts, plants, and birds; a realm of warmth and worldly cynicism, where I was always on the inside of his sarcasm.

My father is more at ease with children than with adults. At twenty-one, I was surprised to find that I could be a *them*—displaced beyond the gates of his prickly emotional garden. Now, at forty-one, I told myself a new story: if my father survived, if he awoke and had some kind of meaningful recovery, then I would have the father from my childhood back.

But I am no longer a child.

When my father regained consciousness, he wouldn't make eye contact with me. I looked at his hands and feet instead. The feet were easy: calluses, freckle on big toe, him. But looking at his left hand was like seeing him naked, like I should have to ask permission first. What was once his dominant hand—his scrawling, gardening, cooking, and hauling hand—now lay limp, with nails overgrown and skin covered in purple blotches. Gently, I took his hand in mine. He allowed me to hold it for a few seconds. Then he pulled away.

"He probably doesn't know who we are," said my sister.

But I took it personally, and in the periods of consciousness that followed, I mounted a new campaign to connect with him.

It had taken me years to see clearly that I was not the cause of my father's depression. Still, I never stopped hoping that I could be an exception to it. Now the accident was a second hurdle to overcome, and I wanted to be the magic daughter. I'd live in that garden once more.

But before I could take root, my father fell unconscious again. This time, I fled to the desert.

I'm here at the Best Western for a week under the pretext of figuring out "the desert section" of my next novel. If I'm honest, I came to escape a feeling—an attempt that's already going poorly, because unfortunately I've brought myself with me, and I see, as the last pink light creeps out to infinity, that I am still the kind of person who makes another person's coma all about me.

TWO

I chose this desert town as the scene of my escape because it's the fictional home of a cartoon bighorn sheep that enchanted both my father and me in my childhood. Whenever I see the town on a map, just north of the Mojave Preserve and south of Death Valley (in the valley of Death Valley, you might say), it makes me smile.

According to Google, the town now has two non-chain restaurants—a '50s diner and a Mexican automat—plus a Wendy's, a Jack in the Box, and other highway fare. There's a general store and trading post, an alien-themed gift shop, a small Route 66 museum, a dinosaur park, and a Target. There are five motels.

I was pleased to discover online that one of the motels is a Best Western. I love a Best Western, so much so that I'm a rewards member (though I've never earned enough points for a free night). It's an underrated motel—rivaled only by the Holiday Inn in terms of bang for your buck, plus the satisfying in-room comforts you'd find in more upscale hotels: soft sheets, fluffy towels, square lampshades. The Best Western is cozy but anonymous; simple, yet not depressing. Just about the only thing lacking is that they no longer give you the little motel notepad and pen.

Every Best Western lobby has a few unifying design rules, at least as far as I've observed, and this Best Western is no different:

Where wood can be fake, make it fake.
Where linoleum can be used, use linoleum.
If a geometric shape can be incorporated
into any wall, rug, or floor tile, it's going in.

My check-in experience has the efficiency I've come to expect from a Best Western, coupled with a dash of added warmth that I find soothing, even stimulating, without being claustrophobic. This is thanks to the attention of a woman at the front desk whose name tag reads JETHRA. And Jethra is very much my type.

She is shaped like a ripe tomato. Her BEST WESTERN: BECAUSE WE CARE polo shirt exposes so much wonderful cleavage that it's hard to believe there's more breast terrain left to go beneath the shirt. But there they are. Then comes her voluptuous belly.

Jethra's fake lashes show their glue. Her nose is jolly, mouth wide. To her waist hangs a mass of hair (extensions, I think)—jet black—with half an inch of solid gray showing at the root. This I forgive her immediately, as she looks to be about my age—and I know how hard it is to keep it all together.

Using one very long pink nail as a dispatching tool, Jethra slides a small pile of forms across the fake wood counter that divides us. On her inner wrist is a tattoo with the name VIKTOR, and I wonder whether Viktor is her husband, or an ex-boyfriend, and if she could also possibly be into women (maybe it's her son).

"Now," she says. "These are your Grab N' Go breakfast bag selections sheets."

She has a throaty accent, something Eastern European-sounding.

"Make sure to fill one out every night and bring back to desk before nine p.m."

"Okay."

"Nice breakfast. I don't want you to miss."

"I won't."

"You get a choice of fruits: apple or orange. Breakfast sandwich I don't recommend. Kellogg's cereal with milk better, or bagel with cream cheese. Bagel okay, not great. I'd stick with Kellogg's. Then a yogurt. You like yogurt?"

I nod.

"Not me," she says. "I like blueberry muffin instead. It's a good muffin, if you like blueberry muffin."

"I like blueberry muffin."

"Get the muffin."

"Okay."

"Maybe you do muffin tomorrow and see how it is. If the next day you don't feel like muffin? You do granola bar."

Jethra's BECAUSE WE CARE shirt doesn't lie. She really does care. I feel warm inside—like when I get a massage or go to the gynecologist and I know the person is just doing their job, but I can't help but feel turned on by the attention.

"Room 249," she says, handing me a key card. "Down the hall and make a left. Wi-Fi password is on key slip. Indoor pool is open twenty-four hours, nice pool. You need extra towels, blanket, sheets, anything, you call desk. Do you like aliens?"

"What?"

"Do you like aliens?"

"Totally," I say, though I'm really more alien-neutral. "You?"

"I love them. We're only two hundred miles from Area 51. We get a lot of UFO-seekers; that's why I asked."

"Oh—"

"Don't forget. Grab N' Go breakfast bag selections sheets by nine."

I thank her, then make my way down the hall to my room, taking note of the ice machine and vending machines for later. I also pay close attention to the art lining the hallway walls, because this is where every Best Western establishes its individual flavor.

Best Western artworks are always photographic in medium, but the subjects chosen for representation depend on the geographic location of each motel. In this way, the art serves as little winks—reminders that we are *here*, not just in a Best Western, but in a Best Western in a *place* (in this case, the California high desert).

On my way to the room, I pass a sun-dazed mesa, a sand-dune panorama, one cowboy, two buttes, and a pack of coyotes.

Once inside the room, the desert theme continues, but with more of a "disco Negev" flavor to it. On the walls: a shiny square-and-rectangle pattern (geometric shapes)—less wallpaper than gold wall laminate. On the rug: same pattern, but make it camel. The glossy blackout curtains take a different turn with concentric circles and curlicues in shades of lime green and olive. But the whole motif comes back together with several framed close-up shots of botanic desert puffballs (healthier-looking than any desert puffballs I saw on my drive in).

It's less neutral than I'd like it. I prefer blank spaces—like I'm living on a cloud, or nowhere. Aesthetically, I feel pretty at home in my father's ICU room: the empty white walls, a single window looking out at the sky. Yesterday, the nurses even had the lights dimmed and quiet, classical music playing over a speaker system I'd never heard them use before. Spa-like.

I thought, *This is kind of nice.*

I felt envious, then immediately ashamed of the envy (who envies a man unconscious from pneumonia?) the way I do when I see this one woman nodding out on the sidewalk in front of Ralphs supermarket. Whenever I see her there, absorbed in a beatific inner world, I can't help but stare—like I'm trying to siphon off some of her heavenly high through my eyes. It's a good reminder that I'm still an addict, actually, because a normal person probably wouldn't look at this poor woman covered in sores and think, *Wow that looks amazing.* But I see past her sores to the memory of a feeling now lost to me. I see surrender.

This is how it was for me in my father's hospital room yesterday. I wanted a sickbed of my own. I wanted to be laid out in white sheets, everything taken care of for me, and let go. Unconsciousness-envy.

I kept imagining my father saying the words, *Cool and comfortable. Cool. Comfortable.* I don't know where those words came from, but I felt as ashamed of the words as I did of the envy feeling—like it's wrong to give language to a dying man. But I couldn't stop thinking it. *Cool and comfortable. Cool. Comfortable.*

Room 249 is, if overdecorated, definitely cool and comfortable. The air-conditioning unit is already humming, set to a generous sixty-eight on the wall thermostat. I like that the bed is a king, and that there's a tiny kitchenette with a mini refrigerator, microwave, and coffee maker with little pods of coffee. It dawns on me that I feel good.

Maybe because I feel good, I give myself a doom check, and of course, the moment I do this, I don't feel good anymore. A surge of fear moves through me, and I feel my chest tighten up, heavy and tight at once, like I'm wearing a bra made of lead. I take three very deep breaths, and each one is harder to draw in. I can't tell if I'm getting enough air.

To center myself, I focus on one of the puffballs on the wall. The puffball goes psychedelic in my anxious vision, zooming in, then out. I cannot remember why I am here. It's an alien feeling (an aliens feeling?). It's a loneliness, dark blue. I came to the desert because I wanted to be alone. Now that I'm alone, it's not what I want.

I need to talk to someone. Who? I guess I have people I could call, but I can't think of anyone who won't hold me to a feeling. People are such a commitment. I would "reach out" more often if everyone promised not to check in again later. That's how they get you. Your tragedy = their ticket to texting every day. Then it becomes about their drama. It's always the people you don't want to be there for you who are there for you.

I could call a customer service representative. I have the 1-800 number for GoDaddy saved to my phone. Recently, my author website got hacked—taken over by an ad for dick pills. At first, I felt violated by the hacking. Then I forgot about it. Then the publicist who works on my books asked if I knew that my website is now an ad for dick pills. I lied and said no. She sent me a link to a $250 GoDaddy software program. It's supposed to stop bad things from happening to your website. I bought the program and installed it. Nothing happened.

I pick up my phone and immediately soothed by the light of the screen. I call the 1-800 number and prepare my spiel: *dick pills, software, nothing.* A computer answers the phone. The computer welcomes me to the system. It asks me to start making choices: my customer ID, my PIN. Do I look like someone who knows her customer ID and PIN? I begin hitting the number zero repeatedly on my phone. Every time I hit zero, the computer says, "Entry not valid."

"Talk to human," I say.

"What can I help you with?" says the computer.

"Talk to human!" I say louder.

"I'm sorry, I didn't get that."

"Hu-man!"

The computer remains unfazed. But as though I have summoned him, I receive an incoming FaceTime call from my husband.

My husband is a human.

Do I want to talk to my husband?